Every Which Way

Brand of Justie
Book 11

Lisa Phillips

eBook ISBN: 979-8-88552-266-3

Paperback ISBN: 979-8-88552-267-0

Published by: Two Dogs Publishing, LLC. Idaho, USA

Cover Design by: Sasha Almazan and Gene Mollica, GS Cover Design Studio, LLC

Edited by: Lost Canyon Press Editing, Janice Boekhoff

Every Which Way

Chapter One

Kenna Banbury had gone into some dark places in her life, searching for the lost and forgotten. Solving cases. Catching bad guys. But there weren't many places worse than corporate America. Wearing a pantsuit and low heels. She had her hair in braids and wore thick-rimmed glasses to somewhat disguise herself.

She stood at the front of the conference room, where the employees had filed in. "Okay, ladies and gentlemen. I'm sure you're all eager to get back to work."

A rumble of chuckles spread across the crowd. Maybe fifteen people, in rows of six chairs, all faced her.

"For now, there are donuts on the side table, and we have coffee. Just in case you'd like a treat."

Half the room got up.

In her earpiece, Maizie said, "Set your phone somewhere closer to the west wall."

Her tech support guru, nearly an adult but not quite, had been raised as the captive of a deviant man with the power to keep her hidden from the world. Now that she was free, Maizie was thriving. Partly because she was in the van outside, being protected by Ramon, so that she was "part of the team" for this mission, out in the field working with them. Trying to take down an international organization, or at least the US arm of it. From what Maizie had figured out, the organization had funneled money through this finance company, laundering illegally obtained funds and making themselves look legitimate.

Maizie said, "You need to be nearer, or I won't be able to establish a connection."

Kenna got her phone from the table behind her, where she'd set it because the pockets in these pants might fit a sticky note but not much else. She moved it to another table against the wall, which held flyers and leaflets about respect, kindness, and the supposed reason they were here— sexual harassment.

As she walked back to the front of the room, Stairns crossed from the far wall to meet her in the middle. Her former boss from the FBI—a lifetime ago now—unofficially worked for her. The retiree looked about as happy to be back in a suit as she was.

"Please take your seats." Kenna smiled, keeping her posture open so she'd come across as being here to help. Not to hack their network from the inside and trace the money the "company" laundered through this place.

"Thank you for coming, even if you didn't have much choice." She scanned the crowd, pinpointing the ones she'd be able to make eye contact with so that she could feel as if she was connecting to someone and not talking to blank expressions or bowed heads because they were on their phones. "But this is a topic I'm passionate about as a survivor."

She wasn't going to lie, so she couldn't tell them an untrue story about sexual assault. But Kenna had been the victim more times than she liked. That much would be true. And she *had* been touched in the wrong situation in ways she didn't want by someone who had ill intent. Up close and personal with a monster, a killer. Even if she didn't consider it sexual assault. Sometimes, it was just the job.

Where it *didn't* need to be the job was here.

"Thank you for listening to me. It's part of my healing journey that I get to share my experiences with you here today, and while I'm not going to go into detail that might make some of you uncomfortable, I can say this. Any of us can find ourselves, at any time, in a situation that makes us nervous or scared. Or one that we realize too late we want out of."

One of the young guys in the crowd glanced at the donuts, like he wanted to go get one. Slender. Probably five-foot-six tops, and maybe mid-twenties but only barely.

The woman beside him, taller at the shoulder, reached over. Did she pinch or poke him?

The young man winced and returned his attention to the front. He realized right away that Kenna had seen that.

This woman was bold, doing that in a situation like this. Or she was so accustomed to it she barely even noticed when she did something to...what? Keep him in line?

"Have any of you been in a situation like that?"

The whole thing had happened in a second, and now the young man didn't raise his hand. He sat there, kowtowed into silence. Kenna might be wrong or reading more into it than there was, but her instincts didn't usually fail her. These days, those instincts were wrapped in the kind of discernment Paul urged the Philippians to have.

A few people in the room raised their hands, and she smiled warmly at them. "Whether we're prepared to admit it in front of others or not, the pain—or the fear—can still be real. Often, it's stronger when we keep it to ourselves. When we speak what happened aloud, the thing loses its power. It loses its hold on us."

Before they concluded she was going to ask them to share their darkest experiences, Kenna said, "Let's all stand and push the chairs to the wall. Maybe stack them. Let's do a little self-defense scenario, and hopefully, you'll go away with some tools to protect yourself."

While everyone stacked the chairs, and a couple of the men got another donut, Kenna tried not to be distracted by the young man. After all, he could be on a diet, and the woman simply had a habit-breaking way to hold him to his promise not to eat donuts. It might not be a relationship or a power imbalance between the two of them.

She turned to her papers on the table at the front and whispered, "Are you in yet?"

Stairns gave orders behind her, directing people to pair up and spread out so they wouldn't swing their arms and whack each other.

Maizie said, "It's not close enough. I'm only getting an intermittent signal, but I'm going to try and get into their system with this. Standby."

Kenna turned back to the group. "All right, everyone has their partner?" She glanced around, clocking more than she let on. The young man had paired up with the woman who'd been sitting beside him.

Kenna walked over to Stairns in the center. "The biggest threat you face is the one you don't see coming."

Stairns whipped out his arm and grabbed the back of her neck, forcing her head forward. Her body bowed under the pressure behind her neck.

Kenna reached back and grabbed his shoulder. Then she kicked out with her left leg but didn't make contact. She held it up, touching it to the back of both of Stairns's knees. His loose grip on the back of her head, mostly just the weight of his hand now, lessened, and she straightened enough to look at the group. "What happens if I swipe his legs?"

Someone said, "He falls back."

"But so do you," a woman at the back said.

Kenna nodded. "It's possible he could take me down with him. If we both fall back, but it was my action that got us there, I'll have an extra split second to think while he's surprised. So there's a chance I can get away."

A chance that had saved her life before.

She straightened and tipped her head for Stairns to step closer to her.

"I'm going to regret this, aren't I?" He moved in front of her.

Kenna grinned and several people chuckled. She put her arm around his neck, feeling the usual twinge of pain in her forearms. She'd been working on physical therapy the last few months, giving her injuries time to heal so she could lift more than her cell phone and open all doors, not just the ones that weren't heavy to pull on.

She wrapped her arm farther around his neck from behind and grabbed her own wrist, holding loosely to everything. "I can trap my opponent, and he'll never see my face. Once he's immobilized, I could do whatever I want. This is something we're going to practice because I'd like for you to know how to get out of a choke hold. It's important that, in the heat of the moment, you don't panic. So if we practice these things, you might, for a second, be able to have a cool head."

She looked at the group over Stairns' shoulder. "One partner get the other into a loose hold. I don't want anyone getting hurt or passing out. But here's your first tactic. The second you realize your partner is moving to choke you, I need you to do two things. First, tuck your chin as far as you can before the hold hits. Second, get your stance strong."

Stairns said, "If they can get you on the ground, it's harder to get out of the hold. You need to stay standing." He shifted. "Plant one foot slightly back and keep your knees soft."

The pairs each got into their stances. Most of the pairs were two men or two women. Considering the size difference between some of them, that was good. Interestingly, the young man was the victim, and his female friend was the attacker.

Kenna said, "Okay, all of you turn so you can see me."

The young man winced, turned by the force of the woman's hold.

"Make sure you're not holding tightly on your choke. The goal is not to hurt your partner."

The young man's face remained impassive, maybe even resigned. She'd seen that look before on the faces of victims who didn't believe they had any power to change a situation. It might be a stretch, and she might be projecting based on the kind of people she usually associated with, but if there was even a chance this guy needed help, she wanted to help him.

"If they're close enough to choke you, you're close enough to hit back. Anyone have any ideas of things you can do?"

"Jab their eye with your thumb!"

"Elbow their side."

"Stomp on their foot."

Kenna said, "Anything you can think of. If your airway is cut off, you have ten seconds before you're going to pass out. That means you need to work fast. First, you have to *decide* that you're not going to be a victim. Right here, right now."

She had an idea.

Kenna let go of Stairns and started to walk around the room. "A choke hold is a threat to your life. So, what are you going to do? I want all of you who are in the position of the victim to say this out loud."

She took a breath. "I'm not going to be a victim."

A couple of people murmured it.

"Louder!"

Her friend Ramon, tucked away in the van, chuckled in her ear, but he didn't know what was going on in this room. He thought she was only pretending.

A few of the "victims" repeated her statement. She went to stand in front of the young man. "Let me hear you say it."

His jaw flexed, determination on his face. "I'm not going to be a victim."

"You don't have to be." And so he didn't think she was singling him out, Kenna looked around the room. "Any situation you're in, no matter what it is, you can make that choice. You can say, 'I'm not going to be the victim.'"

She glanced over in time to see him push the woman's arms away and step out of her hold. The woman frowned, but Kenna didn't give her the chance to start a conversation.

She clapped. "Okay, time to switch places!"

Now that he'd chosen to not be the victim, it was time for the power balance to shift in his favor. "Again, we're not trying to hurt the other person. We're working on tools you can use to get yourself out of situations you don't want to be in."

Stairns took over, walking them through when a person

has grabbed them by the wrists and immobilized them. A few quick ways to break a hold and get free.

Kenna walked back over to the table and said quietly. "Update."

Ramon, whose only function in the van was to protect Maizie, said, "She's pulling information in pieces. We might not know if we have everything, but we'll have...a lot?" He paused. "Enough, at least."

Maizie had to be furiously typing away to communicate through Ramon without speaking up herself. But then, she said, "If you can get to the server room and plug in, that'll get us the best result. It's the only way to know if we have everything."

"I'll see what I can do."

Stairns had everyone in their pairs, jerking their wrists out of the other person's hold. The young man looked a lot more determined. The woman with him didn't look so happy. She had to be at least forty, so if they were in a relationship, there was already a power imbalance with her being older than him. A lot of people made that work, but sometimes, one party subjugated the other. To what extent, Kenna couldn't know from only an hour or so of observation.

"Let's everyone take a break. We've made some great progress." She walked into the center of the room. "I've had too much coffee, so I'll be looking for the bathroom. We'll meet back in ten."

Hopefully, by then, the seminar would be over.

Instead of coming back and continuing this farce, they would leave with the information Maizie had gained from their system.

She retrieved her phone and took it with her, wandering through the halls. "I need some help."

"I'll pull up schematics," Ramon said in her earpiece.

She smiled at a couple of people and found a hall with less traffic.

"You're close," he said. "Second door on the left, toward the end. That's their server room."

Kenna checked that no one was watching her and ducked into the room, lined with floor-to-ceiling racks, all humming. Lights blinking.

"Now we're talking," Maizie said. "The signal is way stronger."

"How long do you need? I could leave my phone and come back for it."

"Only a few minutes," Maizie said.

Ramon added, "Hang tight and then you guys can leave that place."

"It's just an office."

"Don't remind me," he said. "Corporate offices give me the hives."

Kenna smiled. "Makes me wanna tell you that you have to wear a tie to my wedding."

"You wouldn't dare."

She glanced down at the ring on her left hand. Jax had proposed in Greece months ago, under the warm Crete sun. The trip where everything had changed for her. Kenna had learned so much about where she came from and who her parents really were.

She'd even met her grandfather, though due to his illness, he'd passed away a couple of months ago. The old man's guardian had given Kenna a book of her father's that was never published. *The Constantine Initiative.* Constantine was the family name the old man had passed down to Kenna's mother and the two women who were her aunts—one of whom was actually technically her mother.

She'd been trying to wrap her head around it ever since.

Amara was her aunt, but she'd married Malcom Banbury, and they'd been determined to raise Kenna together as her parents. She'd considered Amara her mother. The woman had been shot when Kenna was a toddler.

Or so everyone believed.

This was no time to get distracted thinking about that unpublished novel right now or the questions it had given her when she read it. Namely, where her mother was. If she was alive.

Why hadn't she made contact?

Kenna shook off the thoughts and paced around the server room.

"Okay, got it," Maizie said.

"I'll pack up." That was Stairns.

Ramon said, "There's an exit door at the end of the hall, Kenna."

She went to the door. "Meet you downstairs." Kenna slowly eased the door open and looked at the end of the hall.

The young man stood there in heated conversation with the woman. "No." He tugged his arm from her grasp. "Don't touch me."

She bristled with aggression, every muscle in her body tight.

Kenna didn't like the look of it.

"It's over." The young man walked off.

Kenna said a quick prayer for him, that he'd be safe and make even more changes to his life that would bring him peace. That the woman wouldn't retaliate.

She stepped out.

The woman whirled around only to find Kenna in the hall. "This is all *your* fault."

Kenna faced her. "Excuse me?"

"Putting ideas in his head!"

"About what? Not being a victim?" She was going to play dumb until this woman incriminated herself. "About having a choice to *not* be in a situation?"

The woman blustered, stuttering but not actually saying anything.

"Why would he feel the need to break it off with you after hearing that? Is there something your manager needs to know about your relationship?"

People started to gather at the end of the hall, witnessing the intense conversation between Kenna and this woman.

Kenna lifted her chin.

The other woman came at her, those long talon nails bared. Kenna planted her foot, turned her upper body, and slammed her shoulder into the woman. She yelped, knocked back. Kenna hadn't even laid a hand on her. She just blocked the woman's attempt to...what? Claw her eyes out?

The other woman stumbled back.

"Don't touch me." Kenna stood her ground. "You don't have my permission. I'm not going to be another one of your victims."

Someone behind the woman started to applaud. Then others joined in, most of whom had been in the seminar.

Before the woman could turn to see the result of her actions, Kenna said, "We're done here."

She walked to the exit and pushed her way through to the stairs. At the last second, she spotted the young man at the end of the hall, barely visible by the corner of the wall.

She thought she saw him mouth, *Thank you.* But she

didn't stick around long enough to find out. "Stairns, we're leaving."

He responded over comms. "On my way."

In her earpiece, Ramon said, "Can't help yourself, can you?"

Kenna jogged down the concrete stairwell. "Just be ready to go when I get down there."

"Yes, ma'am."

Chapter Two

"You really think it did them any good?" Ramon glanced over from the driver's seat for a second, then back at the freeway in front of them. Good thing since it was clogged with traffic even though it wasn't lunchtime.

The downtown skyline stretched out in front of them, a blue sky above it. It looked warm out, but looks were usually deceiving. Plus, this was Denver, and this time of year, it could snow in the morning and be seventy degrees later.

"All part of the service." Kenna grinned. "And I actually *do* think it did them some good. A person who has never taken a self-defense class might go seek one out now. At least one person was inspired to stand up for themselves, and we got what we went there for."

Ramon left the freeway, racing down the exit ramp to the light at the bottom. Kenna looked at her phone so she didn't have to be aware of his driving. The guy was like a teen boy—too fast, too reckless. Maybe some drove sedately, when someone was watching. But who hadn't pushed it on occasion? Tested the limits.

Behind her seat, Maizie tapped away on the keys of her laptop.

Kenna checked her messages, emails, and the contact inbox for her website. Nothing new. Jax knew they were in Denver working on getting more information about the dangerous "company" they'd found out about on their last trip. An organization responsible for crimes going back more than a century. They'd profited from war, subverted justice, and believed they could manipulate global politics.

She'd run into them in the UK a few months ago, and since then, she'd read that book her father wrote that was never published. Now she had more questions than answers. Despite the fact she wasn't invited to participate in the investigation, even in the US, she wasn't going to let this lie.

"Thinking about your mom again?"

Kenna glanced over at him. "Will you just drive to the coffee shop?"

Maizie said, "I can give you an update on the hunt for where your mom might've been hiding for the past thirty-however-many years, but there's nothing new."

"She doesn't want to be found." Kenna stared out the window, remembering a letter she'd been given in the UK. *Don't believe anything they tell you.* Great. Solid advice, but it had her doubting everything and everyone, except the people in her inner circle. "I know she doesn't want to be found because I have no idea where she is or how to contact her."

Ramon pulled into the parking lot for a coffee shop in the center of a strip mall. Some independent place that had a wide seating area and probably half a dozen kinds of milk —maybe more. "Maybe there's something about her in the stuff Maizie got from that company server."

Kenna got out and slid the back door open. "Coming inside?"

The teen closed her laptop lid. "Yep." She looked excited to be out of the van, which was understandable.

Their lives were a delicate balance of letting Maizie feel like she was free and making sure she was protected. The teen had to be coming up on eighteen soon enough, but it wasn't like she was going to leave home anytime soon.

She stepped out of the van in jeans, Converse sneakers, and a zippered hoodie, which was a lot like the style Kenna had—not that anyone had mentioned it. Maizie could adopt whatever style she wanted when she settled on something. It might mirror Kenna's, and it might not.

Long blond hair that hung loose over her shoulders. A little makeup. Huge blue eyes and delicate features. One day, she was going to stop a guy's heart, and Kenna prayed Maizie would be healed enough to be able to accept healthy affection. That she would be free enough to keep the way she'd been raised from corrupting every relationship in her life.

"You're staring."

Kenna said, "We really should find out when your birthday is."

Maizie set off after Ramon, toward the door to the coffee shop. Their friend scanned the parking lot around them, keeping watch. A car pulled into the lot with Stairns driving. Good, he was here. Their other friend wouldn't be too far behind.

Ramon held the door, watching the parking lot while they went in.

Maizie asked, "When's your birthday?"

Kenna eyed her young friend. "I'm not the one about to turn eighteen."

Maizie shrugged. "Someone other than me can find my birth certificate. I might need it, so it's probably a good idea to know how to get it."

"But you don't want to see it?"

She only shrugged again in answer to Kenna's question. They ordered at the counter and found a table.

Stairns settled between Ramon and Maizie, but closer to Ramon. The two of them couldn't be more different in appearance. Where Ramon was younger and Hispanic, Stairns had that grizzled ex-marine look to him. Now that he was retired, it seemed he only wore jeans and checkered shirts. His cabin was a couple of hours from here. Maizie lived in his backyard in an Airstream that belonged to Kenna's father.

Stairns glanced over at the door.

Ramon pushed his chair back. "I'll grab the drinks."

Maizie had her laptop open and was typing away.

"This is where I say something about teens and too much screen time."

"It's work, not play."

"I know," Kenna said. "Since I'm the one who pays your salary." In cash. In nonsequential bills. Maizie would have to get on the grid at some point, but that was another thing they'd need her birth certificate for. Ramon had suggested she get a fake ID, but Kenna wanted the girl to live an honest life—once she chose a name for herself.

She couldn't be Maizie Smith forever.

"You're thinking way too much." Ramon set the mug of coffee down in front of her. "Bruce is here."

Kenna glanced over at the man walking across the seating area, heading in their direction. "Uh-oh." She'd met the guy in England, a burned CIA agent who'd helped her out when she'd been cut off from her friends and on the run from the police. He wore his typical tan slacks and Hawaiian shirt, canvas shoes on his feet, but the expression on his face had her asking, "What's wrong?"

Bruce slid into a chair. "I need a drink stronger than this place makes."

Maizie looked up from her laptop screen.

Bruce said, "Hey, trouble," almost absently. Like there was far too much on his mind.

She smiled and went back to her work.

Kenna sipped her coffee. "Start talking."

Across the table, Ramon had his phone out. Stairns looked like he wanted to pester his old friend but said nothing. That wouldn't last long.

Bruce tipped his phone over and over on the table. "I went to look up an associate of mine. Catch up on old times since I'm back home."

He'd been out in the cold, stuck in England with no way to get back to the US. Until Kenna and her friends pulled some strings and got him home. "What happened?"

"So, the guy takes one look at me, flips out, and he splits." Bruce worked his mouth back and forth, pursing his lips for a second while he thought. "All signs of a guilty conscience."

Ramon set his phone face down on the table. "I could track him down. Get him to talk to me, or rough him up and then he talks."

Kenna frowned.

Stairns said, "You and this guy worked together at the agency?"

Bruce nodded. "Partners as much as you can be in a business like that, where it's all secrets and lies. Now, he's sitting pretty living in a penthouse apartment a block from here and working as the CEO of some finance company."

Maizie lifted her head. "A finance company that's connected to the one we just accessed?"

Bruce asked Kenna, "Your mission was good?"

"We got what we went in there for." But if their enemy was moving money through it, and the company was connected to a former CIA agent who had a reason to run from Bruce, that could mean they got a lead on top of all the information they got.

Ramon said, "And Kenna maybe even changed some lives in the process. For good."

Bruce lifted his chin. "I'll pass you the info, Maizie. You could tell me if they're connected, these two finance companies?"

"Sure." She went back to her typing.

"Thanks, kid."

Ramon said, "The offer is still open to rough the guy up."

Kenna just scowled at him. How Bruce chose to solve his problem was his business, but she didn't want Maizie involved.

Stairns shifted in his seat. "So this is it? The job in Denver is done. We have everything from their server, and we're free to go home?" He sounded disappointed.

Ramon grinned. "Cases with Kenna never go as planned." He rubbed his hands together. "I'm waiting for something to kick off."

She shot him a look, then asked Stairns, "When does Elizabeth get home?" His wife had gone on a cruise with her best friend.

He pouted over his black coffee. "Monday."

Ah. "Guess we should find something to do for the weekend." Kenna smiled.

"I have an idea about that," Maizie said.

Kenna's phone pinged. She looked at the screen and found an email Maizie had just sent her. "A wedding show?"

"Denver's biggest wedding show of the year," Maizie said.

The three men at the table busted up laughing.

Kenna's cheeks heated. "You're all fired. Except Maizie." She turned her sweetest smile to the teen. "Thanks."

"I forwarded the email to Jax's mom a couple of days ago. She said those things always give out loads of free samples."

Kenna's jaw dropped. "You...what?"

"She said it's a great idea. She'll be here tomorrow, and she's going to bring Laney with her."

Jax's mom, Adrielle, was coming here? And she was bringing his sister too? "Laney has kids. She can't just pick up and—"

"Her husband is gonna take a few days off and stay with the kids so she can come."

Kenna didn't look at the rest of them. They had to be staring at her, though. Probably wanting to watch the show when she erupted into an epic freakout over the fact Jax's *mother* was coming here for a *wedding show*.

What could she say?

Maizie had no remorse in her expression whatsoever. "You need to find a wedding dress. It's a good way to get ideas and figure out what you like...or don't like."

Kenna lifted her mug and sat back in her chair, internally so off-kilter she felt as if she was going to fall off the chair. Outwardly, she projected an air of complete calm. Maybe a little bit of ice-cold rage because Ramon actually shifted in his seat.

"Great." She managed to get the word out.

Mrs. Jaxton was already on her way here. What on earth could she do now to avoid this?

"Sounds great." Kenna sipped her coffee, trying to decide whether to get out of it or not.

"Sweet." Maizie went back to her typing.

Kenna stared at her coffee mug.

"Heads-up." Stairns tapped two fingers on the table.

She set her mug down and glanced over her shoulder. Both Ramon and Bruce had stiffened, for different reasons, based on their history. Neither of them would ever be comfortable around law enforcement. Two uniformed police officers walked up to the counter, and all of them relaxed. Maizie pulled up her hood so that less of her face was visible.

"We need something from that network," Kenna said. "I'm not trying to pressure you, Maze, but we really need a lead to chase."

From the other end of the table, Bruce said, "I've got my own thing to work. I might not be available."

"Need any help?"

He said, "I'll let you know."

"This is a team now. If I have to accept that, then so do you. We're a package deal."

Ramon chuckled. "You make it sound like the best thing that ever happened to you. We're so blessed."

She balled up her napkin and threw it at him. "Someone give me a bad guy to catch. Something that sends me on a case to find a serial killer or a missing person. Anything. I'll be unfortunately busy for a couple of days. Jax's mom and Maizie can scope out the wedding show thing with his sister, and they can just get me samples or whatever to look at later."

Stairns shook his head.

Maizie said, "Not happening."

"Good luck with that." Ramon chuckled. "No cases for you until after you make nice with your future mom."

Kenna groaned, leaned forward, and banged her forehead lightly on the table.

Bruce nudged her shoulder. "You need me to kill someone."

"No." Her voice was muffled by the table.

"Is this woman really so bad?"

Kenna sat up. "We met a few months ago, almost right after Greece." She cleared her throat. Someone had shot at her and Jax on the day they got engaged, but Bruce killed the assassin. Unbeknownst to them, he'd been there watching their backs. "Jax ambushed me into meeting them because he knew I'd drag my feet. His mother is...an interesting woman. Lovely, well meaning. She's impeccably put together, so I'll need to find shoes other than the ratty pile of Converse in my RV closet."

To be fair, Jax had been correct. She would've probably put it off forever, but he'd figured out how to make it happen.

"Did you meet his dad as well or just his mom?"

"Both." She shook her head. "His dad doesn't really engage. He answers the questions he's asked, but aside from that, he sips his whiskey and smooths down his tie." And he did his best to look disapprovingly at everyone. "I'm interested to see if she's different on her own, with Laney."

It could be that Jax's father set the tone when he was around.

How two kids from those uptight, one-percenter parents managed to be so down to earth was a mystery. Jax was... Jax. Best boyfriend ever—now her fiancé. Laney had an air that was just settled. Peaceful. She loved her husband and her kids, and she handled the family drama like a pro. Like it didn't bother her at all that she was the peacemaker.

Kenna had been raised by a single father after her mother died—or so she thought.

They'd driven all over the country in his Airstream while he'd solved cases as an investigator, and she'd home-schooled herself.

Two things she knew now were that her mother wasn't her mother and that she wasn't dead. Not that Kenna had proof of either. All she had were stories. The book that woman in Greece had given her. But she also had an overbearing team in her life and an international organization to take down.

It was enough to make her bang her forehead on the table again.

She needed a case to work before life got too real and forced her to do something insane, like choose a veil for her wedding dress.

Chapter Three

Kenna and Maizie stood beside each other, descending the escalator at the convention center into an ocean of people—mostly women. A lot of them wore veils, or sashes, indicating they were the bride-to-be. "Kill me now."

Maizie giggled.

If Kenna looked around, probably behind them, she would find Ramon somewhere. Bruce and Stairns were working on whatever Bruce's thing was today—digging into the life of the man Bruce had confronted yesterday, the guy who'd been his colleague in the CIA.

And she was here. At a wedding show.

"Anything on the company from yesterday?"

Maizie waved at someone across the lobby. "I'll tell you later." She wound her arm through Kenna's and pretty much dragged her through the crowd to where two women waited for them.

Jax's mom, Adrielle, had a long pixie cut and wore gray slacks with a pink blouse and a cashmere shawl. Her shoes were flat black with a gold buckle. She smiled widely and, when Kenna got near enough, kissed her cheek. "Kenna, how are you?"

"I'm good. How was your flight?" Better than asking how their impromptu trip had gone.

Adrielle shrugged one slender shoulder. "No turbulence, and our bags arrived at the same time we did."

Laney got between them. "Kenna." She gave her a hug, squeezing tight. "This is fun."

Kenna shot her a look.

Laney laughed. "It's been ten years since I got to peruse any of this. I'm excited."

Kenna said, "This is my friend Maizie."

"Right," Adrielle said. "Your assistant."

"She's going to be my bridesmaid as well."

Maizie whirled around to Kenna. "I am?"

"Who else would it be?"

"Uh...Dixie? Forrest Crosby—"

Adrielle said, "You know the author, Forrest Crosby?"

Kenna nodded, and Maizie continued, "Laney. Elizabeth Stairns. Valentina Ryson."

"Okay, fine," Kenna said. "But I only need one, right? So that makes it you."

Maizie blushed, looking nervous.

"Besides, I have an 'if I have to suffer, then we all have to suffer' policy about the whole thing."

Laney busted up laughing. "I love it."

Jax's sister wore dark jeans and canvas shoes with a white button-down shirt and a white undershirt in the open collar. She had on a simple gold necklace, and her dark blond hair was long and loose. Kenna had liked her the first time they met, over the holidays a few months back, and even her husband had been the kind of person who allowed Maizie to relax—at least to an extent.

At their meeting, they'd explained to Laney and her husband about Maizie's background and how they'd met her. They hadn't done the same with Adrielle Jaxton or Jax's father. Neither needed to be privy to what Maizie had suffered.

"Sounds like we're going to need cake samples." Adrielle smiled wide. "Otherwise, what's the point?"

Kenna said, "I like your style."

Laney led them through double doors into the big convention auditorium, with huge chandeliers hanging from the high ceiling. Floral carpet. Rows and rows of vendors selling all kinds of things.

Adrielle said, "I already made an appointment with one of the dress designers. I think you're going to like her style."

Maizie glanced over.

Kenna said, "Sounds great."

Adrielle and Maizie got distracted by stationery, comparing paper color and fonts. As if Kenna was going to send out actual invitations.

Laney slowed to walk with her. "I know you and Jax had that plan where you go to the beach and you both have bare feet."

Kenna smiled. "It was a nice idea at the time. But this thing isn't going to get out of control. I'm not getting talked into four hundred people in some huge church I've never been to just to impress a bunch of people I don't really know."

Laney's eyes widened. "I'll help wrangle Mom. I promise I won't let her lock you into anything, but she knows you don't have much family. I think she's trying to fill a gap."

Kenna sidestepped a lady pushing a stroller. "I actually found out that my mother might be alive."

Laney gasped. "Are you serious?"

"It's crazy, right? Because if she really is alive, then where has she been for thirty years? You'd think she'd have contacted me and let me know she wasn't dead." Kenna shrugged. "Don't get me wrong, I understand having to fake your own death. But the book made it seem like my dad knew."

"What do you mean?"

Kenna slowed at a vendor for matching luggage, which was pretty safe as far as this whole convention went. Did they need Mr. and Mrs. monogrammed suitcases? Right, probably not. She looked anyway, and Laney stuck beside her. "He never published the book, which is probably because it's about the hero investigator and how his true love faked her death. And how they met up a few times over the years or sent letters to each other, then later, emails."

Laney frowned. "Can you find the email account and trace it somehow? Isn't that what Maizie does?"

"We've got a lot of things going on." Kenna continued walking. "Maybe when she has some downtime, but right now, she's working on data we got from a finance company yesterday. There's a lot of that to go through."

They'd caught up to Adrielle and Maizie, who glanced over. The teen seemed hesitant, maybe even nervous.

"Everything okay?" Kenna didn't usually find herself in the middle of such a thick crowd of people. She had an itchy feeling on the back of her neck.

When she glanced around, the reason for her nerves became clear. They were live on someone's social media channel. The "influencer" took up the whole aisle, gesturing with one hand and holding a tiny microphone to her lips with the other. Evidently "so excited" to be here.

She kept talking, but Kenna barely understood half of what she said.

She glanced at Maizie, tugging her elbows around so the girl's face was away from the camera coming toward them. "Is she even speaking English?"

Maizie smiled.

"I feel old just listening to her."

Adrielle said, "How do you think I feel?"

Kenna winced inwardly, but when she glanced at her future mother-in-law, she spotted humor on the woman's face. "We definitely need cake."

"And champagne with our lunch. This is a celebration!" Adrielle whirled around and continued on.

Maizie didn't move right away, so Kenna wound her arm through Maizie's, and they walked together. "You okay?"

Maizie said, "Weird memories. But you should know I looked up that woman you ran into yesterday."

"At the company?"

"Sheryl Nolan." Maizie bit her lip. "I just got a couple of pings on my phone. She's posting on how she lost her job this morning and ranting about how it's all your fault."

"Does she know my name or where to find me?"

"She has your picture from their security system. Don't ask me how she got it." Maizie ducked her head and whispered, "She's calling you out on socials."

"Thanks." She wasn't too worried—at least, not until something happened.

"Having fun yet?"

Kenna eyed her suspiciously. "Maybe it's not so bad."

Maizie chuckled, and it was good to see her laugh. She'd ventured out of the Airstream more and more over the past few months, since the trip to the UK. But it couldn't be denied that this was a huge step for the young woman.

"We should throw you a big birthday party when you turn eighteen."

"What if I'm already eighteen and we missed it?" She shrugged.

"We could start planning for your next birthday."

"Do you care about *your* birthday?"

Kenna frowned. "Okay, fine."

"I guess you're raising me the way you've been raised. To not need a fuss made about me and to not want to be the center of attention."

"That's not a bad thing. It's good to live a quiet life you're happy with. No flashing lights. No notoriety. Seems like everyone wants to be famous, like having people notice you is the most important thing in the world. What if I don't want anyone to notice me?"

Maizie said, "It's easier to stay under the radar if no one notices me."

"Plenty of jobs prefer the employee to have no social media accounts. They're a breach of security."

"So I should go for one of those?"

"You can do whatever you want."

Maizie said, "You know that's not really true. I mean, you can't do everything. I can't either. I'll never be an MMA fighter or an Olympic track star. I'll never be a nurse because it's too gross, and I don't think I could be a therapist."

"We should work out."

"You know what I mean."

Kenna said, "But if you want to get stronger, we can have Jax make us a workout plan and get a gym going at Stairns' place. When I'm on the road, we can touch base, keep each other accountable. And in the meantime, you can choose whatever field you want to work in."

"How about yours?"

Kenna would've objected even just a few months ago. "You're already doing that. But you don't have to do it forever if you decide to switch fields or move on. Maybe I'll make it a requirement of your job that you have to get a college degree."

"I've been thinking about it. I can do an online school, right? I'll be able to work around cases."

"Sounds like you're on the right track."

"Which is why you should listen to me." Maizie stopped, turning to face Kenna.

So suspicious.

"I found a church."

Kenna started to object.

"Hear me out."

This could get awkward. Especially since Adrielle and Laney had also stopped and were close enough to hear.

"It's in Colorado, in this tiny town. A small white country church. The old kind with the spire, and it's been there for two hundred years."

Maizie paused long enough for Kenna to say, "Go on."

"The pastor is Elizabeth's uncle, and she said he's quiet and kind. And *suuuuper* old."

Kenna smiled.

"The church only holds about fifty people. So, it's not like a whole lot of Jax's friends and family will come, and we can tell everyone to sit wherever. That way, you don't have his side of the church packed and you've only got me and Stairns and Ramon and like five other people."

"Elizabeth's uncle?" First Kenna was hearing about this.

Maizie nodded.

"What else have you figured out?" Kenna narrowed her eyes. "You know I don't like surprises."

"Searching for the church has been keeping me from flipping out about heavy white dresses."

Maizie was having flashbacks?

Kenna moved closer to the girl and touched her cheeks. "We can leave right now. Or Ramon can come over and take you outside, let you get some air."

"I know why you like the RV."

"That's the nicest thing anyone's ever said to me." Kenna smiled. "You want Ramon to take you?"

Maizie shook her head. "I want to see you put on a dress."

Kenna gave her a quick hug. "Who says I'm wearing a dress?"

Adrielle gasped.

Laney's eyes widened in a panic.

Maizie said, "You wouldn't dare!"

"My wedding." Kenna folded her arms and fought the smile that pulled at her lips. "My rules."

And, on top of that, it was pulling Maizie out of her funk.

"Well...well..." Adrielle sputtered. "What's the alternative?"

"Crisp white slacks, a white bodice made out of wedding dress material, so I get the top part. White Converse."

Laney started laughing. "That's oddly specific. Almost as if you've thought extensively about this."

Adrielle started to fan herself like she was going to faint.

"But I *suppose* we could try some dresses on. Just in case." Kenna bit the inside of her lip. She was going to murder Jax.

Okay, maybe not.

But still.

Adrielle smiled widely. "Let's at least go look at some. Who knows, you might be inspired."

Laney looked like she thought this entire thing was hilarious.

Kenna turned to Maizie. "Sure you're okay to be surrounded by dresses?"

The teen said, "As long as you're around, and Ramon is close by."

Except that the threat wasn't here. It was in Maizie's mind, locked in her memories. Everyone had things they wanted to forget or parts of their past they chose not to recall. One person couldn't say their experience was worse than anyone else's—except that Maizie's had been as bad as things could get.

"I need my wingman." Kenna nudged her. "That church is a pretty good idea."

Didn't mean that was how it would go down. She preferred Jax's idea of the two of them with a few people— she was thinking five max.

Him in slacks and a white shirt, not even tucked in. Bare feet. Her *maybe* in a white sundress or her idea of white pants and a wedding-dress-like top, also no shoes. Loose hair with a flower in it. On the beach, but not when it was hot.

Quiet.

Gorgeous.

The perfect day.

Fanfare was *not* her thing. They all knew it, and Adrielle was going to catch on.

Kenna didn't usually think about her former fiancé, Bradley, who had died in the basement of a serial killer's house. Watching his life slip away, Kenna had watched her dreams die with him—and their unborn child. She'd lost so much and since then gained more back than she'd imagined she would have.

Some people might think she should recreate the wedding she was supposed to have had with Bradley, but that wouldn't be fair to his memory. And it wasn't what she wanted.

The designer had set up in a room off to the side of the auditorium. Adrielle introduced them all to a four-foot-eight woman with some Asian in her ancestry. Her dark hair was cut into choppy angles, and the ends were pink. The room had fairy lights strung up all around and even a few racks of bridesmaid's dresses in all colors. Shoes. Jewelry. Kenna's head spun just taking it all in.

Akira scanned Kenna from head to toe. "I have just the thing!"

The room had a changing area behind a screen. A pedestal step and trifold mirrors to look at the dress from all angles. Slender glasses of bubbly apple cider to sip while they perused the racks of dresses.

Akira raced to a rack at the far end and started rummaging.

Kenna glanced over at Adrielle. "You were right. These are fabulous."

Laney, one row down from her mother, looked relieved. Oh good. Kenna had said the right thing.

The door opened, and Maizie quickly ducked down between rows of dresses. A blond woman stepped inside wearing casual street clothes and holding a cup of Starbucks, which was one of the most innocuous things in the world. With a cup of coffee, you blended in at a place like this *immediately*.

Akira held up one hand. "We have a private appointment in here!"

The woman closed the door behind her. "So do I," she said in a British accent and glanced at Kenna. "I need to speak to you."

Just when she got used to wedding dress shopping.

The door opened again, and Ramon stepped in, grabbed the woman, and backed her against the wall with his arm across her throat. The Starbucks cup fell to the ground, and the lid came off. It was empty.

Adrielle gasped.

The woman glared at him.

Ramon said, "Start talking."

Chapter Four

"As I said"—she cleared her throat, Ramon's forearm still pressed up against it—"before you so rudely grabbed me, I need to speak with Kenna."

Ramon didn't move. "Kenna?"

"Maybe later. I'm busy right now."

Who knew where Maizie had ducked down to hide? But wanting to be out of sight was her choice. Adrielle watched the situation, glancing back and forth between Kenna and the two by the door. Laney had her phone out.

Akira came over. "No fighting in my shop!"

She seemed to speak entirely in short exclamations.

Ramon backed off a fraction. "She said later."

The woman shifted, brushing off her clothes. She had on wide leg jeans, black boots with low heels, and a gray T-shirt, over which she had pulled a jacket. "Fine." She glanced at Kenna. "I know how to find you."

Wasn't that nice for her, being able to find people whenever she needed. Nice skill set. Shame it might be a problem for Kenna and her family.

She stared at the woman, refusing to back down or

acknowledge any interest in what she had to say. At least, not right now.

Ramon held the door open, and the woman stepped out. He closed the door and turned to Kenna. "I was late."

"Only a second or two."

"It won't happen again." He glanced at the racks. "*Hermanita.*"

"I'm okay." Maizie stood up. She glanced at the three nonteam members in the room and said, "I tripped."

Ramon looked back at Kenna. Guilt. Determination. Fear.

"We're good now." She nodded. "Thanks to you."

He went to the door.

"Not so fast!" Akira eyed him like a specimen, walking over and drawing a tape measure apart. She held it across his chest from shoulder to shoulder and muttered something in a language Kenna didn't speak. "I have the perfect suit for you."

Ramon shook his head. "I don't wear suits."

"You model for me. I have just the thing that will change your mind." She reached for his shoulder and stroked a hand down his arm. "I can be very persuasive."

Kenna pressed her lips together and glanced at Maizie. The teen's eyes practically bugged out of her head, making Kenna laugh aloud. "I mean...he could stay."

Ramon ducked over to the door and flung it open. "I'll be outside."

The door slammed shut.

Akira said, "Shame."

"Yes, it is," Adrielle said. "That was exciting."

Behind her, Laney had the same expression on her face as Maizie had just a moment ago. If only Kenna could hide in the dresses like the teen had done. Or run out and catch up to that woman. Find a case. Search for a killer. Locate a missing child.

Something.

Anything.

It wasn't that she was necessarily avoiding the inevitable —her wedding and all that was going into it—but surely, there were more important things to be done right now.

"Why didn't you hear what she had to say?" Adrielle asked. "That woman."

Because she was supposed to be able to go a day without a major case landing in her lap? Or was it that she'd been addicted to the rush of helping people for a long time? It had been a compulsion, doing what she believed she was put on this earth to do.

"You don't have to tell us. It's not really our business," Laney said.

Adrielle looked like she wanted it to be her business.

"Apparently, I'm supposed to have healthy boundaries." Kenna looked at the closest dress, but there was way too much lace. "If I keep getting pulled away to solve cases, Jax and I aren't ever going to get married."

There would always be a reason to put it off. Making it happen was more of a challenge than maintaining the status quo—even with all the ways her life had changed in the past few years. Plus, it sounded good that she'd rather be here than running down a dank hallway chasing a murderer.

At least this wedding thing only happened once in her life.

Then she could get back to work.

"Healthy boundaries are good," Maizie said. "But we're gonna find out what she wanted later, right?"

Kenna nodded, aware of Laney striking up a conversation with her mom and Akira.

Maizie leaned over and whispered. "You think she's one of their assets?"

"She didn't try to kill us."

Maizie said, "Someone from the resistance?"

"That would be my guess." Kenna shrugged, keeping her voice low when she said, "I don't know how to tell the difference yet."

"Me either." Maizie seemed to want to say something else but didn't.

"What?"

Maizie whispered, "We need a forensic accountant to go over what we got yesterday. It's too complicated for me."

Kenna gasped. "You don't know *everything*? Shocking. What do I pay you for?"

Maizie grinned. "Answering your emails and telling people you're unavailable."

"I should give you a raise."

Akira came over to them. She seemed to have shaken herself out of the Ramon-induced daydream. She ran to the end of the rows and came back with a dress. "Try this on."

"How can I resist?"

"And give me that yummy man's phone number."

Maizie sounded like she had a frog in her throat. Once she cleared it, the teen muttered something in Spanish.

Kenna had to say, "I can ask, but he might say no."

Akira sighed. "This is my life. Gorgeous men everywhere and none will let me dress them."

Good thing Jax wasn't here right now.

"But of course, that isn't your problem. You're getting married!" Akira leaned in and spoke quietly. "Is he gorgeous?"

Kenna felt her cheeks heat. "Yes, ma'am."

Akira tipped her head back and chuckled.

Kenna went to the changing area behind the screen. "Maizie, I'll need your help in a minute." She'd have to get the thing zipped up, and that would be impossible even with arms that wouldn't hurt when she bent them behind her back.

No way she could get around them seeing her forearms, knotted with lines of ragged red scars. The doctors had tried to consolidate with each successive surgery, but it wasn't always possible.

That was probably part of the reason she shied away from the idea of a big wedding with lots of people. If she kept it small, then it was contained to people who either knew what had happened to her or who had seen her scars enough times they wouldn't create a spectacle.

Kenna unlaced her Converse and kicked them off, then stepped into the dress and pulled it up. It was simple, Victorian-style draped layers in a slightly off-white color. Some pattern on the bodice but understated.

"This whole thing is ridiculous. I'm not going to wear a dress."

Maizie grabbed the zipper at the back and eased it up. "Aren't you supposed to want to see the look on his face? You're gonna make him choke on his own tongue."

"Why do I care about 'supposed to'?" There were plenty of those in her life that she'd never experienced. A house with a fenced yard and a dog to grow up in. A mother to drive her to school. A baby that lived. A career and a life, a family.

She turned around.

Maizie's eyes widened. She said nothing, just backed up.

"This thing is poofy. I have to kick it out in front of me, or I'll trip on it."

"It's not that poofy. You just never wear anything like it." Maizie smiled like she had a secret while Kenna emerged from behind the screen. "It's called a dress. I'm gonna choke on *my* tongue now."

Laney and Adrielle both had their hands over their eyes.

Akira waved her to the podium. "Stand here and we will do the big reveal."

Kenna didn't look at herself in the mirror. It didn't make that much difference what this thing looked like. She was sticking with her slacks and bodice idea, thank you very much.

She fluffed the dress so it draped instead of tangled. Fine, the skirt wasn't that poofy. She fluffed it out some more so that it draped over the podium.

"I'll need to take it up a little." Akira stepped back. "Look now, ladies!"

Laney and Adrielle lowered their hands from over their eyes, and both gasped.

"Is that good?" Kenna asked.

Laney nodded. "It's *so* good."

All Kenna could think about as she stared at their reactions was how she'd never done this with Bradley. They'd been engaged when he died, but really only because she was a few weeks pregnant. Barely engaged, hardly pregnant at all.

They were about to tell the FBI about their situation. Working on what they were going to do about it. Making plans for the future that never got this far because he'd died. She'd lost everything and managed to continue.

Their chance had been over practically as soon as it began.

Kenna felt the burn of tears in her eyes and turned away, but that gave her a look at herself in the mirror. She didn't recognize the woman looking back at her. She'd never met this version of herself, the one who was going to be a wife. Maybe a mother.

Her gaze zeroed in on her arms and how awful they looked. Everything else clean and tidy, except the skin of her forearms. Ragged and red.

Moving on meant carrying the horror of the past with her because it had been carved into her skin. She couldn't leave it behind. It had been washed away, but the evidence was still there. Like Jesus after He'd been crucified. Not that her situation was *anything* like His. Just enough that she could understand a small part of what it meant to see the scars and remember what happened. Every day it was there.

She would never forget.

She'd read that verse recently about having fellowship with Him in His suffering. At the time, the meaning had eluded her, but now that she'd had a tiny glimpse of it, she was humbled by the immensity of what He'd done for her.

A tear rolled down her cheek.

"You don't like it!" Akira rushed over. "We find something else for you to try."

Kenna shook her head. "Sorry. It isn't the dress." She took Akira's hand. "The dress is beautiful. It's kind of perfect, actually. There's just a lot of things going through my head right now."

Akira stood beside her, on the floor instead of the podium. She barely came up to Kenna's waist but still reached up and took Kenna's hand. "White silk gloves that go to your elbows?"

"I didn't even think about that." Maizie came over to stand on Kenna's other side. "I don't even notice them now."

That probably wasn't true, but she appreciated Maizie's attempt to make her feel better. "Thanks, Maze."

What was she going to do about her forearms?

Maizie said, "When you marry Jax, will you guys adopt me so I can have his last name?"

Kenna flinched. She flipped the end of the dress around so she could face Maizie, touching her cheeks again. Drawing her close. When had it become this kind of day? She leaned in and smiled. "Yes."

Maizie's eyes glistened with tears. "Thanks, Kenna."

She whispered, "We need a case."

Things were getting far too real. Too emotional. Too... everything, and Jax wasn't even here! Secretly, she was a little overwhelmed by the idea of getting married. Some people might think their relationship had progressed slowly, but all she could do was try to figure out how to slow things down.

Maizie laughed. "You're the one who sent that woman away."

"She was interrupting this." Kenna swept her arm down at the dress. And it was a lot. It was enough.

But in the story of her life, this wasn't the way she'd thought it would go.

Not yet.

Maybe not ever.

"If we're lucky, maybe something crazy will kick off at the wedding show." Maizie chuckled.

Kenna's phone started to ring, tucked in her clothes. She stepped off the podium and glanced at Adrielle and Laney. Both of them had red noses. Laney sniffed, and Adrielle dabbed a tissue under her eye.

"It's Jax!" Maizie ran out from behind the screen.

Kenna answered the call and put the phone to her ear. "Hey."

"It's going well?"

Kenna glanced at herself in the mirror, and from this angle, she could see both Jaxton women still sitting.

Maizie sat on the floor crossed-legged beside them and said, "This happens a lot. Sometimes, she talks to him for *hours.*"

"Kenna?"

"Huh?" She cleared her throat and focused back on the call, trying to remember what they were talking about. "Things are good."

"That's good. I got a call from local law enforcement there in Denver. I guess someone watches the news, and when your name popped up in their system, they called the FBI office in Phoenix to ask for me."

Kenna frowned. That was going to start happening more and more in the future. Even if the wedding happened quietly with not many people in attendance, word would get out within the law enforcement community.

Jax said, "The Denver PD has a crime scene they're working, and the DNA left behind came back as a familial match...to you."

"Me? That makes no sense." She didn't have any close living relatives except... "My mom?"

"I guess it's possible."

"It's insane is what it is."

"They want to know where you are so they can pick you up for questioning." He didn't sound all too happy, and she didn't blame him, but she figured it wasn't for the same reason she was unhappy about this. "But we have no information on this, so you'll be going in with no idea what the case is or whose DNA this might be. It could be a cousin, for all you know. Or your dad's DNA from years ago."

"So I'll find out. Then we'll be back to what we're doing." She glanced at Maizie and saw the teen had a bunch of questions. Kenna mouthed, *Get Ramon.* Then she said to Jax, "Don't worry. We're all good here."

He was all the way down in Phoenix. No need for him to be distracted by what was happening here in Colorado. After all, if anything did go down, he'd be too far away to help.

"Right." Jax dragged the word out.

Kenna ducked her head and smiled. "I've got this."

"I know you do."

"But?"

"Nothing."

If she pressed him, would he tell her he was ready to quit his job so he could be around her all the time? Working together. Solving crime. "We need you in the bureau."

Jax chuckled. "I might not quit today. Ask me again tomorrow."

"I'll find out what they want."

"Good. Call me later."

He hung up.

Kenna turned to Akira and said, "We'll take the dress."

Chapter Five

Kenna stepped out into the hallway rather than heading back into the auditorium. Ramon was already out there, talking to Maizie. Kenna held the door for Adrielle and Laney, who both stuck near her to say goodbye.

Adrielle gave her a gentle hug.

"Didn't go the way I thought it would." Laney gave her a hug as well. "But you got a dress."

"We cried. We laughed. We shopped."

"Dinner tonight? I can find a place," Adrielle said.

Kenna nodded. "That would be nice."

The two of them wandered off, and at the end of the hall, Kenna spotted the woman who'd come into the room earlier. She watched Jax's mom and sister but didn't follow them. Instead, she turned to stare at Kenna.

Who waved her over.

While the woman walked to them, Kenna crossed to Ramon and Maizie and caught their conversation.

"She did?" Ramon looked like a proud uncle.

"It's gorgeous." Maizie grinned.

Both of them looked like they'd won something.

"We might have a case."

They snapped around to face her.

"If you two aren't busy."

Maizie didn't quit smiling. Ramon's facial expression was more like a smirk. Their body language told her everything—both of them were enjoying themselves immensely.

As the woman drew near, Ramon shifted slightly in front of Maizie, who leaned against the wall behind him. The woman had seen her. But they already knew their enemy was aware of the teen's existence, where she'd come from, and where she lived now. It was up to them to protect her because they certainly couldn't change the fact she'd been exposed by them.

Their enemy had been watching all of them.

The question was, what did they want?

And what did this woman have to do with it.

"I'm Kenna." She motioned to him. "This is my associate, Ramon."

He said, "The empty Starbucks cup was a nice touch."

Neither of them introduced Maizie, and it looked like the woman might've been expecting it. "Roxanne. Nice to meet you all."

Sure it was. "You wanted to talk to me?"

The first inkling of a frown appeared on her face. "I have a problem, and it requires your help."

"Does it have anything to do with a police crime scene?"

Roxanne seemed surprised Kenna knew. "Actually, yes."

"Okay, then." Kenna tipped her head. "Let's go check it out." She glanced at Ramon.

He said, "Later."

Maizie had said that only a forensic accountant could

help make sense of the information they'd gained yesterday, so she may as well get started with that. "Call Jax and ask for a recommendation for what you need."

"Bye."

Kenna kept her smile to herself, figuring the two of them wouldn't be walking through the wedding show getting ideas. They were more likely to head back to the RV where Maizie could get to work while Ramon protected her.

The guys—Stairns, Ramon, and Bruce—had obtained a Class C, which they stayed in. Parked in the spot next to hers at the site. They'd opted for that so they could be nearby, but who would get custody of it when the trip was done remained a mystery.

"I can drive." Roxanne glanced after Ramon, similar to the way Akira had looked at him.

Kenna figured ignoring it was best. His personal life wasn't part of their working relationship, and if he wanted to start something, he could figure it out himself. He seemed content protecting Maizie when she was in the field, but that wouldn't last forever.

Roxanne walked with her to a set of doors, through which was a concrete half a dozen steps that led them outside to a breezeway between the hotel and the parking lot structure. From there, they headed through another set of doors. She drew the rental keys from her jacket pocket and waved to the far side of the structure. "That way."

After wearing that wedding dress, and the emotional upheaval that came with it, she'd changed back into her cotton cargo pants. The ones with huge pockets and some stretch for maximum door-kicking.

At least the wedding dress had that going for it. If she had to, she could fight in it.

Not that she was planning to do that.

Roxanne clicked the button on the key fob and started the car. Kenna slowed to stand by the back bumper.

"Now that we're out of earshot of anyone, why don't you tell me what this is about?" Before she got in the car. If it came to that, Kenna had plenty of weapons on her, but if Roxanne turned out to be an asset of the company, then Kenna would have to be careful. Assets could be lethal.

Roxanne turned to her. "You probably know who I work for."

"Depends. Are you part of the resistance or loyal to your Grand Master?" At the least, this woman was bred to be genetically superior than the average person. Smarter. Faster. Kenna had been as well, but with her arms, she would be at a serious disadvantage.

"You think I'm going to incriminate myself?"

Kenna shrugged. "Wouldn't it be nice to tell someone the truth for a change?"

Roxanne laughed. "And have you turn that information over to the wrong person? The company takes me out, and your hands are clean because they did the dirty work for you."

She really thought Kenna would give her enemy information on its assets who were members of the resistance? "You think I'd purposely end the lives of good people trying to do the right thing in a horrible situation? Even to reduce the number of assets in the world?"

"I don't know." Roxanne mimicked her shrug. "Would you?"

She wasn't likely to accept the argument that, in a way, those men and women were Kenna's brothers and sisters. Who knew what Roxanne would think was a believable response?

"I guess you'll find out," Kenna said. "Now, tell me who it is that has familial DNA to mine." For all she knew, it could be any of them—all created in a lab with donated cells.

"One of our assets."

"Resistance?"

Roxanne hesitated a second, then said, "Yes. That's how I know."

But she wasn't going to admit it aloud, in plain language. Kenna figured that was probably what had kept the resistance alive so long.

And her mother.

"Who is this asset to me?"

"I guess DNA testing will be able to tell you. Things within the company are far too compartmentalized for me to know one person and their situation."

"Okay, so what *do* you know about this one?"

Roxanne glanced around. "Get in and I'll tell you on the way."

"Are we going to be able to look at the crime scene? The cops will have it locked down."

She tugged open the driver's door. "I figure you can talk us in there."

Not too likely, but showing up at the scene was a sure-fire way for those detectives—or whoever had called Jax asking after her—to find her.

Because she was coming to them.

The real test would be what Roxanne did when the cops showed up.

Kenna buckled her seat belt, shifting so her phone and a weapon were within reach. The last thing she wanted was to miss out on her wedding *again*. Wearing that dress brought up so many thoughts about Bradley and some great spiritual revelations she hadn't considered before.

Right now, she needed to focus, though. Being all twisted around internally wasn't going to help her make sense of familial DNA at a crime scene.

If Roxanne didn't plan to tell her who this person was in relation to Kenna, the only alternative was to guess. The one person in the world she knew of that was connected to her genes, at least for certain, was Amara Constantine.

But if her mother was an asset for the company, then that meant not only had she faked her death when Kenna was a toddler, she'd also gone back to work for them. Either for the resistance or because she had no other choice. Though there was another option—that Amara had changed her mind and agreed with the company's endgame.

More likely, she was a double agent, using her position of trust to undermine them. Pretending she'd changed her mind. It might even be what had kept Kenna's father, and Kenna, alive for so long. Her dad had passed away years ago now, but he was still a huge part of who she was.

Roxanne pulled out of the parking structure.

"Start talking." Kenna glanced over, glad to not be the one driving so she could focus on assessing this woman.

Different clothes and hairstyles, and she could come across as all kinds of thirty-something women from a number of walks of life.

Roxanne said, "Two weeks ago, we lost contact with our asset here. I was sent to find you and gain your assistance in helping to find her."

They probably figured if she thought the missing person was family, she'd be all on board to help. But what if the missing woman didn't want to be found? "What do you know about her?"

"Not a whole lot, actually. Things are so compartmentalized I only have a code name. Chimera. As for what she was working on, she'd checked in that she was meeting with someone, but that was the last we heard."

"You must burn through a lot of assets letting them go out on their own like that. Seems like you'd do better to keep track of them."

Roxanne glanced over. "I'll submit that as a suggestion for the future. You know, because the higher-ups are so good at taking constructive criticism."

Kenna didn't smirk since Roxanne likely wasn't trying to be funny. "I already know they don't care much about the value of a life. But if you had any information about the extent of their operation here in the US, that would help me fight them."

"You mean clean up the mess *you* made."

"What's that supposed to mean?"

Roxanne took a corner way too fast. "You took down the Rosenburgs. Now the company has nothing to push back at them, they can take all the territory they want and get a foothold here in the US."

"So, it's my fault for creating a power vacuum for people looking to steer society where they want it to go?"

"You said it, not me."

"The Rosenburgs had their hooks in every level of US society. Private stockholders, government lobbyists. Healthcare. The media. Higher education. They even had someone in the FBI. That kind of corruption isn't something I'm going to allow to continue if I can help it. The alternative to us being in a war against this 'company' as you all call it is that people like the Rosenburgs have the country in a stranglehold. So I'll pass."

"Except now you have to fight us whether you like it or not. And the company is so much worse than one family."

Kenna said, "That's life, I'm afraid. You take down a bad guy, and another comes along. Sometimes, they're worse. Not exactly where I thought I'd be when I set out to catch killers and find missing people, but if taking them down makes it safer for ordinary people to live their lives, then that's exactly what I'm going to do."

No matter that the president had effectively told her he had it under control. And he'd asked Jax to sign a nondisclosure about his mission to connect with the resistance so the US could help them. She was up against an international organization. No walking away.

And thankfully, she wasn't alone.

She continued, "But it's always been about finding a missing person. That's the core of all of this. It's about protecting lives. Especially when it's family." Making sure no one else had to go through what she went through the night Bradley lost his life. Not as far as she could help it, anyway.

So, if this organization wanted to manipulate her, they'd pressed the exact right button. They knew what tune to sing to get her to help Roxanne without even really thinking about it.

They'd made it about family.

Roxanne said, "Then this is right up your alley. And you could get the answers you're looking for."

That was what she was afraid of. "She's your asset. Why don't you find her?"

This woman had to be trained. There was no way she wasn't. Whether she was here officially or under the radar, she had skills. Why involve Kenna? Unless they needed a scapegoat.

Kenna had to tread carefully with this, or it would blow up in her face.

And sometimes, that happened literally.

Roxanne said, "Aren't you the one looking into the operation, trying to find a way to fight back? At least, I figure that's why you broke into that finance company and copied all their files the other day. Finding this woman and uncovering what she was working on will be another blow. The resistance might even...owe you."

And how did she know all that?

Regardless, it seemed they didn't understand Kenna and what drove her, but she wasn't going to let on about that. Instead, she said, "I guess the resistance needs my help, after all."

"You can't blame them for being insular, given the threat. Or for being wary of outsiders. Proud and wanting to do it themselves."

"They've been at this a lot longer than I have. Even as long as I've been alive, someone has been fighting. Trying to regularly deal a blow to the organization's operation. If I wasn't a threat to the company, then that woman wouldn't have tried to shoot Jax and me in Greece."

She watched Roxanne for a reaction to that, which might be telling one way or another. Or not at all.

Her expression shuttered. Roxanne pulled onto a side street and into the parking lot for a low-budget motel. Good place for a clandestine meeting.

Not many cars were in the parking lot, probably due to the crime scene tape across one door on the upper level.

Roxanne said, "You wanna live a long and happy life, that's your business. The rest of us want to stop the company from hurting people. And if you'd like to help, this is how we're gonna do it."

Chapter Six

Kenna pushed open the car door and got out. Smoke lingered on the air, along with the earthy tang of something else. Trash littered the parking lot in a few places. The cars were either older high-end models or the kind of rusty compact that looked like the engine was about to fall out.

An unmarked police car pulled into the lot at the far end. Antennae for their radios on the roof was a dead give-away, along with the unit for a blue-and-red flashing light at the bottom of the dash window, though it was currently dark.

The engine revved in the car she'd just been in.

Roxanne pulled away from the space and left the parking lot in a hurry.

"Great." Kenna turned back to the cop car and watched them pull up by the stairs. Two detectives got out, a male and a female. Both wore dark-colored suit pants and a white shirt, over which the woman had pulled a dark green cargo jacket.

They both had short hair, though the man's was about

as rumpled as his suit. The woman had gelled her pixie cut to lay close to one side of her face.

Instead of going to the stairs and up to the crime scene, they crossed to her.

Kenna asked, "Who ratted me out?"

The woman said, "Your boyfriend told us to wait an hour, then try the crime scene. Lo and behold." She waved at Kenna.

"He told you where to find me?" At least it was intel that gave them something to do. He'd probably figured if she didn't want to be found, then she wouldn't do the obvious thing—come here. "I guess that means I have nothing to hide."

The male detective eyed her. "We're the ones who'll make that determination."

"Kenna Banbury." She held out her hand to the woman. "I'd love to know where you got that jacket."

The woman grinned. "Detective Naomi Langford. Give me your info. I'll send you a link."

Kenna shook hands with the other cop as well. He said, "Detective Sebastian Davis. Nice to meet you and all that."

"What can I help you with?" It was better to act like she knew nothing and needed the information from them rather than having these people think that, somehow, she knew more than they realized.

Davis sized her up. "Have you ever been to this establishment before?"

"No."

"Do you have any close relatives, a sibling or cousin, parent or aunt or uncle who might have?"

"I would have said I don't have any of those things. No living relatives that I'm aware of. But I guess that's not true anymore, is it? I mean, it can't be." She channeled a little of her feelings about the fact her mom was alive, when she'd believed for years that the woman was dead, into her words.

"So there's nothing you can tell us about this?" Detective Davis shut down, realizing there wasn't much more that Kenna could offer to his investigation if she knew nothing.

Which would mean she was shut out, barely a witness or someone they could tap for information. "I'm sure I could tell you a lot since investigating missing persons cases is what I do."

A lot of cops didn't want private investigators in their business at the best of times. This guy was probably one of those and had no intention of asking for her help. Any minute, he'd explain that to her in no uncertain terms, and then Kenna wouldn't be able to do anything without defying direct instructions and winding up in trouble.

Fortunately, Detective Langford said, "So tell us."

Kenna wasn't sure Naomi was ready for the conversation about genetically altered kids born every generation, operators and assets, an international conspiracy, and an underground resistance. She barely had a grasp on it herself. She would do what she could to fix the problem, though she didn't want to be blamed for opening the door for the company to start encroaching on US territory.

After she'd taken down the Rosenburgs, the company exploited the power vacuum, where they hadn't been able to get a foothold before, which was just part of what happened. Evil would keep trying to win ground, and good people would continue working to bring justice.

Instead of getting into all that, she asked, "Two people were in the room? And they're both missing?"

"Presumed dead, given the amount of blood," Davis said. "And yes, they're missing."

"Suspects?"

"This is an ongoing investigation." He lifted his chin.

Langford said, "You can understand that."

They were testing her to see how cooperative she was going to be. Kenna said, "I've learned in the last few months that I may have siblings, or cousins, with DNA similar enough that one of them would be a familial match. But I believed they were all in Europe. At least, for the most part."

"But you don't know?" Langford seemed suspicious.

Kenna didn't blame her. "It's a long story, but I believe one of these women might be the one who was here. It might actually be my mother."

She hadn't quite acknowledged it yet, but it made sense now. After all this time, though. Why would her mom be here, so close? Or working for them...

The resistance.

She must have never left that group. Which meant she'd never intended to devote everything to protecting her family, because if it had been Kenna, she would never have gone back. She'd have taken her husband and that baby in her care and never looked back. Saving one life—and making a family—was surely more important than going up against an organization like that.

Only wasn't Kenna doing the same thing? Making a family and resenting facing the organization.

There were international groups, intelligence agencies, and governing bodies whose job it was to fight that fight. One operative couldn't possibly do it all.

Rather than do it all alone, Kenna had her family to help her.

They were all going to do this together.

"We can take your information," Davis said. "Keep you apprised of what we learn."

"Can I see the scene?"

Langford glanced at her partner. "It has already been processed. Anything to find has already been found."

Kenna waited for the two of them to agree.

Davis said, "I'll go talk to the manager about the security tape. You take her up there." He looked at Kenna. "No touching anything."

She nodded. "I know the rules."

Kenna and Langford headed for the stairs and up to the second floor. She glanced over at the female detective. "How long have you two been partners?"

"Six years now." Langford stowed her cell back in a clip on her belt. "First time in Denver?"

"You know what?" Kenna said. "I have no idea."

Langford glanced over.

Kenna shrugged. "Maybe we came here when I was a kid. My dad and I drove around a lot, and he worked cases. We pretty much lived on the road."

"I've heard a little. Davis is the one who knew who you were the minute your name popped as a familial match. He'd never tell you this, but he's a huge fan of your dad's books. He's in this group on social media that speculates about the true cases behind the ones your father wrote about. I guess it's like a fan club."

Kenna said, "If you say so." She had no interest in notoriety—or speculation. The truth was hard enough to grasp. And that was without a group of people she didn't know going down rabbit trails of guessing.

"Nothing? No social media?"

"I guess not nothing." Maizie had set up some accounts to funnel people in the right direction if they genuinely needed help. "But there's enough going on in the real world to keep me occupied."

Langford chuckled. "That's true." She drew out a set of keys and unlocked the padlock on the door, then pushed it open.

Kenna had to duck under the crime scene tape.

"Stick by the door. Don't make me go get my booties from the car."

"Got it," Kenna said. "I just wanted to take a look."

"No photos."

Kenna glanced at her. "How about a light?"

"The switch is to your right."

Someone had replaced the regular bulbs with red ones, casting an odd glow across the room. "Interesting."

"That's what I thought," Langford said. "Tell me what else you notice."

Kenna shone her camera flashlight around. "The bed was largely untouched. Maybe they weren't here for long enough or weren't here for that. Did you get an ID back on the second set of DNA?"

"Male, a few parameters other than that. But nothing popped as far as an ID. He isn't in our system, the federal database, or military."

"Hmm." She kept shining the flashlight around, scanning the room where she could see it. Definitely not a full picture, given she couldn't walk through the place. "Bathroom?"

"Untouched."

"Security video?"

"That's what Davis is getting. Whoever was in here was incapacitated."

So they were subdued, apparently in a way that cost them a lot of blood, and then taken away? Perhaps for the killer to bury them elsewhere. Or they were going to continue the party.

Kenna said, "Maybe they needed them together, and this was the only way to manage it. Or these two were just unlucky."

They might have been specifically targeted or chosen completely at random. Most killers who intentionally set up a death chose the victim because they fit the need. Stalking them. Preparing. Incidents like this weren't usually random, but the mess with this scene could indicate something went wrong.

"You think they fought back?" She didn't see any destroyed furniture.

"You know what I think?" Langford asked.

Kenna ducked under the tape and stepped out. "What's that?"

"I think he was the target. More blood loss. Her DNA was in minimal amounts." Langford leaned against the balcony rail and folded her arms. "His was more extensive. Maybe she lured him under false pretenses with the intention of taking his life."

"You think she might've been the perpetrator?" Kenna also leaned against the rail and saw Davis leave the main office. "It could just as easily have been the male who lured her there, and he was injured when she defended herself."

"There's certainly no evidence a third person was here."

"That only means that if there was a third person who took them both, they're smart."

Langford nodded. "I guess the security tape will tell us if they left on foot of their own accord or if they were carried out of here." She glanced over her shoulder as Davis approached them.

The look on his face didn't bode well, but perhaps that scowl was normal.

Langford asked, "Footage?" with a little hesitancy in her voice.

Davis stuck his hands in his pockets. "There's nothing. Someone came in and took a copy, claimed they were police. Had ID and everything. Any files that remained have been mysteriously corrupted. If there was anything on the security footage, we'll never see it."

Kenna asked, "Can the employee describe the person who came in?" If they were pretending to be an officer, that was a serious offense, and interfering in a case was even worse.

"They're asking the person to come in so they can tell us." Davis stared at her. "Any idea who it might've been?"

"It wasn't me or anyone I work with. I can tell you that much." She'd barely been in Denver a couple of days. "All I know about this case is what the two of you have told me. When Jax called and said you were looking for me and why, it was the first I'd even heard about it."

Davis didn't look convinced, but it wasn't up to her to change his mind.

It was only up to her to have integrity in her life and her work—and the living out of the faith she'd claimed.

People could believe what they wanted to believe.

"I should be going. Thanks for your time." Kenna didn't want to seem too interested, and she needed to find out where Roxanne had gone. It wasn't a stretch to assume she was the one who'd taken the footage, and if she had, then Kenna wanted to see it. Whether it was anonymously delivered to these two detectives later would be between her and Maizie. Roxanne didn't need to know.

She shook both of their hands, exchanged business cards, and headed for the stairs, aware that they watched her head down and then away from the front office. On purpose. They didn't need to believe she was fishing for information so she could run a simultaneous investigation.

Even if she probably would be.

Kenna slid out her phone at the corner and dialed Ramon's number.

"Yep."

"It's me."

"Obviously."

Kenna rolled her eyes and heard a car behind her. She glanced over her shoulder and saw the same vehicle approaching, Roxanne in the driver's seat. "I was gonna ask for a pickup, but my ride just showed."

"We're at the campsite. All good?"

"I'll be there."

Ramon said, "Bring chips. We just ran out."

Kenna hung up and waited for Roxanne to pull up. As she slid in, she said, "Didn't want them to see your face because you're the one who has their security footage?"

"Among other reasons. I need to maintain a low profile, okay?"

"To keep from being arrested?"

Roxanne shrugged one shoulder. "Finding our asset doesn't happen if we're constantly interrupted by law enforcement. Or waylaid by them. Did you see the crime scene?"

Apparently, she'd been too far away to see Kenna go in. "I did."

"And?"

"The cops don't have much."

Roxanne said, "Envelope behind you on the seat."

Kenna reached back for the thin manila, stuffed with several sheets of paper. "What's this?"

"Other cases with the same MO."

She slid the papers out. "Here in Denver?"

Roxanne shook her head. "This is the first one in this city. The others are all over but concentrated in Wyoming and Utah motels on highways that are major travel routes for crossing the west."

Kenna leafed through the pages. "Where did you get this information?" Some of these cases went back years. "And why has no one put it together that they appear to be the work of one person who likes to keep their activity to a discernable pattern?"

"You tell me. You're the top-notch investigator." Roxanne glanced over. "I guess you've got a serial kidnapper on your hands. Or a serial murderer."

"One that took one of your assets. How is that possible? You guys are supposed to be the best of the best."

"Even the mighty fall," Roxanne said. "You should know that better than anyone."

Chapter Seven

"Did you put some feelers out to the contacts we've made?" Kenna pulled the car into one of the few spaces in this little public parking lot. It was going to cost a fortune for the privilege of leaving the car here during dinner at the restaurant Adrielle had chosen.

She glanced over at Maizie in the passenger's seat, wearing her nicest black jeans, boots, and a white T-shirt and denim jacket. Her hair was loose and curled because she'd been watching videos on how to do it.

The teen said, "I'm waiting on a reply from the resistance about Roxanne."

"Trust but verify."

"I should write that down. Start a notebook. Kenna's rules for investigation."

"By the way," Kenna said, changing the subject, "you look like a rock star in that outfit. Oh, I know! You actually look like you got famous as a child star, and now you're trying to keep things low-key so no one recognizes you."

Maizie chuckled. "You're weird. And you look like you, by the way."

"That's a good thing."

"Yeah." Maizie sighed. "It is. You look like you'd be ready to chase a guy through the bayou or search through a compound that belonged to a cult in Washington state. Or fly to England and crack a case wide open."

"What about dinner at a fancy restaurant?" Because that's exactly what they were about to do. "Should I have worn the slacks?"

"You're supposed to be comfortable and not care what anyone thinks."

"Some places have a dress code, and it isn't sweats."

Maizie said, "You look fine. Those are your nicest door-kicking pants."

Kenna figured this confusing conversation was probably par for the course with a teenager. Maizie developing her own—sometimes strong—opinions about the adults in her life was a very good thing. No matter what, she would take every drop of normalcy she could.

"I'm going to wear that dress to get married."

Maizie grinned. "I can't wait to see Jax's face."

Kenna grinned right back. "Me, too." She caught the time on the dash clock. "We need to go in. They're probably waiting for us."

Maizie waited until they were out of the parking lot and on the sidewalk before she asked, "What am I gonna say if they ask me where I grew up and stuff like that?"

"Laney knows where you came from. At least the high-lights, enough to know what not to ask because it would make you uncomfortable."

"What about Jax's mom? Don't you want to tell her the truth?"

Kenna said, "Kids have opinions about their parents. And in my life, I have levels of trust. It seems like Jax trusts his sister implicitly. That's why they were invited to Stairns' place last Christmas. But it seems like he keeps his parents a little more at arm's length."

"Like he doesn't tell them everything."

Kenna glanced over. "Most kids don't tell their parents everything even when it's a good relationship."

"Huh. Don't they trust them?"

"It's more about privacy. Or autonomy. You don't have to share all of yourself with someone if you don't want to. Does anyone share every thought they have in their head?"

"I do sometimes...with Elizabeth. But less now than a year ago, I guess."

"Right. Sometimes, we need to be honest because we need to get something out, and then after that, it feels better. We could go back to that level of sharing later, for accountability. Or stick with this. Depends on what's happening, like the seasons. You always wear shoes, but they change depending on the weather. Like how much of your foot they cover and how insulated you want them to be."

Sometimes, it was about protection.

Kenna continued, "I've had seasons in my life where I saw no one for days and rarely talked to anyone unless I was on a case. Look at me now. This season, I've got more people than I know how to handle."

Maizie chuckled. "Deal with it."

"So much compassion." Kenna wiped a fake tear from the corner of her eye and approached the door to the restaurant, aware they were being watched. Probably by Ramon, but it might not be only him. Far as she knew, Bruce and Stairns would be around later to be on hand. Whatever Bruce was working on wasn't happening tonight.

Hard to tell if the itch between her shoulder blades was down to her friends keeping her and Maizie in their sights or someone with a far more nefarious intention. Either way, there was plenty of protection surrounding Maizie. Kenna was going to have to get used to the teen being exposed—out in public where anyone could see her.

Tomorrow, she was going to have Bruce and Stairns sit down with her and explain the whole of what Bruce was working. The last thing she needed, when there was likely a case here, was for her to be distracted by their thing. Worrying if they needed help. Or needing their help when they were tied up. She'd rather work on one case at a time than split her focus.

The maître d' stepped out, holding the door for them. Inside was remarkably warmer than outside. She scanned the place, looking for Jax's mom and sister.

"Table for two?" He was older, probably in his sixties, and wore a black waistcoat over his crisp white shirt. He slid a couple of single page, embossed menus on white cardstock from under his podium.

"I see them." Maizie pointed.

"Thanks," she told the guy. "But we see our friends."

"Have a wonderful evening."

"Thank you." Maizie headed across the room with zero hesitation. Kenna watched her, in awe of how far the girl had come out of her shell.

Adrielle and Laney got up. They both kissed Kenna on the cheek, and Laney gave Maizie a hug. Jax's mother smiled endearingly at the teen.

"This place is supposed to have fabulous sea bass." Adrielle slipped some dainty gold glasses on her nose and looked at the menu.

"How was your afternoon, Kenna?" Laney asked her.

Kenna shrugged. "Not too exciting. I do need to call Jax

later, though. Fill him in. It's nice to be in the same time zone."

Laney seemed disappointed. "I guess there's always tomorrow."

"Looking to get swept up in a case?" The woman was in her thirties and had two elementary-age kids. Maybe she wanted some excitement. Too bad. The last thing Kenna wanted to have to explain to her fiancé was that his sister had been sucked into something dangerous. "I can't say I'd recommend it."

"My husband said the same thing."

Kenna smiled at her. "What about an adventurous vacation? Somewhere exotic."

"That could work." Laney tipped her head to the side. "Oh, maybe a murder mystery cruise!"

Maizie said, "That sounds like fun. But I don't think I want to be trapped on a boat for that long."

"It's a ship, dear," Adrielle said with a slight smile. "A floating tin can with four thousand other passengers onboard, and it's been two days since they ran out of shrimp."

Maizie grinned. "I prefer my Airstream. It's a tin can, but it won't wash away."

"Agreed," Kenna said.

Laney asked, "Have you and Jax talked about where you're going to go on your honeymoon?"

"Not yet." She'd figured some quality RV time. Or they'd head to a cabin somewhere with no cell signal and no way for anyone to track them.

Laney said, "You should go on a murder mystery cruise. You'd win, if they make it a competition."

"With my track record," Kenna said, "we'll end up in the middle of some kind of international smuggling operation or somehow finding a killer who uses the cruise ports to cover up his activity and throw the local police for a loop."

Adrielle glanced at her and blinked.

"I'm thinking that having no one around, just us, might be a whole lot safer." She wanted to explain more, but Maizie's cheeks had reddened.

Adrielle said, "I'd normally hesitate to suggest this, but have you thought about Canada? Somewhere remote, like the coast of British Columbia."

Kenna smiled at her future mother-in-law. "That sounds like a great idea. I should add it to the list."

Adrielle looked back at her menu, smiling. "Happy to help."

Kenna tried not to stare at the woman, but when she'd met Jax's mother earlier this year after they got engaged, she'd seemed a lot different than this. She'd deferred to his father, let him set the tone and steer the conversation. His father was curt and clearly saw things only his way. Adrielle seemed to come out of her shell when he wasn't around.

This woman was one Kenna could grow to love. She didn't have a whole lot of experience with maternal figures in her life but figured they might be able to make this work.

"Thank you."

Adrielle must not have heard her because she didn't look over or say anything. Meanwhile, for Kenna, having something in her life she didn't have to worry about was a breath of fresh air. This woman wasn't a source of stress. Kenna's marriage wouldn't have to be a nightmare when it came to her extended family.

She glanced around and caught Laney staring at her. They shared a smile, and Laney said, "Seemed like you went through something profound putting on that wedding dress, if you don't mind me saying."

Kenna didn't want her to worry. "I did. But I'm good." Another thing to debrief with Jax about, along with telling him about the possible serial killer. "How long will the two of you be in Denver?"

"Trying to get rid of us already?" Laney grinned.

Kenna glanced at Adrielle, who was still studying the menu. She mouthed, *Serial killer*, in Laney's direction and watched her expression change to something more like fear. That was good. Some healthy fear could give Laney a little more levelheadedness. "It's been wonderful seeing both of you."

"And getting all those samples at the wedding show," Maizie said. "What's a remoulade? Did I say that right?"

"Fancy salad dressing." Laney glanced at Kenna. "We have our flights booked for tomorrow morning, unless there's another altercation with a mysterious woman or life-changing moment we should stick around for."

"Might be better to get out of harm's way."

Laney looked at Maizie, then back at Kenna. "You guys be careful, okay? Y'all make me nervous with the crime fighting."

"Honestly, Laney," her mom said. "Y'all? Is that how we address people?"

Laney grinned. "I'm having the steak and pasta. I feel like splurging."

"Oh, good idea." Maizie dropped her menu to the white tablecloth in front of her. "I hope it's as good as Stairns' steaks."

Kenna's phone buzzed in her pocket. She only looked at it long enough to see who the notification was from, not intending to pull it out at dinner.

The text was from Bruce.

> I'm hungry. Y'all are talking about food too much.

She replied.

> She's married.

His response came back almost immediately.

> I have eyes, don't I?

Kenna stowed her phone. When she looked up, she saw someone get up from a table across the room and head toward the bathroom. For a second, she got a look at the woman's face. Her hair was dark brown, the same color as Kenna's, but threaded with some silver strands. Her skin was not quite Caucasian, a little darker, and not just from spending too much time in the sun. As if she might have Greek in her ancestry.

She walked away, winding between tables, and disappeared down a back hallway. Probably the location of the restrooms.

Kenna drew her phone out and stood, making her call at the same time.

"Yo," Bruce answered.

"Back door. Now."

She glanced at the three women at her table. "I'll be back." To Maizie, she said, "Don't move."

Kenna walked as slow as she could without running. She tried to keep the fast walk from drawing attention to herself and finally pushed through the door to the back hall. She'd been right that the restrooms were back here.

And a door that led into the busy kitchen.

A guy glanced over and frowned at her.

She continued walking, and at the end of the hall, the

exit door clicked shut. Kenna didn't bother with the ladies' room since it was far more likely she'd left out the back. A dine and ditch? The restaurant might have security footage to keep them from losing money over that.

Kenna unsnapped the latch on her gun that kept it in the holster, but she didn't draw it from the small of her back. She pressed down the bar and looked outside.

Bruce ran from one end of the building at the back. She let the door shut behind her and scanned the parking lot behind the restaurant, a spot for customers of the neighboring building to use. A few dumpsters overflowing with trash. Stairns ran from the other end of the lane.

They met her in the middle, and she asked, "Did either of you see a woman?"

Both shook their heads.

Stairns said, "The same blonde from earlier, Roxanne, wasn't it?"

"Not her." Kenna gave them a description of the woman.

Bruce shifted his weight from one foot to the other. "You think it was your mom?"

"I'm not sure." Now that the moment was over, she didn't know what to think. "I really only saw her for a second. Maybe she went in the bathroom."

Stairns opened the back door for her. "We'll look around anyway."

"Thanks, guys."

Bruce said, "Enjoy your dinner."

She glanced at him, wondering what that tone was in his voice. He turned away before she could ask, so she went to the ladies' room and found it empty of people. She needed to get back and tell Maizie everything was fine but caught a flash of something as she turned. A plain envelope had been left on top of the towel dispenser. It couldn't have been there long, or someone would've noticed it.

Kenna eased the flap open and tugged out the folded paper.

Lines of text followed each other down the page—what looked like a back-and-forth conversation. A transcript, or an internet-based chat, something like orders given and received. Instructions. She folded it and slipped it into her pocket, leaving the restroom at a walk since the contents of the note hadn't been information about a terror threat or someone's life in danger. Unless it was in code. But it could wait—she needed to let Maizie know everything was fine. That was her first priority.

Her phone buzzed with a message from Stairns.

> Didn't find anyone outside.

Kenna went back to the main dining room. Had that actually been her mom or just a trick of the light? Memory from a photo that had given her a sense of something familiar about the woman.

All for a note that wasn't even a note.

The photo she'd been given at the US Embassy in London months ago had said, *Don't believe anything they tell you.* It was written on the back of a photo of Kenna and the woman she'd believed for most of her life was her mother—Amara.

So, was the novel *The Constantine Initiative* full of truth or lies?

Or was it something else entirely?

Chapter Eight

K enna stood by the sink in her RV because, aside from being closest to the coffee pot, it was the one place not occupied by another person. Ramon, Bruce, and Stairns sat around her table, located between the kitchen and the two front seats. Maizie was back in the bedroom, sitting up on the bed with a tray table desk over her lap and her laptop on it. Cabot, the mutt Kenna had rescued years ago, lay beside her favorite person on the bed.

"Okay, someone start." She took a sip of her drink. "What do we have?"

Bruce shifted in his seat, blocked in by Ramon. The former spy said, "Stairns and I spoke with the restaurant management company. What footage they have is useless. She never looked at the camera."

"She doesn't want to be ID'd." Or found.

Kenna wasn't looking for her, even if she was the woman Kenna considered her mother. If she'd ever wanted to be a part of Kenna's life for the long term, she could have been. At any point.

Kenna hadn't yet written the whole thing off as being too late, but it was close.

She'd had nothing and no one. Now, why would she need a family when this RV was already full of people?

Ramon sat on the edge of the seat beside Bruce, his legs stretched across the aisle. "The asset is getting orders. Doesn't look like CIA stuff to me. They only speak in code. So, are we thinking this is that company? They're telling their asset what to do? She might be part of the resistance, but she's not going to let on to them that she's some kind of double agent."

Across the other side of the table, Stairns lifted one knee onto the seat and leaned back against the window. "That's what I'd guess. If it is her. Could be someone else talking to them. If it isn't the victim, then it might be the lady you met at the wedding show." He raised his voice and called down the aisle, "Maze, did you confirm with the resistance whether they sent that Roxanne woman?"

The teen called back, "They said no one was sent here. They don't currently have any assets in the US that are anywhere near us."

Kenna glanced at Maizie, then back at the guys. "So she's with the company and came to me specifically because I'll want to find this woman. Find her *for* them."

And if the missing woman wasn't Amara—because she'd been at the restaurant—then who was it?

"Maybe they figure you know the terrain," Ramon said. "This is what you do, so you're the fastest route to locating this woman they need to find."

"And she's one of them? Or an enemy I'm going to locate so they can take her for themselves or kill her?" Her stomach turned at the idea of any of those things happening.

"So, you're gonna let her be a victim?" Maizie asked.

Kenna knew that tone. "If she is one of them, I have no reason to want to find her. Except that she's family by DNA. But for all I know, they could've manipulated that to get me to help them."

As far as she was concerned, her family was here. Plus, she was marrying into another family. None of them were related to her by genetics. Kind of like the man she'd grown up believing was her father, the only one who'd taken care of her.

"We're not taking the case?" Bruce asked.

"Of course we're taking the case." Kenna wasn't walking away from this mystery. "I want to know if there have been any similar cases. Everything Roxanne told me needs to be confirmed. The company doesn't want the police looking into this, so they've stalled the whole investigation and given the detectives little to work with."

Bruce said, "Maybe your girl Roxanne is the one who did it, and it's a cover-up. A way to string you along so you're distracted investigating this case that'll go nowhere, and they can do whatever they want in the meantime."

Ramon glanced at him. "You're a very suspicious person."

"I'm astute."

Stairns looked over at his old friend. "It's not paranoia if they really are out to get you."

Bruce chuckled.

"I feel like I'm in a sitcom about grumpy old men." Ramon shook his head, his attention on his phone. "Pizza is on its way."

Kenna tugged out her phone, but she hesitated. Her mind spun with all the questions she had surrounding the missing woman, the person responsible, and how she was going to find them. Not to mention the woman from the restaurant and the company. But she didn't call Jax. Yet.

Better to think through the implications of what was happening first.

Maizie was here with all of them only because Elizabeth had gone on a cruise with a friend of hers. With Stairns here, the teen understandably hadn't wanted to stay home alone with only the dog for company.

Now, she would get what she'd been saying she wanted since almost the first time they'd met. To be in the field with Kenna, working a case.

The time they'd spent in England didn't really count since they hadn't been tracking a killer.

If her team accepted this case, then they might be.

"I'll go outside and wait for the food." Kenna grabbed the door latch before anyone could object, carrying her phone and her coffee mug. She stepped out into the still night, stars visible overhead but not many. They weren't all that far out of Denver, so light pollution from the city meant the full spread of natural light was hidden.

She sank into one of the plastic chairs on the rug she'd laid under the step. Maizie had insisted they put up the awning, and she'd strung fairy lights around the edge so that Kenna could sit in the yellow glow of those lights.

The phone rang once and then connected with the hum of being on speaker. "Hey."

"Driving home?"

"Finally." Jax sounded tired. "But it was all meetings about new procedures for logging time spent working on a case."

Kenna leaned her head back on the chair. "Sounds exciting being the boss."

He chuckled, the sound warm against her ear. "Tell me

about your day. From what I heard, it was a whole lot more interesting than mine."

She recounted the wedding show, crime scene, dinner story. Her mom. The note. The case, and how it might be connected to other disappearances.

"A serial?"

Kenna bit the inside of her lip. "That's what I'm afraid of."

"Are you really?"

"It's an expression. I'm understandably cautious, as opposed to the rest of them who think this is business as usual."

"Isn't it?"

Kenna said, "You're supposed to be on my side."

"Oh, I thought I was challenging you to be a better person."

"That, too." Kenna blew out a breath. "Maizie is here. This morning, she said that when you and I get married she wants us to adopt her so she can have your last name. Am I really going to let her go chase a killer?"

"I'm more worried about the rest of you than the one person all of you are determined to keep safe. And adopting her is a great idea."

"I didn't ever say my worry was gonna be rational."

"Ah." He paused for a second. "Laney said wedding dress shopping might not have been a light and breezy experience."

Kenna was about as excited to talk about that as she was to talk about Maizie helping chase a dangerous person who could target them. "I'm good."

"It can't be easy to be reminded of things you've already grieved. Reminding you of what you lost."

"It was more like realizing what I have now," she said. "And realizing what I was supposed to have had."

"You lost a lot. It has to hurt, and there might never be a day when it's gone."

"I was supposed to have Bradley here. It's not a loss I want to be okay with, but I have you now, and it's a circumstance I'm content with. Otherwise, I'd still be alone." She watched a car drive by slowly, a single occupant in the front. "Is it weird for you? You were married before, and now you're doing it again."

"I'd love to say that was a disaster from start to finish, but there were good times in the beginning."

"There had to have been something, or you wouldn't have married her."

"Everyone was so excited—more excited than me. It was weird."

Kenna said, "So because this time we're taking a more measured approach—"

"You might be." He chuckled.

"Fine, I am. And your mom isn't totally convinced about me. Your dad certainly isn't."

"Green flags," he said. "And for the record, Mom came around. She's a hundred percent Team Kenna."

"Really?"

"You were worried."

"No, I wasn't."

"It's cute."

"I'm not cute. I catch killers." She smiled to herself but refused to let the humor bleed into her tone.

He said, "We all change. We grow. New experiences and new people in our lives leave an impression on us."

"I was fine on my own."

He didn't argue because he knew how she felt about it.

Solitude wasn't a character failing, and it hadn't been about licking her wounds. It had been about having her own space to carve out her own life after she'd lost everything. Slowly, she'd built that back up to where she was now. It didn't mean that time was half of a life or something she needed to "fix" about herself.

He said, "I'm never going to object to you having backup on hand."

"How about pitching in and helping?"

"You want to tap me for my FBI access?"

"Absolutely," she said. "Or I'll need another confidential informant in the bureau. I'll have to cozy up to someone else and get them to spill federal secrets to me."

"I don't think so."

Kenna laughed aloud. "Roxanne, the company asset. Not sure whose side she's on right now. She told me this is one of several cases that are similar."

"You want to know if the FBI is aware. Or even investigating."

"There's not much to go on."

He said, "I'll see what I can do."

"Thanks."

"If you find something concrete that they can run with, pass it to me, and I'll send it over to the Denver office. They'll want to open a case if it needs investigating."

Sure, she was going to just turn everything she had over so the FBI could have her case and do the investigation themselves? Right.

"Kenna."

"Concrete evidence. Of course, no problem," she said. "Pizza's here, so I've gotta go." She did the "love you" thing they did now and hung up so she could use her phone to pay for the food.

Kenna carried the stack of three boxes into the RV. "Why did we need this much pizza?"

At the same time, Bruce said, "You only got three?"

She set them on the table. "While you eat, you can tell us about your old friend."

Ramon slid off the bench and took his slice to the front seat, which had been rotated so it faced in. He sat eating where he could see the whole RV. Like the way a dog in a pack would take his meal away from the others so no one tried to steal it. Whatever issues he had with food didn't matter now. He had money and freedom, so he could eat whatever he wanted whenever. He would figure it out.

But she still prayed for him to find the kind of deep peace she'd found in Jesus. They could use some of that.

Bruce swallowed a huge bite. "My thing doesn't matter. Revenge takes time and planning. If we have a case, then we're gonna work that. I can figure my stuff out after."

Stairns glanced at him. "That's all you're gonna say about it? All that bitterness is going to eat you alive."

Bruce shrugged. "Doesn't matter."

"Whiskey isn't going to solve your problems," Ramon said. "Trust me, I know."

"Maybe not, but it's a decent distraction." Bruce took another huge bite.

Kenna grabbed a slice for herself because fancy dinners were always tiny. She took what was left in the box to Maizie. "The dog doesn't eat pizza." She set the box on the bed.

Maizie looked at Cabot, then at her. "Um, sure."

Kenna frowned. She pointed at Cabot and said, "No pizza," then went back to the guys. "Bruce, what did this guy do to you anyway?"

When Bruce didn't immediately answer, Stairns said,

"The guy is shady as heck. He's probably the one who got Bruce canned from the CIA."

"Guess every time he said he had my back, he didn't." Bruce's expression had a darkness to it that looked deadly. "If we can verify the theory."

"Which is what will take time," Stairns told Kenna.

"I'll think on it while we work this case," Bruce said.

She didn't need to think about that one. "As long as you're not distracted when we need your focus."

"I'm good."

"You do that, and as soon as we're done with this case, all of us can help you. We'll dig into this guy, find everything he's ever done, and take him down."

Ramon said, "There won't be anything left of him when we're done."

She frowned. "That's not exactly what I meant."

Before she could continue, Bruce said, "But it's how I like it."

"Okay, then." They could figure out how to mitigate the fallout of that later. Kenna leaned back against the counter. "We're gonna work this like any other case. We find evidence and witnesses, we narrow our suspect list, and we find this person—and his victims."

Maizie came to the door of the bedroom where the slider sectioned that room off from the rest of the RV. "You're going to let me work a case?"

It could be that Maizie was only standing there to keep Kenna from seeing Cabot eating pizza out of the box, but Kenna didn't ask. "Despite the fact it fills me with abject terror, yes. You're here, so you can work with the rest of us."

"I'll have three bodyguards," Maizie pointed out.

As if Kenna didn't know that. "But when Stairns goes home because Elizabeth is back, you go with him. Deal?"

Maizie lifted her chin. "Fine."

"That means we only have a few days to solve this case before the two of you go back home. So I guess we'd better get started."

The first thing Kenna was going to do was pray this wouldn't turn out to be a giant mistake.

Chapter Nine

"You can't leave me in the van this time."

Kenna pressed her lips together. The teen was right because Kenna was the one who'd sent Bruce and Stairns to follow up on a couple of the other cases Roxanne had given her. Related. Not related. Whether it was a ruse or not, the blood in that motel room hadn't been faked. Someone close enough to Kenna to have a familial DNA match was out there, maybe hurt, and probably in danger.

Maizie smiled. "Besides, I'll need physical access to the computer if I'm going to try and retrieve the deleted security footage."

"Fine." Kenna pulled her jacket on and grabbed the keys to her car, the one she towed behind the RV.

Maizie shoved the laptop in her backpack. Kenna held the door for her, listening to her tell Cabot she'd be back later.

Ramon came out of the Class C in the next spot carrying a thermal cup and rolling his shoulders. Wearing jeans and a Henley, black cowboy boots, and a dark gray jacket with red checkered lining.

Kenna glanced over at Maizie. "We need to find him a girlfriend."

The teen said, "Wouldn't that be weird? What if we don't like her?"

"That's why *we* find her."

Ramon got within earshot. "Find who?"

Kenna wasn't going to lie, so she shrugged. "Who do you think? We should get going." She headed for her car. "I'm driving."

"Right." He sipped his coffee. "Great."

It didn't take long for them to make the drive to the motel. On the way, Ramon said, "So, what are we thinking? Private investigators? Police consultants? Concerned citizens?"

At least he wasn't suggesting they pose as law enforcement. That would open them up to getting arrested. "What about guests checking in? We need to get the layout. See if we can distract whoever is at the desk long enough for Maizie to slip in."

She hadn't been in the main office. She'd been in the room with Langford when Davis went to get the security footage. For all she knew, the computer could be on the front desk or in a back room.

Ramon sipped his coffee. "I could start a small fire in the trash. He'll run out."

"The fire department will show up, take one look at it, and agree it was deliberate."

He shot her a look. "You think I don't know how to make a fire look random? I could slash his tires. Or tell him someone did. Draw him outside."

Kenna wasn't taking the bait on any of that. "You can't guarantee it'll be long enough for Maizie to do her thing." She shrugged one shoulder. "We could pretend we're from corporate and she's an IT tech here to install new software or an update."

Maizie asked, "Will he believe that?"

"You could look older," Kenna said. "We'd have to hit a thrift store and get a change of clothes. It's easier to be guests and do some recon. We need to get into the office but also talk to some of the guests about what they might've seen or heard."

"Wouldn't they have already talked to the police?" Maizie asked.

Kenna pulled into the parking lot of the motel. "Some people will be more inclined to talk to us than the cops. They won't want to open up about why they're here or what they were doing when it went down. They'd rather not incriminate themselves. We're... I was gonna say less threatening, but I don't know if that's true."

Ramon said, "I'll grease some wheels with the desk employee. You knock on doors and find out who was staying here the night those folks were taken."

"I want to hear you do interviews." Maizie leaned forward between the front seats. "I can find out who was staying that night if I get into the computer."

"Let's go." Kenna got out. "Bring your cash, Ramon."

He spoke over the roof of the car, closing the door. "Pretty sure it's your cash."

Maizie got out, grinning like she just got everything she wanted. Kenna let go of a long sigh. "You know, things don't always go smoothly or simply. It can turn out one of a hundred different ways. We might succeed, and we might fail. You have to prepare yourself."

Maizie glanced over as they crossed the parking lot. "I know you've found victims who didn't survive."

"Sometimes, I'm too late, and sometimes, there was nothing I could've done."

"What about people you've never found?" She seemed nervous now.

"It's part of the job. You don't win every time."

Ramon turned back at the entrance. "I want copies of those case files. The ones you couldn't solve. I wanna take a look." He hauled the door open and went inside. "What's up, my man?" Ramon sauntered up to the front desk.

"Good morning." The guy had a middle eastern accent. His hair was cut short, and his dark beard was thick but threaded with silver. "How can I help you?"

"Gotta room for me?" Ramon bellied up to the counter. "Need somewhere to stay a coupla days."

Kenna and Maizie hung back by the door. The office had a counter with a window that slid back, separating him from the lobby, that was big enough it might hold eight people max. Through an open doorway on the side, she could see a hallway with a couple of side rooms and an exit door at the end with a window in the middle, letting light in through the opaque glass. A woman came out of one room, wearing a long black dress draping from her shoulders and a black hijab that covered her hair but left her entire face visible. She had applied her makeup with precision, noticeable but simple.

Kenna crossed to the end of the hall. "Hi."

The woman shot her a guarded look.

Kenna indicated Maizie. "Is it okay if she uses your restroom back here? We've been driving for a few hours, and she needs to...freshen up. If you know what I mean."

"Oh. Of course." She waved at the first door on Kenna's right. "It's in there."

"Thank you."

The woman nodded. "You are welcome."

Maizie slipped past Kenna into the hall, and Kenna turned to lean against the frame, blocking the view back here. From this angle, it didn't seem like the guy could see behind her. Maizie would have a chance to look around a little, and if Ramon distracted the guy long enough, she might be able to get into the computer.

Hopefully, she could remotely access it from the bathroom, though.

Kenna's phone buzzed with a text from Maizie.

Get me the Wi-Fi password.

Kenna smiled because it was such a thoroughly teenage thing to say. She found the guest Wi-Fi displayed on a sign on the far side of the room and sent it to Maizie. Adrielle had messaged her about going shopping today, which meant they had changed their flights, and now she wasn't sure when they would leave.

The last thing Kenna wanted was for either of them to get caught up in this. She'd rather they were on their way back to California right now but wasn't going to order them. Maybe Jax could convince them.

"Thanks, my man." Ramon stepped back and glanced at her. "Your turn, ma'am." As if they hadn't come in together at the same time. "I've gotta use the restroom."

"It's occupied."

"Well, I've got to *go*."

"Go in the room you just booked."

"It's on the second floor."

The desk employee stepped out from behind his counter, into the lobby. "Everyone, be peaceful. This is not a place to argue."

Kenna heard the door behind her and turned to see

Maizie step out. The teen swung her backpack on her shoulders, and her expression shifted to something Kenna had never seen before—a look of teenage disgust that nearly caught her by surprise.

Maizie said, "Are we really gonna stay here?" She practically curled her lip.

Kenna had to keep from laughing. "I guess not." She matched the teenage attitude in her tone. "Let's go."

They headed outside.

As soon as the door clicked shut, Maizie said, "I got the footage. They deleted it, but it's never completely gone. I restored the file and emailed it to myself."

"Did you watch it?"

Maizie said, "Yes. We need to talk to Roxanne."

Kenna turned to her. "Why?" They slowed their walk and stopped in the lane between rows of parked cars.

"I checked the security cameras for the timestamp just before someone deleted the files, and she's the one who took the footage."

Behind Maizie, Ramon stepped out of the office with his key card and came over to them.

Kenna spotted the woman from the hallway. She exited a side door with a bag of trash. "I want to speak to her, see if she remembers anything. Will you send me the image of Roxanne?"

When Maizie indicated she would, Kenna handed her the keys.

Ramon said, "I'm gonna check the crime scene."

Kenna looked at Maizie. "Lock the doors." Only when the teen nodded did she jog over to speak with the woman she assumed was the wife. "I'm sorry to bother you." Her phone buzzed, and she opened the image. "I'm a private investigator looking for some missing people. Have you seen this woman before?"

The wife frowned at Kenna's phone screen. "A private investigator?"

"You know that two people were abducted from your motel?"

"I don't know anything about that." She started to turn away.

"One of the victims was my sister."

The woman stalled.

"Do you have a sister or children?"

She looked over Kenna's shoulder. "Was that girl your daughter?"

Kenna said, "She was the prisoner of a very bad man, but she managed to escape. I found her, and now she lives with me because it's a safe place to heal."

The woman shifted just a fraction. "Show me the picture?"

Kenna held up her phone again.

"I have seen this woman. But only once. I was house-keeping, cleaning one of the rooms. I see her walk past the door." She paused. "That is all."

"Do you know when it was?"

"Before the people were taken."

"Did you see that happen? Do you know who took them? Anything at all could help me find them. Even the smallest detail that you think might not help."

The woman hesitated. "I see nothing."

"Even a tiny glimpse would be helpful. Anything at all." Repeating herself might be redundant, but it might encourage this woman to give in and talk to her.

She started to shake her head, but a commotion on the upper floor drew her attention. Kenna spotted Ramon at the rail with his hands raised. She couldn't make out what they were saying, but she didn't need to.

Kenna ran over and up the stairs. At the top, she spotted a man coming out of the room beside the taped-up one. He held a shotgun pointed at Ramon's chest and wore jeans that hung low on his hips. No belt. No shirt. A chain around his neck and unlaced boots. Hair askew.

She drew her weapon but held it at a forty-five. "Put it down! Put the gun down!"

A woman leaned out of the room and looked at Kenna. "No, he will not!" She wore a tiny skirt and a tube top, her stringy hair hanging nearly to her waist.

"Then I'm calling the police, and they can sort this out."

Thankfully, Ramon didn't move or argue.

The guy with the shotgun, however, said, "You ain't gonna call the police. I'll shoot him if you do!"

"Because you wanna go to jail for life. You'll never see her again."

"What do I care about her? I'm gettin' paid."

The woman gasped. "You said we was gonna go to Florida!"

Kenna said, "You might wanna make your own way there. Your man's goin' to jail." She was guessing possession of a weapon would be the charge or some version of it, depending on how things played out. "I'm calling the—"

"She said it wouldn't go down like this!" The woman shoved her man, who whipped back around to her with a frown. Ramon grabbed him from behind, his bigger size enough for him to get a good hold on the weapon. He kicked the back of the guy's knees, and the man fell to the ground through Ramon's arms, crying out from surprise.

Ramon asked, "She?"

The woman backed up, probably because Ramon now held her man's gun. "What?"

"You said *she*. Someone told you to pull a gun on me?"

Kenna said, "Start talking."

"That's what she said! Eric just got carried away."

The guy was still on the ground, looking disoriented. Perhaps he was high on something. She kept an eye on him. "Keep going. What did she say?"

"She said to tell you what we saw. But how do I know we're not gonna be next? I watch true crime shows." She gasped. "I don't want to get stuffed in a barrel."

"What did you see?" Assuming it was the truth. The woman who'd concocted this might have fed them false information to pass on.

But was it Amara or Roxanne or someone else entirely?

Chapter Ten

Kenna took two more steps. The woman backed into the room a little. Kenna got in her space with all that police "command presence" they had. "What did you see?"

The woman decided to go on the defensive rather than cower. She stuck a hand on her impossibly slender hip. "She said to tell you we saw the guy carry them out. One in the passenger's seat, like it was meant to look like he wasn't alone, and the other on the back seat."

"Anything else?"

The woman shrugged.

"Where's the money she paid you?"

The woman scoffed. "We already spent it." She waved an arm at debris that would usually be associated with a narcotics case.

Kenna said, "Enjoy the rest of your party." She turned and stepped out of the motel room, glancing over the railing to see someone in the passenger's seat of her car. Not Maizie.

Maizie was in the front seat, holding onto the wheel.

"Maizie!" She took off running toward the stairs at the

end, moving fast. Grabbing the rail and swinging herself around the corner to stumble down even though it hurt her arms. She didn't care. The only thing that mattered was Maizie.

The car engine revved.

"No, no, no!"

Maizie hit the gas, and the car lurched forward fast, but she didn't turn the wheel. As Kenna jumped two at a time down the stairs, she could only watch while her car raced at the next row of vehicles and slammed into an SUV head-on.

Almost as soon as it had set off, it was stationary again.

The passenger's door flung open, and Roxanne stumbled out, scrambling to stand before she took off in the direction the car had come. Away from Kenna.

Ramon said, "I'll get her." He raced by her and off the bottom of the stairs to sprint after Roxanne.

Kenna jumped down the last step.

Above them, the shotgun ratcheted and exploded. Kenna ducked her head and angled right, running under the level above so that the guy couldn't aim at her. Ramon raced away, not caring one bit that the guy fired again. Buckshot sprayed out in his direction.

Fully focused on the woman who had just tried to abduct Maizie, Ramon didn't even care that he could get shot.

Don't get shot.

She ran to the far side of the SUV and along the driver's side, keeping her head down. Above her, she could hear the two of them fighting. The front desk employee came out of the door, talking on a phone. Hopefully, calling 911.

Kenna got her front car door open, reached under the airbag, and shut the engine off. She eased Maizie back from the airbag and watched her blink.

"I don't think you need to learn to drive just yet."

Air puffed out from between Maizie's lips.

Something clattered to the ground behind Kenna. She turned far enough to see the shotgun lying on the sidewalk. Above, on the balcony, the partly clothed guy and his stringy-haired girlfriend were making out, and he had her pinned against the wall, her legs wrapped around his waist.

Kenna could not even. "Gross." She turned back to Maizie, her priority here. "Hi." She touched the teen's cheek. "You're gonna have two black eyes, and tomorrow, you're gonna feel like you got hit by a truck."

"Hurts."

"We're gonna get you taken care of. Don't worry." She had a million questions, but all she needed to do was keep reassuring Maizie...and find her ID.

A black-and-white police car pulled into the parking lot, lights and sirens flashing. An ambulance followed it.

Kenna waved them over. The cop had her step aside and explain what'd happened. His partner went to the stairs to talk to the couple, and she stayed with him. Kenna glanced at the EMT, easing Maizie from the car so she could climb onto the wheeled chair they'd unfolded. After a brief assessment, they handed her an ice pack for her face.

The girl looked dazed and not entirely aware of what was going on.

So long as they took care of her, Kenna didn't care about much else right now. She watched for Ramon with part of her attention.

The cop, a guy with blond hair and a soft voice, said, "I'm going to need her ID and yours."

Kenna retrieved it from the car, noting Maizie's laptop was still in there. She tugged the backpack closed over it and tried to figure out why on earth Roxanne would be here. Paying those people to distract Kenna and Ramon, all so she could slip into the car. And...what? Kidnap Maizie so she could coerce Kenna into doing whatever she wanted?

Whatever the reason, Maizie hadn't let that happen.

She handed the driver's license to the cop, holding the backpack close to her front.

"She's over eighteen, then?"

Kenna nodded, assuming that's what the ID said. She actually had no idea. Right now, she could barely even think, which didn't bode well if he was going to ask a bunch of questions.

Another car pulled into the parking lot. One she was familiar with. Langford and Davis. All she wanted to do right now was keep Maizie safe. That took priority over everything, eclipsing even her need for justice in a way that surprised her.

She leaned against her car and spotted Ramon jogging back to them. He caught her gaze and shook his head.

He'd lost her.

Kenna winced. The cop saw it and proceeded to ask her a bunch of routine questions. Was she staying at the motel? What was her business here?

Detective Davis went upstairs, presumably to help the other officer with the two who'd been shooting that gun. Langford came over. She told this officer, "I've got it from here."

Kenna said, "That's the shotgun over there on the concrete. The guy up there"—she pointed to the upper level —"shot at my colleague and me just to distract us."

The officer headed for the weapon.

"They could've killed us." She muttered the words, but Langford heard it. Kenna looked over at Ramon now by the ambulance. "I need to go with her."

"I have questions." She shifted in a way Kenna took as *don't leave.*

"And I'm that young woman's guardian, even if she is eighteen. She isn't going in that ambulance alone. She was nearly kidnapped except that she kept her head and resolved the situation. You can speak with my colleague now and catch up with me at the hospital." Kenna took two steps around Langford, who stepped back and held out her hand.

"Is this about my case?"

Kenna wasn't going to tell her that she had the surveillance footage now. She swung the backpack onto her shoulders because holding it for a minute was fine but longer than that was gonna start to ache. "Ask those two." She waved at the balcony and saw the officer and Detective Davis talking to the couple. "They were paid to distract my colleague and me so that the person who paid them could try and kidnap my friend who'd stayed in the car."

Langford just stared at her.

"The suspect ran off." Kenna took another side step. "Come and find me at the hospital."

Langford nodded, clearly not satisfied. But Kenna wasn't sticking around.

Langford said, "I will."

Kenna strode over to the ambulance. "Maizie!"

She tried to sit up, but the EMT touched her shoulder. "Stay right there, missy."

Maizie lay back down. "I'm fine." She sounded like she had a stuffy nose and was holding an ice pack over her face still.

"I'm coming with you." She turned to Ramon, who was overseeing the whole thing with his arms folded. Looking like every inch the big brother, standing at the open door of the ambulance.

Ramon said, "I'll clean up here, and then I'll be there. Got it, *Hermanita?*"

"Yeah," Maizie called out. She lifted one hand and gave him a thumbs-up.

Ramon motioned with his head for a second. When Kenna moved a couple of steps away with him, he said, "Just confirming, she got away. She ducked down a side street and disappeared. Must've jumped the fence or something."

"It was Roxanne, for sure?"

He nodded. "Get going."

She climbed into the ambulance and moved along the bench seat all the way until she could see Maizie's face. "Hey."

The teen lowered the ice pack, revealing a red and swollen nose and two swollen eyes.

"Ouch."

Maizie said, "It hurts."

"Let's get you to the hospital so we can get you some meds, okay?" Kenna glanced at the window. The driver was a woman. She had dark brown hair pinned back and a ball cap on.

The driver pulled out of the parking lot. Kenna turned her assessment to the male EMT. "Is there something you can give her for the pain?"

"Sorry, the hospital has to sign off on it. She's not critical, so I have to wait until a doctor is available. We'll probably be there by then." He shrugged one shoulder, wearing that big neon jacket. T-shirt under it. Dark blue cargo pants and black boots.

Kenna ran her hand over Maizie's forehead and the top of her head.

The teen said, "I figured you'd be telling the police you want in on the investigation now."

She shook her head. "Not when that just happened. Roxanne paid that couple to shoot at us and to tell us what she wanted us to know. Probably lies. We can talk about this later." Questions about what Roxanne had said to Maizie could wait.

"She told me to drive. So I did."

Kenna smiled. "I really should teach you."

"I wanna drive the RV."

"Yeah...we can talk about that later, too."

The EMT chuckled. "That usually means no."

Maizie lifted the ice pack. "I don't really wanna drive it, so it's fine."

Kenna shook her head. She glanced at the front slider window that had been shut. "How far is it to the hospital?"

"Not far."

"Okay. How far is not far?"

He said nothing.

Kenna kept Maizie in view and scooted to the window. It wouldn't slide open. She knocked on the panel. "How much farther?"

The ambulance bumped over something, and they all swayed. Maizie nearly rolled off the bed. Kenna slid her phone out so she could dial Ramon.

The EMT pulled a gun out and held it pointed at her. She reached for her own weapon.

He said, "Don't. Hands where I can see them."

She held her hands up, using her phone to call Ramon.

"Put the phone down."

It connected. "Fine." She lowered it to the floor with the

call connected. "Where are we going? Because it certainly isn't the hospital."

He stared at her.

"Put down that gun. Even if you're not an EMT, you're still not gonna shoot me." Too many people wanted her to find that missing couple.

The ambulance bumped something again, pulling onto a road that was far less paved. The vehicle shifted and jolted. Kenna held Maizie steady, kicking her phone away from the man. They'd probably disabled GPS in the ambulance if they were smart, so she didn't figure anyone would be looking for it.

"Who says I'm not going to shoot you?"

Kenna shot him a look. "If you wanted us dead, you'd have killed us already." But that didn't tell her who he was or why this was happening.

"Unless we're taking you somewhere so we can kill you without making a mess in the bus."

"Then why didn't Roxanne take care of us? Save you the trouble."

"All part of an elaborate plan."

"Right." More likely, he wasn't with Roxanne. So what did that mean? That he was part of some other group or maybe the resistance. "Whose plan? Yours?" She scoffed, as if she didn't think much of him. Sometimes, that induced a person to share more than they meant to just to defend themselves.

He was about to speak when the ambulance jerked to a stop.

Kenna stood up, reaching for a cupboard. She pulled the door open and rummaged. Nope. She pulled open the next cupboard.

"Sit down."

"Give her pain meds, and I won't keep messing up your *bus*." She threw a few packages on the ground for good measure. Then she found the unlocked cabinet with high-dose pills of normal over-the-counter meds. "Here we go."

She handed Maizie the packet and had her sit up.

"Here." The EMT sighed, then threw her a bottle of water. As if her defiance was inevitable and not that big of a deal in the grand scheme.

So he thought.

"Put that gun down." She sat so she could focus on Maizie while uncapping the water. Or trying to. Kenna gritted her teeth and got it open even though it hurt. "Take the meds."

Maizie put the pill on her tongue and swallowed a mouthful of water.

The back door opened, and Kenna didn't even look. She might've flinched a bit to keep from turning to see but kept her focus on Maizie. "Okay?"

Maizie stared at the open back doors. "It's her," she whispered. "The photo."

"Amara?"

The guy EMT shifted out of the ambulance. She heard him jump onto the ground.

"Yes," Maizie whispered.

Her mother.

Kenna touched Maizie's shoulder. First things first. "Listen to me, Roxanne was going to take you, but you stopped it."

Maizie pressed her lips together. "I crashed the car."

"I'm so stinkin' proud of you right now." She turned her head slightly and spoke louder, still not looking at the doors. "We're supposed to be going to the hospital. In case you didn't realize, she needs to see a doctor." Kenna didn't look over.

From over by the door, she heard, "That's all you have to say to your mother?"

Kenna looked over at the tall woman standing just outside the open doors. "You can't be my mother. She died a long time ago."

It was her. After all this time, the woman holding her in the photo taken back when Kenna was a toddler. The one her father had married, who had claimed Kenna as if she intended to raise her. Then she had "died." Shot to death after a family trip to get ice cream.

Leaving Kenna's father heartbroken for the rest of his life.

Kenna moved then, turning so she could sit on the end of the stretcher. Protecting Maizie from view. "What do you want?"

Chapter Eleven

Kenna had been waiting all her life to have a mother, but right now, all she could think about was the child in her care. Maizie.

"You got my note," the woman said.

It was definitely her. She looked like the photo—Maizie had been right about that. Dark hair with a few silver strands. Smooth skin with not many lines. She hadn't lived a life of laughter. She'd aged well or employed other means to slow time. She wore black khakis and a heavy jacket, her hair loose over her shoulders.

If Kenna didn't know better, she'd think this woman was worried.

And she'd mentioned a note. Kenna frowned. "In the bathroom? That wasn't a note; it was intel."

The woman's expression softened a little.

Until Kenna said, "You think I'm gonna act like we're friends?"

"We're family."

Kenna felt Maizie's hand on her sleeve. "You left me. You didn't want to protect me."

"I died to protect you!"

The outburst made Maizie flinch. Kenna could feel the shift behind her. She just stared at the woman standing in the open door, whose face betrayed nothing of the stress they were all under here. Like she was a spy who could keep her face completely impassive.

If she hadn't just yelled, Kenna might wonder if she cared at all.

According to the novel, *The Constantine Initiative*, it was true that Amara had opted to die to keep the family safe. She had faked her own death to return to the company as a double agent. Always working to safeguard the family she'd left behind. But her father had embellished nearly everything he ever wrote.

So how was she supposed to believe this was the first truthful thing he'd ever written?

This woman wanted her showdown. Or reunion.

But Kenna had to get Maizie to the hospital.

She thumbed at the teen over her shoulder. "She needs to be checked out. So talk, Amara. If that's even your name."

"No one has called me that in a long time," the woman said. "I like to hear it. I've wanted to see you for a long time, Kenna. To let you know I'm alive." She looked past Kenna. "And to meet you, Maizie. I hear you are a remarkable young woman."

"You know," Kenna said, "when people say stuff like that, it just sounds like a giant red flag. A security breach."

Amara looked at Kenna. "Leave this alone." She paused. "Just take care of that woman, the company asset."

"Roxanne?"

Amara tipped her head to the side. "That's what she told you her name was?"

"Any information you have that will lead to her would be helpful. But I'm working the missing couple case." Probably that was what Amara referred to when she'd said, "Leave this alone." But Kenna was only guessing.

Amara lifted her chin. "I don't need your help to find them."

That kind of determination? This wasn't just a job to her—it was personal. The kind of personal it would be if Kenna lost Maizie today or if anyone she cared about was taken. She'd be all set to burn the world down to get them back. Scorched earth wasn't just an expression. It would become reality.

"Who is she to you?" Kenna asked. "Because if there wasn't a personal connection, you wouldn't care so much, I'm guessing."

She felt Maizie shift behind her again and then heard the teen whisper, "Hello?"

Kenna figured she'd picked up her phone and was talking to Ramon. She kept her focus on the woman who was supposed to have been her mother. Who had chosen to be dead rather than raise her. Who'd put the fight for the world in front of family.

The choice had already been made, so there was no point berating this woman for it.

But that didn't mean it hurt any less now than it had every day when she'd been growing up, knowing she had no mother and never would. Seeing other kids with a mom and realizing what she would miss.

Amara finally said, "The missing woman is my daughter."

"And I'm your niece?" She wanted confirmation. She wanted to hear it from this woman's mouth even though she already knew the truth.

"And she's more your sister than anyone has ever been. Or could be."

Kenna frowned. "What? Her father was Malcom Banbury?"

Maizie gasped.

Amara said, "Perhaps you could tell her what it was like to be raised by him. When I find her, that is."

"I don't know what it's like to have a father." Kenna shrugged. "He was barely mine."

"He took care of you."

"He lied to me." She wasn't going to resolve the point with this woman. Maybe she'd been holding on to some things recently, and they'd just spilled out. Fears she'd harbored and hadn't even had the notion to say aloud. "But yes, he did take care of me. Funny how things seem different when you look back."

"I don't need help to find my daughter, and Roxanne only wants to use you to get to *me*."

"What is her name?"

Amara stared at her. "Zeyla."

Kenna repeated the name in her head. *Zeyla.* "Thanks for the heads-up about Roxanne. It was helpful. It didn't stop her from trying to kidnap Maizie, but it helped."

Amara said, "She would've kept her to force you to find Zeyla."

"I was already going to find Zeyla. And the man." Wasn't that a good thing? Despite her words, this woman surely wanted help to find her daughter.

Amara made a face that indicated she didn't think much of the man. "She'd have forced you to find her...faster."

"Tell me how to take down the company."

Amara laughed, but it had a hollow sound. "You can't take them down. All we are is a nuisance, and that only barely." Her British accent, softer earlier, grew in strength now. "None of us can take them down."

"Okay, so how about all of us working together?"

Behind her, she heard Maizie whisper, "Okay." Talking to Ramon on the phone, or so Kenna assumed.

Amara shook her head. "We do what we can. It has to be enough."

Behind her, a pickup truck pulled over on the road, kicking up a cloud of dirt as it came to a sliding stop at the back of the ambulance.

"Your friend, I presume."

Maizie said, "His name is Ramon." She didn't sound nervous. She sounded determined to stand up for herself, even if it was only because Kenna stood in front of her, and it was the two of them against the world right now.

Amara smiled slightly. "I know who he is. You both have some interesting...friends."

He jumped out of the driver's seat, immediately confronted by the male EMT. "Kenna!" He had his gun out and a thunderous expression on his face.

"We're good," she called out. Assuming these people were going to let her and Maizie go, however, and that remained to be seen. "As long as we're free to go."

Amara took a step to the side, leaving the way open for her to get out with Maizie. She grabbed the teen's hand and the backpack, and Maizie brought her ice pack. They stepped carefully out of the ambulance, and then she looked at her mother, not really knowing what to say.

Amara said, "Don't interfere. You'll just get hurt."

Kenna led Maizie to Ramon and slid into the pickup between them. Huddled on the bench seat, Maizie held her hand.

The teen put her head on Kenna's shoulder. "Sorry."

Kenna shook her head. "Don't worry about it." But a tear slipped down from the corner of her eye.

She closed her eyes and let Ramon drive, knowing he wanted a rundown of what had just happened but determined to give herself some time first. For once, she didn't need to process it. She felt almost numb about the whole thing.

Ramon pulled up at the curb in front of a hospital. He left the engine running and came around to open her door. "Maizie?"

The girl stirred, moaning.

"Picking you up, okay, kiddo?" He slid his arm under her knees and behind her back, then drew her out. To Kenna, he said, "Slide over and drive. Call Stairns." He stepped back. "I've got this."

She nodded and found her phone on the seat and the backpack on the floor.

"Go." Ramon slammed the door shut.

Despite his order, she found a parking space and shut the engine off. Gave herself a second. If only she could call Jax, but he was at work and busy, and she probably didn't have it in her to reiterate all of it.

She called Stairns' number. They had gone to investigate another case that was supposed to have been perpetrated by the same kidnapper—killer—who had taken her sister and the man she'd been with.

Her sister.

Kenna couldn't believe her father had not only seen Amara after her "death" and not told Kenna about it, but he'd also had a child with her.

A child who was now grown up and in danger.

Had she been raised in that world, trained to fight the

resistance in the way Kenna had been trained her whole life to be an investigator?

"Hey."

Kenna pushed the thoughts of her sister aside. "Yeah, it's me. What's going on?"

"Found another motel, same kind of incident, but the manager was looking out the window and saw the whole thing. Two people carried out the couple and put them in the back of the vehicle. A small SUV. They just laid them in the trunk. When he ran out the door after them, not thinking but determined to stop them, one of the assailants swung around and stabbed him in the shoulder. They left him for dead in the parking lot."

"He told you all this?" That meant they hadn't been successful.

"Yep. It was a year ago, and the couple was never found."

Kenna said, "The victims or the perpetrators?"

"Exactly. But he saw her face."

"Her?"

"Yep, says one of the two was a woman."

Kenna frowned. "A couple kidnapping couples? That's a new one."

"Got ourselves a murdering Bonnie and Clyde," Bruce said in the background of the call.

"Regardless..." Stairns actually sounded a little nervous. "We should figure out how to find them because no one else is looking."

"Except my mother."

"Huh?"

"I'll explain later. But the resistance wants us to take care of Roxanne and let them find the missing couple."

"And we're going along with that?"

"Of course not." Maybe he was just checking they were on the same page.

"Good."

In the background, Bruce said, "Good!"

"We need to ignore all this international company business and focus on what we know how to do. Solving missing persons cases."

"Agreed."

"We need to know who the guy was and find out what was going on between him and the woman." Her sister. "Figure out how they were targeted."

Stairns said, "You think this Roxanne person knows more than she's letting on?"

"I think Maizie's laptop probably has more information on it than any person we can ask." She reached over and dragged it out of the footwell on the passenger's side. "We need to run everything on the victims. Figure out where they went during the last couple of weeks before they were taken and see if we get any matches."

If each of the victims used a particular gas station or visited the same location, it would be a big clue as to how the perpetrators were selecting them.

"There's someone I need to talk to. See if they have more information than they want to admit." And bonus, they were a couple. "Call me if you figure anything else out."

"Got it."

The line went dead.

She sent a message to Detective Langford, then to Ramon about what she was doing and got a thumbs-up in return. A second later he texted.

They're treating her now.

And looking at me like I did this to her.

Kenna replied that she would get the case file number for him from the police since that was where she was headed. Fifteen minutes later, she pulled up at the police station and went to the front desk. She showed her ID and asked for Detective Langford.

She didn't have to wait long before Langford came through a side door and waved her over. "This way."

Kenna went with her and was led through a series of halls to a bullpen area. She spotted Davis across the way, a few other detectives, and through the glass window on the side, an older woman she presumed was their superior officer standing up while on the phone, gesturing wildly.

"Figured you'd be at the hospital with your friend," Davis said.

"She's covered." Kenna wasn't going to explain about the ambulance. It wasn't relevant to their search for Roxanne, and despite how it had shaken out, she didn't actually want to get the resistance, or Amara, in trouble.

She had Davis give her the report number from the crash so Ramon didn't have to deal with a social worker or the staff calling the cops thinking Maizie had been beaten. Then she said, "Can I have a word with the couple from the motel?"

"Serious charges." Davis leaned back in his chair.

Langford sat at her desk opposite his. That left Kenna to sit in the chair a suspect would use at the end of their desks. She pulled it out and turned it to face them, effectively blocking the aisle. But no one would confuse her for the criminal in this situation.

Langford's lips curled into a slight smile.

Kenna asked, "They have priors?"

Davis nodded. "She has a couple of arrests for prostitution. He's got some assault and battery charges. Five years of time served between them. Neither is going to skate out from under this."

"Are they talking?"

Langford said, "The DA won't offer them a deal, even if they have information that would lead us to the woman who tried to take your friend. You know who she is?"

Kenna said, "Sort of. I know the group she belongs to. I met some of them overseas. They're pretty hardcore. Like they think they're assassins. She's trying to find the victims of the motel kidnapping, but she's going about it by every means except actually looking for them."

Langford looked at her partner, a question in her expression, and when Davis indicated she proceed she slid a file over the desk and held it out to Kenna. "We finally got a match to the man's DNA. It hasn't officially been logged into the case file yet because the minute it gets inputted, someone is going to see it, and the word will get out. Right now, we need to figure out how to control the fallout."

Kenna said, "You know who he is." And the information was significant enough the public would certainly react—likely with an uproar. Whoever the guy was, the fact he'd been taken was newsworthy.

Langford said, "We know who he is."

Kenna opened the cover of the file folder and looked at the image. His name. "Oh boy."

Chapter Twelve

Langford hung back by the wall. Kenna approached the interview table and pulled the chair out and sat down. They'd run it by their lieutenant, but she didn't have a lot of leash here. She wasn't a cop, and they hadn't opted to bring her on as a consultant. If the district attorney found out Kenna had interfered, things wouldn't go well.

"You're more than welcome to have your lawyer come in and be here for this." They were recording, so Kenna figured she'd make this as official as she could. "It's up to you. This is all voluntary."

Ms. Miniskirt Tube Top from the motel had been given a cup of coffee and a sweater that was far too big for her. She turned out to be Sally Morris from Aurora. Nineteen and she'd already done two years in county lockup. She sniffed, holding the coffee cup with one hand on the table in front of her. "What do I care?"

"Perhaps you should, as that would be the decent thing. But we're not here to debate where your life went wrong. Or how you wound up in this situation. You're an individual. You want to change your life? Do it. It's your choice."

Sally sniffed again. "You people always say that."

"Once you start to actually believe it, then things will start to change."

"That's why we're in here? So you can pretend to be my therapist or whatever?"

Kenna shook her head. "I try to help anyone I come across. In whatever way I can help them. But from you, I'd like something in return."

"Figures."

"I need the truth. What happened to those people?"

"How should I know?"

Kenna leaned forward slightly. "Were you in the motel the night they were taken?" She studied the woman for a few seconds. "Maybe you're glad it wasn't you."

"They wouldn't take us. They like us." Given her expression, that didn't seem like a good thing.

Kenna held herself still. "You've met them?"

"Partied with them." Sally brushed her thumb back and forth on the outside of the paper cup. "Until it got weird, and I told Eric I didn't like it. We packed up and left. Gave it a few weeks before we came back to the motel."

Kenna spoke gently. "Who are they?"

"You think we gave each other our real names?"

"But you can ID them."

"They wore masks." Sally bit her lip. "Hers slipped off at one point, so I saw her face."

"Is that typical, hanging out like that when you don't get to see someone's face? Would you be able to describe her to a forensic artist?"

Sally shrugged one shoulder.

"You met them at the motel?"

Sally nodded.

"Did you ever go anywhere else with them? Or meet them anywhere else?"

"They wanted us to come to their house, but we said no."

"What about the car they drove? Can you tell me about that?"

"It was silver."

Kenna could press her but figured there weren't many more details about that to be had. "The police here need your help, Sally. They want to find these people before they hurt anyone else, and you have more information than anyone. That makes you an asset to the police. They might not be able to do this without you."

"How? I don't know who they are."

Kenna shrugged. "Sometimes, we know more than we think. Or we don't want to admit to ourselves what we remember."

"Thought you were gonna ask me about that British woman."

Roxanne. "I'd like to know about her, but the police need to find a pair of killers, and that's more important than me settling a score."

Sally stared at her.

"How did you find the couple? How'd you hook up with them?"

She didn't move, just kept staring.

Kenna waited because this broken young woman, who was most likely facing more prison time, needed to decide whether Kenna could be trusted. And whether the information could be used to buy herself currency with the district attorney.

But was that the reason for her hesitation?

Maybe it was something else. Sure enough, the question was answered when Sally stood up.

Langford shifted but didn't leave the corner.

Sally turned around and lifted the sweater, tugging down the hip of her skirt to reveal a tattoo on one side at the small of her back. Close to a long jagged scar that ran vertically down several inches.

Langford muttered a curse word and came over to stand at the corner of the table. "Is that what I think it is?"

"A QR code." Kenna stared at it, thoughts racing through her mind.

Langford pulled out her phone, opening her camera with her thumb.

"Hang on." Kenna put her hand in the way, behind the viewfinder on Langford's phone.

The door opened. "Find out where it goes." Davis strode in, determination on his face.

Kenna shook her head. "Get a picture of it, but don't click the link. We have no idea who these people are or what they're into. If you use a department phone to get the information, you could be opening your network up to a hack. You need a secure connection that doesn't touch your server."

They needed Maizie.

But considering what this was likely to be, she didn't want a former victim anywhere near the website. Probably a dark web forum or membership portal.

Langford snapped her camera. "I got a good picture of it. Thank you, Sally."

The younger woman turned.

"Davis is going to take you to the forensic artist so we can get an image of this woman. I'll have my lieutenant call the DA's office and explain how helpful you're being," Langford said. "And will continue to be, hopefully."

Sally shrugged. "Whatever."

Davis led the woman out.

Kenna turned to Langford. "You aren't going to ask her about it, where it goes? What she knows about its meaning, or who put it on her?"

"We have a meeting." Langford shook her phone. "The fire department commissioner is expecting us."

They'd had to make the approach using official channels. "And the missing chief?"

"Let's go find out from his colleagues why no one has reported him missing." Langford stepped into the hall, and Kenna walked with her to the main entrance.

"I'll follow you."

"Actually, I'll ride with you. I can find my way back here later."

Kenna said, "That pickup truck."

"New car? Your other is totaled, right?"

"You tell me."

"I guess I'll pass the officer your number so he can give you the tow company info. See where they dumped it."

"This one belongs to a friend." Kenna pulled out of the parking lot. "Tell me about this fire chief, the one who is our victim."

"Chief Hadley. First name Carlton. Married for nine years. No kids. He's forty-two; she's thirty-one. And no one reported him missing? That's crazy."

Kenna said, "This is more interesting than his family and colleagues having no clue and being totally in the dark. There's got to be a reason they don't think anything of it. Which means there might be something to find out from them."

"Huh."

Kenna found a spot to park outside the fire department building, not far from the main police headquarters in downtown Denver. A gleaming building with glass windows all the way up to the top floor. From down here, it looked like the building touched the sky.

Langford walked beside her up the rise of concrete steps.

"I don't miss cities when I'm not in one." Kenna figured it was as good as talking about the weather.

"You know, I looked you up."

"Guess you're not so surprised I like to roam around, then?"

Langford smiled a little. "I guess not."

"Have you lived here your whole life?"

"Born and raised. I'd go other places but the altitude, I'm used to it." She shrugged. Seemed like she knew it wasn't such a good excuse. "Plus, what else do I need? I've got city amenities and mountains to look at. All four seasons, sometimes in one day."

Kenna grinned. "A beach. I prefer them in winter, though. When it's windy and you have to wear a sweater."

Langford frowned, tugging open the front door to the building. "You're an odd one."

Kenna's phone buzzed in her pocket, so she pulled it out. Ramon had texted that Maizie was good, checked out, and ready to be discharged. "I need to get to the hospital after we're done so I can pick up my friends."

"Probably won't take long since this is the last place we're actually going to find Chief Hadley." Langford got them signed in, and they went up to the top floor where the commissioner's office was located.

Derek Shannon was at least seventy but looked like he kept fit. Not just because he had a treadmill in his office.

Langford explained who they both were but nothing about the case.

"Have a seat, please, ladies." He waved them to the two chairs in front of his desk, making the gold ring on the pinkie finger of his left hand reflect the light. He smoothed down his tie and sat in his chair. "You're asking after Chief Hadley? I've made some calls. It's been at least a week since he came into the office, and that doesn't necessarily indicate foul play."

The door opened.

Commissioner Shannon waved in that direction. "This is Chief Martin. She works with Chief Hadley. She will, hopefully, be able to shed some light on the situation."

Chief Martin's uniform was crisp and buttoned up. Her hair pulled back, and her makeup sedate. "Sir, you asked to see me."

The commissioner said, "Enlighten us about Chief Hadley."

"Sir?" She swallowed.

"Explain to these investigators how a man can fail to show up for work for several days and never be reported missing." Commissioner Shannon laced his fingers together on his desk.

"Oh. Well. You see...it's just not all that...unusual."

Kenna glanced at Langford.

The detective said, "He goes missing regularly?"

"I mean," Chief Martin said. "Maybe a couple of times a year. He blows off steam. We all...well, his stress levels rise, and if it's not a busy time and we can take on his duties, it's better for everyone if he takes some time off."

"Paid leave, Chief?" the commissioner asked. "He books out vacation days?"

Chief Martin shook her head, her lips pressed tightly together. "Um, not exactly, sir."

"I see."

Langford asked, "Has anyone ever called his wife because they were worried about him? Or has she ever called in?"

"I don't know why anyone would be worried. He always comes back a few days later or maybe in a week." Chief Martin shrugged, getting defensive now. Likely as a result of being the one in the hot seat. "It's not a big deal. I don't know how it is in the police department, but in the fire department, we cover for each other."

"So, you aren't worried about him?" Langford asked. "He could be dead, for all you know."

Chief Martin frowned. "But he's back."

Kenna said, "What?"

Langford stood. "He's here?"

Martin nodded. "Chief Hadley is in his office downstairs. I thought this was about him getting a slap on the wrist. He came in first thing and closed himself in his office. He didn't talk to anyone. I figured he was catching up."

Kenna shot out of her chair, a hundred thoughts going through her head. If he was back, did that mean her sister was also? And why did no one know they'd escaped? This made no sense.

Commissioner Shannon picked up the phone. "Get me Chief Hadley. *Now.*" He slammed the phone down. "This is unbelievable. Chiefs going off on benders for days, covering for each other. Heads are going to roll."

"You said you wanted to talk about him." Chief Martin winced but then lifted her chin. "You didn't say you were looking for him. I just thought he was in trouble or something."

The commissioner's office door opened again, and the assistant who'd been out there when they came in stuck her head in, a worried look on her face. "Sir, when I called down to the chief's assistant, she said right after she told him you wanted to see him, he ran to the stairs." She shook her head.

"He's making a run for it." Kenna moved to the door, and thankfully, the assistant got out of the way. She jogged to the elevator and hit the down button with Langford right behind her.

"You really think he's making a run for it all the way down to the parking lot?"

Kenna said, "You think he's down five floors by now?" The elevator doors slid open. She chose a floor below ten, just in case. "He'll slow down at some point, too tired to run."

Langford said, "So we're meeting him on the stairs?"

"That's the plan."

"Thanks for filling me in on it."

Kenna grinned and stepped out of the elevator, heading to the stairwell door. Inside, it was several degrees cooler. She listened. "He's stumbling down." She went up, keeping her footsteps light. Langford went in front of her.

The detective slowed a couple of floors later.

Kenna listened for the footfalls but heard nothing. Then a dull thud, or a tumble. She kept her voice low and said, "Sounds like he collapsed."

Langford nodded. They continued up until they found him, sprawled on a landing. "I'll call an ambulance."

Kenna winced. "Make sure it's legit."

"What?"

"Nothing." She crouched beside the chief, who was lying on his side. She pressed two fingers to his neck. "He's pale, but he's still alive."

"Look at that." Langford lifted the hem of his shirt. Something was visible on his skin underneath. A bandage. She pulled the shirt back more. "He was injured, and someone gave him medical attention. Looks like he ripped a couple of stitches."

Kenna shifted to sit on the stair above them while Langford called in the ambulance. Thankfully, given this was the fire department, help wasn't far. There might even be plenty of firefighters with EMT training in the building.

Langford peeled back the bandage. "Whoever did this isn't a pro. Looks like battlefield triage."

Kenna kept her speculation locked inside. It might have been her sister who doctored this man, but she wouldn't admit she knew anything just now. Maybe later. "How did they escape?"

"Good question," Langford said. "Now he's here just pretending things are fine, back at work like normal. Where's the woman?"

"I'm getting the feeling we don't know much about what's going on."

But Kenna was going to get out there and find answers.

Chapter Thirteen

Maizie slipped her sweater over her shoulders. "Seriously? A QR code." She eased to the edge of the hospital bed and stuck her feet into her tennis shoes without unlacing them, wiggling her foot around until the back of the shoe worked its way out.

Kenna had updated her in reverse order, starting with Hadley, who was now down the hall in the emergency department being treated. "Tattooed on her back. No idea where it goes, but the police are going to figure that out. I cautioned them on what device to use. If these people are clever, they've got a way to see who accesses their site."

Maizie nodded. "Probably hosted on some dark web server, so you can't find it unless you have the code."

"The second the police get on there, they could dump the whole site and start over on another. We'll never find them."

"I want to come with you to talk to Hadley."

"I don't want a guy like that to see you, but you can be nearby. With Ramon."

Maizie almost rolled her eyes but seemed to catch

herself before she did it. "Fine. I know arguing isn't going to make you change your mind."

Kenna grinned. "Rethinking me being your mom officially?"

"Because you'll tell me what to do?" Maizie glanced over. "Maybe I *want to* be parented. Could be fun."

Kenna chuckled. "Good thing neither of us knows what we're doing. We can just be happy doing our own thing, and we'll never know if we get it wrong." She grabbed the paperwork, and they headed for the hall past the curtain. "But we're not getting into that. We have our own things to do."

She had been thinking about Roxanne since meeting with Amara. Thinking about her mother—aunt. Whatever. And her sister.

Especially her sister, and where Zeyla might be right now.

"That way." She waved in the direction of the waiting area, and Ramon showed up behind them. He cleared his throat.

"Maybe if we ask nicely," Maizie said. "He'll get us coffee."

"Not in my job description, *Hermanita*. Unless the barista is a killer."

Kenna glanced at his face and saw no humor there. The man was a hundred fifty percent serious about protecting them and bringing justice to the world. Fortunately, he worked with her because Ramon's brand of justice could potentially be a scary thing.

A nurse and then a hospital staff member glanced at them. They probably made an odd group. Two adults who weren't a couple and a teen that could be their child except she looked nothing like them. Misfits who had become friends—a family.

"What else happened with that woman?" Maizie asked. "And did you update Jax yet?"

"I'm going to tonight. And that woman, Sally Morris from Aurora, is working with the cops to give us a likeness of the woman from the pair who are doing this." She found a few seats in the corner of the waiting room where Langford had said she would meet them. Kenna bounced her knee up and down. "There's just..."

"Something?" Ramon sat across from them and stretched his legs out, crossing his ankles. "The case is starting to have more scope, and you can feel it, but you don't know how."

Maizie shrugged. "We can speculate, or I can get on my computer and find out."

Kenna asked, "What about your financial accountant? Did they find anything yet?"

"Let me log on and see." She leaned forward for the backpack by Kenna's foot and then stopped suddenly, letting out a long groan.

Kenna tugged on her shoulder and drew her back. "Easy, Maze. I'll get it."

Maizie leaned her head back against the wall and closed her eyes just as Detective Langford strode in. "You look better than the last time I saw you, but not by much."

Maizie opened her eyes. Bruises darkened her cheeks and around the inside corner of both eyes. Her nose was swollen but not broken. "I didn't get kidnapped, though."

Langford held out her hand like she was asking Maizie to shake it. When Maizie put her hand in the detective's, she said, "I wish every victim was as resourceful as you in the moment. I've seen a situation like that go wrong a thousand different ways, but you're here, and you only have minor injuries. You did good, kid." Langford let go of

Maizie's hand, leaving the teen with a sheen of tears in her eyes.

Ramon shifted in his seat. "You're good, Maze."

He was about to go to war if she wasn't, given the look on his face. Kenna put her arm around Maizie and put the laptop on her lap. When Maizie leaned her head toward Kenna, she kissed the teen on the top of her head. "She's good."

The detective said, "I'm Naomi."

"Ramon." He stood to shake her hand, possibly so she could see he was taller. As if he wanted her to take in his full measure and decide. Because he was certainly interested in her.

Naomi cleared her throat. "Nice to meet you."

What did that expression mean? She didn't have time to figure it out before Naomi turned to her.

"Kenna, we are due to speak with Chief Hadley."

She stood. "Is he awake?"

"The doctor is meeting us down the hall."

Kenna opened Maizie's laptop for her. "You guys good?"

Ramon said, "We're good."

"Yep." She dove in and didn't even look up from the computer.

Ramon smiled, already on his phone. Kenna followed Langford down the hall. The detective said, "I know that your fiancé is an FBI agent in Phoenix."

More than that, he ran the whole office, but Kenna didn't need to add that tidbit. "That's right."

"So, who is the guy?"

"An old friend of mine. He hangs around to help with investigations." Kenna shrugged, not wanting to get into the fine detail of why they weren't prepared to let Maizie go anywhere without someone watching out for her. "I have a couple of other friends also helping out with the case."

"Here?" Langford asked.

Kenna shook her head. "Another kidnapping, in a motel up by Fort Collins. They found a guy who saw the woman's face."

"That's great. When Sally finishes her description, we can show it to the guy and get him to confirm." Langford's brows rose. "Another nail in her coffin, whoever she is."

"Let's find out." Kenna slid open the door, through which she could see the doctor and a nurse with the patient in a bed between them. Hooked up to all kinds of wires, but it looked like he might have regained consciousness.

The doctor glanced between them and handed the tablet to the nurse. "Can I help you, detectives?"

Langford said, "She's a PI. I'm the cop."

"Doesn't mean either of you can be privy to a patient's medical condition. It's a violation of privacy," the doctor said.

"Were any of his organs removed?"

Langford spun around to look at Kenna, which meant she didn't see the look on the doctor's face.

"I'll take that as a yes."

"Where did you get that idea?" Langford asked.

"The scar on Sally's back. The scars on him, and the hack job sewing him back up. Thanks, doc. No need to violate HIPAA rules." Kenna stepped into the room, where the patient, Fire Chief Carlton Hadley, watched her approach. She asked the nurse, "Is he lucid? Will he be able to talk?"

"He's in pain, and he's been through a lot. If you have questions, you should come back."

"No." Hadley shook his head. "I need..." He tried to shift on the bed, and his eyes nearly rolled back in his head.

"Easy." Kenna leaned against the rail on the side of the bed. "Don't hurt yourself."

She couldn't imagine how much pain he was in, and the bottom line was that if he made himself worse and ended up unconscious, it would delay the investigation for as long as he was out.

Langford came over, her badge in view on her belt.

The nurse said, "If you're still here in two minutes, I'm calling security."

"We are talking to him here and now," Langford said. "We'll make it as quick as possible."

Hadley touched Kenna's arm. "Sit me up a bit." He cleared his throat. "Don't like lying down."

"Bad memories?" She reached for the remote and hit the button to raise the back of the bed. "I get those in a lot of places. Feels like there's something on your chest, and you can't breathe."

"Something like that."

She handed him the cup by the bed with a straw so he could take a sip. "Can you tell us what happened?" She wanted to add *before the nurse comes back and kicks us out* but didn't.

"It's like a nightmare."

Langford stood at the end of the bed. "Start at the beginning. You were in a motel room with a woman."

"Zeyla. Seemed like a good idea at the time. I didn't realize she was expecting them until they came in, all apologetic like they got a key to the wrong room. Then they're suggesting we turn it into a party with all four of us, asking if we were interested."

Kenna said, "You saw both of their faces?"

"Until they shot me up with a needle. I was asking them to leave, and the woman stuck me. After that, it all went blurry. I know Zeyla tried to fight them, and I got in the way. Got myself cut. I remember I was bleeding. I woke up in a basement cell. She wasn't there." His expression twisted.

"What happened, Chief?" Langford spoke softly.

"They came in again, and there was another needle. I woke up in a hot tub full of ice and couldn't feel anything. She got me out. Zeyla. She helped me to a wheelchair, and we hurried out to a side door, then to a truck. They shot at the vehicle, and we didn't make it far before we realized one of the tires was flat. I could walk by then, so she told me to run for it. I don't know what happened to her." Tears spilled down his cheeks. "I didn't think. I just ran. I left her."

"Do you know where you were?" Langford asked. "Or how you got back to work?"

"I wandered through the woods. I could see the mountains. I think I was west of Denver, but I can't be sure without a map and images."

"Okay." Kenna nodded. "When you're stronger, we'll want you to go over everything, describe it all, and help us figure out where they took you."

"I can do that." He seemed to rally at the idea of providing them information.

"Did someone pick you up? How did you get back to Denver?" Langford looked up from her notebook, a pen in her hand.

"A truck driver brought me back to the city. I got a ride from the truck stop to my neighborhood and managed to walk home. I found my wallet at the house since I'd left it and my phone behind. Those were her instructions, anyway. I didn't want to confront my wife, so I put my uniform on and went to work. I guess there were still so many drugs in my system I didn't know how bad it was, and I didn't look."

"Then we showed up at the FD, and you made a run for it." Kenna winced. "You should've called the police."

"I was set up. Do you have any idea how humiliating that is?"

She lifted a hand. "Don't get worked up. You'll put too much stress on your body, and you need to let it heal."

"I'm not gonna *heal*. They took half my liver and one of my kidneys!"

Kenna set a hand on his shoulder. "We're going to find them and shut the operation down."

The nurse came in. "Time's up."

Kenna didn't move just yet. "How did she contact you, the woman Zeyla?"

"She responded to my request on the site. I never tried it before, and the one time I do, it's a set up?" He scoffed. "She was probably part of it. Luring me there so they can steal my organs out of my body."

"You said she rescued you."

"Probably so that I'll believe she's some kind of hero. They never took *her* kidney."

That he knew of, anyway. For all Kenna could confirm with facts, her sister might have been captured trying to get them both out and was currently being cut up.

Langford said, "You used the QR code?"

"That's it. Someone sent it to my phone, said I'd have a good time."

"Okay." The nurse clapped twice, walked over, and

waved them toward the door. "If you're not a patient, come back tomorrow. Or the day after."

They stepped out into the hall, and the nurse slid the door shut, then closed a set of curtains, blocking the chief from view.

"How did we get from one couple being kidnapped to multiple cases and organ harvesting in just a day?"

Kenna turned to the detective. "And the day isn't even over yet."

"I'll admit, I may be in over my head. But there's no way I'm giving this case to the feds."

She might not have a choice. "We need to show them what we have. For all we know, they have intel, and connecting with them could close the case."

"So that's what you do? Give your cases to the feds for help and pretend you solved them."

"Hey, that's a good idea." Kenna walked away.

Langford strode after her.

She kept going, finding Maizie and Ramon where she'd left them. Though Maizie had curled up on the row of seats, and someone had covered her with a blanket. Ramon got up and came over to them. "What's next?"

"We still need to find Zeyla and Roxanne."

Langford frowned. "We need to find the people behind that QR code and the kidnappers."

Ramon said, "Sounds like we all have work to do."

"I need to check in with my partner and find out if they've made progress with the sketch of the female kidnapper." She eyed Ramon, interested but also a little suspicious, as she walked away.

"She likes you."

He said, "You think I have time to date in the middle of a case?"

Kenna chuckled. "Usually doesn't stop me."

"And look where it got you. Marriage." He shuddered.

She shoved his shoulder. "One day, it'll happen to you. Then I'll be the one laughing."

Chapter Fourteen

Kenna lay on her back and stared up at the sky, earbuds in. She'd set her exercise mat on a stretch of grass between the two RV's. She tucked one knee up to her chest.

"Want me to call the police department and request the files be sent to the FBI?"

She liked the sound of Jax's voice in her ear. At least he wasn't torturing her with crazy workouts. "And when they ask how you found out about the case?"

"I want to run that QR code."

"Me, too, but we have to let them work the case."

"I'm gonna email the Denver office, see if they have anything. I'll shoot the breeze with their ASAC and see what they say. Could ring a bell."

Kenna switched legs. "Because you don't have enough to do?"

He chuckled. "Just trying to help."

She smiled. "Sure, sure. I haven't heard from your mom. Did she get back home okay?"

"They were shopping yesterday. Not sure what their plans are."

Kenna sat up. "Why didn't they leave?"

"Eager to get rid of them?"

"They're in danger here. They could be targets. I don't have the personnel to protect them and investigate this case."

Jax said, "I'll call Laney and make sure they know to be careful."

"Thanks." At least that would give him something to focus his extra energy on. "If I need the FBI's help with this case, I'll let you know."

"Organ harvesting." He muttered the words. "That's just crazy."

Kenna said, "I have two women to find, for different reasons. And no way to locate either of them."

"And your mom isn't helping."

"I don't even know how I'd reach her. Except to call the resistance, but I'm not sure if they're aware she's alive. It would be too easy for their enemy to find out she faked her death." The novel had said she went back as a double agent, so maybe they knew she was alive, and it was only Kenna who'd been lied to.

"So she formed her own resistance?"

Kenna sighed. "I suppose. I have no idea, really, and she didn't offer. I can't even worry about that right now, and there's no point wishing for something I don't have. Why would I? Right now, my life is full."

"It's a big case, and it could be a shot at taking down the company."

"That isn't what I meant," Kenna said. "I was talking about you. Maizie. Ramon. Stairns and Elizabeth. Bruce, even. I have a full life and then some with all of you guys."

"Everyone needs a mom."

"Do they? I've never had one that I can remember, and I think I did all right."

"Good point."

Kenna slid her phone into the side pocket on her leggings and got up so she could roll up her mat. "I guess when the case is done and things are quiet for a minute, I'll get a chance to figure out what I want from her. But if she isn't prepared to give it to me, it's a moot point. It's just wishes."

The screen door to her RV swung open, and Cabot hopped out, padding over to her.

"Hi, doggy." Kenna bent over and gave the dog a full rubdown.

In her ear, Jax said, "We should get a cat."

Kenna sucked in a breath and choked a bit. "Say what now?"

"I like cats."

"I'm a dog person. You know this."

Jax chuckled. "We'll see."

The call ended.

"What's going on?" Maizie called through the screen door. "You look like you got bad news."

"Jax is a cat person."

Maizie laughed, moving out of sight and groaning. "Ouch, my face hurts. Cabot needs to pee. When she's done, I have information."

Kenna clicked her fingers and gave her dog a hand signal she'd trained a long time ago. The dog still remembered. Cabot walked with her, and they found some grass. Kenna scanned the RV park, spotting an older man out walking a tiny dog over by the entrance office.

Was Roxanne out there somewhere watching her?

That would be better than her closing in on Zeyla. If Amara found her daughter, then Roxanne would never be able to. Kenna figured Roxanne—and the company—considered both Amara and Zeyla a threat to them.

As much as she wanted to jump in her car, which was busted right now anyway, and go find her sister, that could be the thing that led Roxanne to her. And besides, Kenna's efforts were better spent taking down the whole operation than focusing on one person.

She had to keep working this thing one lead at a time rather than focusing so hard on one person that she lost sight of the main issue—this "company" couldn't be allowed to prosper. They couldn't continue thinking they had all the power and could do whatever they wanted.

Cabot trotted back over to her.

The dog hadn't alerted to anything, which gave her enough peace of mind to turn her back and head over to the RV.

Maizie came out with her laptop and two mugs, holding the door so Cabot could go inside. Kenna took both mugs and set them on the table. "Your face looks better."

"Bruce had a cream, but I think he might've mixed it himself. I have no idea what was in it, and I didn't ask. But my face feels better today."

"It's bruised but not as swollen."

"Thanks. The forensic analyst Jax found us just emailed me."

Kenna sat across from her at the picnic table. "Anything good?"

Maizie nodded, tapping keys on her laptop and staring at the screen. "The highlight of what is a fifteen-page report is that the financial company we infiltrated really only has one client. They hide everything in subsidiaries, foundations, and other corporations, but if you trace them all back as far as they go, then they start to connect. Basically, every single "customer" the company has is exactly one organization."

"The company." Kenna took a sip of her coffee.

"Exactly."

"What about where Hadley and Zeyla might have been taken? Anything about that?"

Maizie said, "Based on what he said about where he was, I ran the county records on all the land in that area."

"That's a huge area." He'd effectively said anything west of Denver. "Who knows how long he was in the truck when he got a ride? He could've been in Utah, for all we know."

Maize said, "Sure...*but* there's a stretch of land owned by one of these companies, and it's west of Denver. Rural, the plans list only a few buildings. Looks like it used to be a hospital, but it was shut down after the Second World War, and it's been empty ever since. The company has owned the land all that time."

"We need to go check it out." Kenna took her coffee and went to the outside wall of the Class C in the space beside hers. She pounded the flat of her hand on the window and called out, "Rise and shine!"

Two hours later, she pulled off the highway in a rental car, Maizie in the passenger's seat and Cabot in the back. Ramon, Stairns, and Bruce were in Ramon's truck behind them.

The two-lane blacktop led them to a turnoff with a broken-down sign for St. Dymphna's Psychiatric Hospital. Two brick towers topped with a light flanked the road. She drove between them, working around a downed tree that must have fallen during a storm. A breeze in the air caused the trees to sway back and forth.

As the expansive building came into view, she glanced at Maizie.

"I don't recognize it."

Kenna said, "That's good."

"Sure, because it means everything in there is going to be a surprise instead."

Kenna almost smiled. The two-story brick building had rows and rows of broken windows. Huge stone stairs going up to the front door. Probably a basement level below ground. "It looks...cold."

"That's the scariest-looking building I've ever seen. It looks like the set of a horror movie I don't want to watch."

She was right.

Kenna pulled up in front of the steps. "Only death lives in this place."

Maizie twisted around to look at her. "Did you have to say that?"

"Sorry. I don't know why that came out just then. You can stay in the car."

"There's no way I'm staying in the car. Staying in the car is bad for me." Maizie pushed open her door, but she definitely hesitated.

"I'm sure the guys brought all their weapons." Kenna grabbed her gun in its holster from the duffel on the back seat. No way was she going inside this building without one. She clipped the holster on her belt and slid the gun out to check it.

Ramon pocketed his keys and drew a gun from the small of his back while the other guys climbed out of his truck. They'd parked on the gravel drive closest to the front of the building. "All the grass is dead."

Bruce came up behind him. "The trees, too."

"Hopefully, the building doesn't collapse while we're inside," Stairns said, eyeing the building. He had a shotgun in his hands, which he handed to Maizie. "It isn't loaded, but it looks scary to anyone who comes at you. Keep it pointed at the ground. It's good practice."

Maizie slid the backpack onto her shoulders and tucked the weapon against her front.

"Your finger goes nowhere near the trigger. Got it?" Stairns said.

She nodded. "Got it."

"I don't think there will be a computer to connect to, so you won't need the backpack." Kenna figured she could go with Bruce while Ramon and Stairns split off with Maizie.

"I'm not leaving it out here. It could get stolen," Maizie said.

Ramon looked around. "Ain't no one here but ghosts."

Bruce grinned. "Who you gonna call?" He turned to the steps leading to the front door.

The teen said, "You guys need to teach me gun safety so I can carry one that's loaded."

Kenna wasn't so sure about that, even if Maizie was about to turn eighteen. "I'll put it on the agenda for our next family meeting."

Stairns said, "Guess you'd better check the law, find out what you can legally do at eighteen. There could be restrictions, and the last thing you need is to get in trouble because you didn't follow the rules about having a gun."

Maizie let out a very teenage sigh.

Kenna stepped up beside Bruce, who had the padlock open. "That doesn't match the age of the building."

"No kidding." He pulled the door open. "Someone was here recently."

"Question is," she said, "how recently?" She stepped into the lobby after him.

Dirt and leaves littered the floor, blown in by the breeze through shattered windows. The air was still and smelled faintly of something chemical, like disinfectant.

A wide staircase curled up to the second floor, and below it was a hall to the left. The entryway continued back under the second floor, with doors on both sides and a closed set of heavy doors that led in the direction of the back. Above their heads, a chandelier hung, the pieces of glass now dark and discolored with age.

Ramon wandered through the empty lobby. "Something was dragged across the floor. Look." He waved at the stone floor where the dirt had been wiped away in a long line.

They cleared the ground floor but found nothing.

Kenna said, "Bruce and I will check the basement level. You guys go upstairs."

"If you say so." Ramon followed her up the steps. Maizie walked behind him with Stairns next to her.

Stairns headed for the staircase with Maizie behind him.

Kenna eyed the girl's hold on the shotgun, even though it wasn't loaded. The fact Maizie wanted training was good. She should know how to handle a weapon. But it would be better if she didn't go anywhere near a situation where she'd have to use it. Kenna would be much more comfortable with Maizie in the office than in the field.

"Kenna!"

She jogged to catch up with Bruce and found him in the hall.

"Coming?"

"Yeah, yeah."

He ducked out of sight through a doorway into a dark staircase that went down and then doubled back on itself. His boots echoed in the quiet. "Remind you of that house in France?"

"Hopefully, none of our friends are in the basement."

Bruce chuckled. "We got them out. How is Preston, anyway?" He clicked on a flashlight and held it under his gun hand, pointing both at the space in front of him.

Kenna turned on the flashlight on her weapon. "He's good. He's been emailing from his house in Washington state. A young woman with a baby that we met in New Orleans also lives there since she needed somewhere safe to stay. He's been helping her find a job and a place to stay and a good daycare. All while he recovers from the wounds he sustained."

Bruce opened the door at the bottom of the stairs. "He's the reason I got back into the US, so I can't really fault the guy."

"Mmm." Kenna had been contending with the fact Preston had lied to her about why he wanted her to go to England. He'd hired Miami Security International, and all of them had withheld information from her about why. They'd known about the company but needed her to discover her personal connection to it. She'd found out a lot that she hadn't known about herself, but the journey to get there had been tough.

"But if you want him to die mysteriously of natural causes..."

Kenna said, "I won't be asking you to do that. Not even with people I hate."

"Fair enough."

"Bruce—"

"It's fine. I get it. Protect the kid, help you do your thing. It's fine."

Kenna followed him down the basement hall. "Can we focus? We can do your job performance review later."

"That's probably a good idea."

She spotted the shift in him. "Why?"

"Because there's someone down here with us."

Chapter Fifteen

Kenna listened long enough she could hear it. Down the empty stone corridor, the faint sound of rhythmic breathing. "I don't hear anything else."

She grabbed her phone and used the walkie-talkie app they all had. "We found someone down here."

She left it open and crept forward, her volume low on her phone. Gun-first. Taking easy steps that made little sound on the floor.

Bruce made no sound. He stepped in front of her as if he had every right to take a bullet for her.

She didn't like it, but she also did. Kenna would do the same for any of them.

He stopped near an open door. There was nothing else down here. The whole hospital seemed abandoned, and if this was where Carlton Hadley had been brought after his abduction, she didn't see the cells he'd mentioned. But they could be in these rooms. Or the rooms themselves. They needed to take photos to show the fire chief to be sure.

If this place hadn't been used for anything nefarious,

why did it sound like someone in the room had a machine turned on?

Bruce stepped inside. She heard the exclamation from his lips, almost silent but not quite.

She stepped around him, and he didn't move. "What..." Her words disappeared as she took in the room.

A cell, the walls lined with stone that had been carved into over the years. Scratches and markings made by people over the better part of a century. In the center was a hospital bed with a patient hooked up to machines on both sides. IV tubes on both arms, and another in his neck. If it was a man—she found it difficult to tell either way.

Bruce let out a curse. "There isn't much left."

Her phone chirped from the walkie-talkie app. "Nothing on the second floor. Going to the first now."

Bruce slid his phone out. "Copy that."

Kenna just stared at the patient, her mind not quite able to process what she was seeing. The head seemed intact, but he had a bandage over his eyes. The chest had been cut open, splayed out, and instead of lungs, a machine beside the bed pumped up and down, delivering oxygen to his body. "Is there a heart?"

"Don't throw up. I'll be disappointed." Bruce strode to the far side of the bed and looked into the open chest cavity. "Heart is still here. Not sure it should be exposed to the air, but what do I know? Maybe they didn't need one of those. Though, apparently, they needed the lungs, his liver, and one of his kidneys."

Kenna let out a breath. "I don't want to know if he has eyes under those bandages."

"Or a brain left in his head." Bruce straightened, shaking his head. "He won't survive either way. Being kept alive artificially like this, the machines are maintaining basic functions. Keeping his heart pumping."

Kenna had a lot of questions. "I don't know where to start."

"How about ID?" Bruce pulled out his phone and took a photo of the man's face. Then a photo of the fingertips on his hand.

"You can get a print?"

"I can do a lot of things," he said.

"I already knew that." They had to keep Maizie out of here. She didn't need to see this. "What are we going to—"

Before she even finished, Bruce reached over and literally pulled the plug out of the wall. Then another plug, and another.

"You're gonna—"

Bruce stepped away from the wall and walked past the now-dying man.

"He's going to die! You killed him!"

Bruce grabbed her arm and tugged her toward the door. "He's already dead. He's gone, and there's nothing you can do."

Kenna sputtered, tripping along with him. Being dragged out. "We can't just leave him here!"

"That's why you hired me. To do the hard things." Bruce wasn't dragging her exactly, but he also wasn't giving her the chance to do anything but go with him. "They left him to prove a point. That there's nothing you can do to stop them. But they also left him to slow you down—or to stop *you*."

He nudged her ahead of him up the stairs and said, "Everyone out."

She figured that wasn't only to her when it echoed from her phone. "Why do we need to—"

"We triggered something, obviously. It's what I would've done."

How could he possibly know... "Bruce—"

"Time to run."

Kenna didn't wait around to find out if he was right or wrong. She pounded up the stairs, taking them two at a time.

When they were in the ground floor hallway, Stairns appeared in the lobby. "Come on."

She raced over to him. "Is this place going to blow or something?"

"We found something out back you'll want to see."

She reached the lobby just as a clang sounded at the front door.

Ramon turned back. "That just locked on its own."

Maizie, at the back door, let out a squeal. "The door!" She had it open and was standing in the doorway. "It's closing!" She turned to push on the door, the weight of it sliding her feet back into the building.

Stairns ran to her and pushed at the door. The rest of them followed, and Kenna slipped between, bringing Maizie with her.

Ramon and Bruce came through, pulling Stairns with them.

"What on—"

Bruce kept moving, his approach causing her to stumble back. "Go. Go."

Thunder erupted deep in the building, the throaty sound of an explosion rumbled through the structure, and it started to collapse.

"Go!"

Kenna turned and dragged Maizie with her. Then Maizie was dragging her.

The ground began to crack between her feet.

Bruce stumbled, and Ramon hauled him up.

Kenna jumped a log and kept going, reaching the trees at the far end of the back lawn before she stopped and turned back. They stood together, and she watched the building collapse in on itself.

"How did you know it was going to blow?" She had to talk loudly over the rumble of the building collapsing.

"Instinct," Bruce said. "And...no, it was just instinct."

Maizie didn't let go of her hand. "Uh, Kenna."

She turned from watching the building fall into the ground. "A fail-safe?"

Bruce nodded. "Most likely. Because, like I said, it's what I would have done. If I knew people were coming after me, I'd leave a tasty morsel, and then I'd wreck them so there's nothing left."

Ramon eyed him. "It's a little scary when you say it like that."

"I did hear a sadistic tone in your voice." Kenna gave herself a second to catch her breath.

"Guys."

Kenna turned back to where Maizie stood behind her. The teen had all her attention on the woods behind them. "What is—"

"Just look," Maizie said. "Otherwise, I have to say it out loud."

Kenna scanned the trees, looking for someone who might wish them harm. She saw no one between the dead trunks—Bruce had been right that nothing was alive out here.

Ramon let out a curse.

"Can we all stop swearing!" Kenna sucked in a sharp breath as the evidence before her began to make sense. The periodic mounds of dirt where the ground was raised, each one between a couple of trees. Two feet by six. "Shallow graves."

"We spotted them from the upstairs windows." Stairns said, "There are so many."

She scanned as far as she could see, spotting the mounds of dirt often. Even at the edge of what she could make out, the graves continued.

Maizie squeezed her hand. "How many people did they bury out here?"

Stairns said, "I'm going to call this in. If you don't want to be here when the local police, state police, and FBI show up, then you should leave."

"Maizie?" Ramon turned back to the building and swept his arm out.

Bruce cleared his throat. "Um—"

"You're good," Kenna said. "Go."

"I can't believe I dropped the shotgun." Maizie winced. "Now someone will find it in the rubble."

Kenna put her arm around Maizie and squeezed her shoulders. "Don't worry about it. One gun will be an interesting find, but we won't get in trouble over it."

"Okay. I'll see you later." She wandered off around the side of where the building had been, which was now a great crater in the ground.

Giving it a wide berth, Ramon led them to the front.

"I hope the cars didn't fall in." They'd parked pretty close.

Stairns said, "Thanks, 'preciate it." And then, he hung up. "What was that?"

She shook her head. "How long?"

"Twenty minutes, give or take. They're sending a chopper."

der. He held his phone up, his thumbs poised to text. "I'll see if she's free."

"Why don't we make it a surprise? How about we don't tell her I'll be there. Then I can have the chance to read her honest reaction."

"Okay." His tone sounded like he thought that was odd, but he'd write it off as a girl thing most likely.

"Sounds fun." They had their differences in the past, and she might never trust him. Even if she'd forgiven him for the hurt he'd dished out after Bradley's death, it didn't mean she would invite him to hurt her again now that her life had some stability—and a whole lot of happiness. But she could help him get out of a situation he'd realize soon enough he didn't want to be in.

"She's had drinks with the guys before. I'm sure she'll say yes."

Kenna smiled. "I can't wait."

Chapter Sixteen

"So, you moved from Salt Lake City to Denver, huh?" Kenna glanced at Miller as they walked in the rear entrance of the FBI building from the parking lot.

"Wasn't that much of a stretch. This is a bigger office, and they had an open spot."

"You like it here?"

Miller shrugged. "My dad is in a rest home in Colorado Springs, so I can see him more."

"That's nice."

Miller smiled, shaking his head. "Don't act like it's so surprising that I can be nice."

"Sure? Wouldn't want to ruin your reputation here. Who do they think you are? The tough guy? The funny one?"

"They think I'm a guy who worked with you, so I should know everything about whatever case you're workin'."

"Sorry."

He led her to the desk where she'd have to check in.

"For making me famous?" He snorted. "Don't worry about it."

She handed over the correct ID and signed all the papers, taking a second to text Jax so he'd know she had entered an FBI office—just in case someone contacted him about it.

"Are those cops you told me about coming?"

Kenna backed out of the text thread with Jax and took a look at her message to Langford. "They're here."

"Great. Let's go meet them at the front." He led her through a maze of hallways to the lobby, where she spotted Davis and Langford.

Kenna lifted her hand and waved so they'd see her.

"Kenna." Davis nodded.

"This is Special Agent Miller, Detectives Langford and Davis." She couldn't rush the afternoon, or someone would realize why she was so eager to get to drinks with Roxanne.

Still, the time it would take them to go through all the details of the case and make some determinations meant there was plenty of time for Ramon and Bruce to scope out the bar. And for Maizie to find any other locations that might be places for them to check out.

Miller took them to a conference room a few floors up. "We can chat in here."

An aide asked if they wanted coffee, which Kenna would never say no to, then disappeared.

There was something about being in an FBI office that smelled and sounded the same as the one she'd worked at in Salt Lake City. In an odd way, any FBI office anywhere in the country would always feel at least a little bit like home.

Or like an old friend who had stabbed you in the back, but you still had to see them.

Or both.

"Kenna, you good?"

She glanced over her shoulder at Miller. "Never better."

Langford didn't buy it. "Where are your friends?"

Miller glanced at her.

She motioned between herself and Miller with one finger. "Our former boss is back at the house, where they're going to start digging up victims."

Davis looked like he was going to be sick just hearing about it.

"And your teenage friend and the Hispanic guy?"

Kenna shrugged. "They probably went out to lunch."

Langford definitely didn't buy that.

Best to distract them all with evidence. "I have photos of a man who was in the building's lower level when we searched it." She explained about the explosion but not that Bruce unplugging all the equipment is what likely caused it. "I'll send them to you."

Miller said, "I'll grab my laptop. We can pass the image to forensics, and they can run it. See who he is."

While he had his head bent to the laptop, she looked at Langford and Davis and mouthed, *Did you find anything on the QR code?*

"Special Agent Miller, we'll need to read you in on the specifics of a related case," Langford said. "We believe they might be connected. It's why we're here."

Davis said, "We had two parties in custody who were integral to our understanding of the case. Both were killed earlier today in completely unrelated incidents."

Kenna's stomach flipped over. "Sally and Will? They're dead?"

Davis nodded. "She choked to death while eating. Evidently, it wasn't noted that she is allergic to sunflower oil. He was stabbed almost as soon as he arrived at county lockup."

"That's unbelievable." Kenna took a sip of her coffee, wondering who could have the juice to pull something like that off, then realizing she knew exactly who could've done it.

Yes, they definitely needed to talk to Roxanne.

The operation, if it had been happening in that house, had been completely cleared out. All except for that one victim—the fail-safe.

Proof of the horrors that were being committed.

A way to rub it in their faces.

Someone didn't want the authorities to find out anything.

Langford said, "Not only that, but the QR code that we believe connects the source to their customer base was a dead end. We ran it through our system and got back nothing. A dead link."

Kenna had to get all that information so she could have Maizie run it but couldn't say that aloud in this meeting.

Miller asked, "A QR code? Was it tattooed on someone?"

Kenna turned to him. "You've heard of it?"

"We have an open case that's been driving everyone crazy. No leads. No movement. Nothing. I'll get the lead agent in here to brief you so we can figure out if this is connected." He seemed energized by the prospect, but she would be as well if she was still an agent and someone had dropped a major case in her lap.

Kenna sat with her coffee while they exchanged case information. Jax had replied, telling her not to let Miller get to her. She asked him if his mom and sister were still in town.

Not that she wanted to be rid of them, but the fewer targets nearby who could be used to get to her, the better.

Her phone rang, and Jax's name appeared.

She heard Davis say, "Taskforce," right before she answered it. "Hey." She kept her voice low and stepped out of the room. "What's up?"

"Easier to tell you than type it all out."

"They're still here?"

"Yeah, and I called my dad to see if he'd convince them to get on a plane and go home, and he said not to worry about them. That he'd already made the necessary arrangements to keep them safe."

"Like flight plans?"

"I don't think so," he said. "Dad told me not to worry about them. That he's ensured they won't be harmed."

Across the room, Stairns stepped off the elevator. He lifted his chin to her and motioned to the boss's office. She nodded, then focused back on her call with Jax. "Did he make the same arrangement with you? Because that could come in handy."

"I have no idea. Maybe he thinks I should handle myself."

"Or you have FBI protection and a way to reach the president."

"I didn't tell him that part." Jax sighed. "I pressed him about who he made the arrangement with and how he knew about them, but he just shut down. Told me to stop asking questions."

"At least it's one less thing for us to worry about," she said.

"Even if it's not reassuring?"

"Just check in with them. Make sure they are good."

"I'm coming up there on Friday."

That was only a few days from now. Not so much time in reality, and yet it felt like an expansive stretch that would last forever.

"I'd like that." Even if part of his visit was to ensure the safety of his mom and sister. "I'm sure the guys have a spot for you to crash in their rig."

"I'll find my own space, but thanks."

She chuckled. "Right, back to work."

"I'll check with my dad later, see if he'll tell me anything else. You stay safe."

"I'm uninjured, and no life-changing things have happened all day. Just normal case stuff with explosions and bodies. So...the usual."

"Well, it's still early."

She grinned. "Love you."

"That's never gonna get old. And I love you, too."

"I know." She hung up and headed back into the conference room. "Did you choose a name for the taskforce yet?"

Davis sat back in his chair. "Ultimate Thunder. I always thought that would be a good taskforce name."

Langford rolled her eyes.

Miller said, "Banbury Fallout."

Langford chuckled, bringing Davis along for the ride.

"Real funny." Kenna folded her arms, refusing to admit it wasn't bad. Not that she especially wanted a taskforce named after her. But it could be cool. "Banbury Thunder it is."

Langford had her laptop open. "Oh, I just got a notification. We got an ID on the man in the hospital bed from your photo."

Kenna would have to explain the man's condition and the extent of what had been done to him because she hadn't included it in the images. "Who was he?"

"Ian Whistleborough. Fifty-two, reportedly in great physical condition. A lifelong athlete. He went missing a month ago. The wife didn't report it right away because it wasn't unusual. He goes on 'trips.'"

Kenna said, "The kind booked via QR code?"

"Or a few days in Thailand. Among other places." Langford scrolled on her mousepad. "She detailed it all in the report, figuring it would be helpful information for the police to have."

Davis said, "She mentioned credit card charges for escort services."

"Classy guy," Miller commented.

Kenna said, "No one deserves to end up like that. No matter what they've done."

Miller glanced at her. "Pretty sure that's why you're the one that goes after victims and I'm the one who takes down the bad guys."

"That means both our jobs are valid."

He stared at her, not agreeing out loud but also not disputing what she'd said.

"Your girlfriend is part of this." Kenna couldn't regret it or question it. She'd already said it. "I wasn't going to tell you. I'd have just quietly taken care of her tonight. But she is an agent for the bad guys here."

"You're serious."

Kenna nodded.

"Part of this...organ harvesting? Mass murder?"

"Trying to keep their operation secret."

Miller looked like he wanted to throw his computer across the room. "And I'm how she keeps tabs on law enforcement? I'd like to see some proof of that."

"If she is guilty, do you want me to kill her for you?" Maybe she didn't always agree with Ramon on everything, but it turned out that in some situations, she *was* Ramon.

The two detectives glanced at her.

"Kidding." Mostly. "We should question her first. She knows a whole lot more about this situation than we do."

"Because she's—What did you say?—an agent?"

Kenna said, "Yes."

"I'm supposed to just take your word for that?"

She almost responded.

"Don't bother. It's probably true."

"Sorry." Kenna dialed Maizie's number, leaving Miller to process the news and the detectives to discuss the case.

"Banbury Investiga—oh, it's you. We're fine. We got back to the campsite, and we're working."

"Copy that," Kenna said. "Can you send me everything you have on Roxanne?" She explained about Miller.

"Are you serious?"

A voice rumbled in the background of the call, then Maizie said, "I'll tell you in a second."

"Send it to my email."

Maizie said, "You got it, boss. Anything else?"

"Find out if Carlton Hadley is still at the hospital. I might want Bruce to sit on him. Just in case."

"Is he in danger?"

"If he is, let's make sure he's protected when something happens."

"Got it."

Kenna turned away, speaking low. "And run a cross reference between Jax's dad, any companies he owns or has dealings with, and the 'company' financials."

"Oh, uh. Okay."

"See if anything pops."

"Got it."

"Thanks, Maze." She hung up.

The worst thing she could find was proof Jax's dad had been involved with these people, but the more information they had to work with, the better. Jax could help his dad get out from under their thumb—and so could she if she worked the case.

If she brought her brand of justice to it.

Chapter Seventeen

Kenna had the Merton Roadhouse up on her maps app so she could see photos and check it out before they got there. "This place?"

Ramon, driving the car, chuckled.

Through the speakers, which were connected to the call she was on, Special Agent Miller said, "We wanted somewhere out of the way for the meet."

Tall pine trees flanked either side of the highway, a desolate road. Empty apart from Ramon's pickup and Miller in his car ahead of them. Who knew where Bruce was, but the guy should be out here with them in his own car.

This was the kind of dense forest that hid shadows, and in the dark of night like this, she almost imagined glowing eyes staring back at her from the trees. They were headed to a roadhouse to set a trap to catch Roxanne via Miller, with Ramon and Kenna going in as a casual couple.

They'd opted to leave out the detectives, who had other jurisdictional cases to investigate, and instead had come out here themselves to take care of this issue. "How did you meet Roxanne?"

Through the speakers, Miller said, "I was working a case on this company that was laundering money for an art forger. I pulled her in for questioning, and we clicked, but it didn't amount to anything on the investigation."

Ramon glanced over at Kenna but said nothing.

"When the case was past that stage, I called her up and asked her out. It was hot and heavy at the start. It became a regular thing." Miller paused. "She's really one of these assets for this 'company' y'all are investigating?"

"Yes." Kenna figured she'd be straight about it. "She was going to abduct one of my team members. It didn't go as planned, so she ran off."

Miller didn't comment on that.

Kenna said, "Maybe she genuinely likes you. She's interested, she's falling for you, so she kept the truth of who she is out of it. That way, she can have something nice that won't get messed up by who she is."

Miller said, "You really think that?"

Ramon shook his head, staying silent.

"I guess we should ask her." Kenna closed the maps app. "We're almost there."

"See you on the flip side." Miller ended the call, and in a half mile, Ramon slowed for the corner. After the bend, the roadside widened. The trees moved back from the shoulder to make way for a river on the west side, and on the east, a parking lot and a squat structure with a wood shake roof that was lit up with neon signs.

"Parking lot is pretty full." Ramon slowed but didn't indicate he'd turn in. "That's a lot of motorcycles."

Trucks and cars also lined the lot.

Miller had turned into the other end of the parking

area, so they went the opposite way. Better to make it look like they had nothing to do with each other.

"Now we know why he switched his FBI clothes for jeans, boots, and a leather jacket over his T-shirt." Kenna frowned. "Maybe he was undercover, and he liked it, and that's why he turned from a pencil-pushing, uptight city guy into some backcountry, roadhouse guy out for a beer and to meet his lady."

Ramon chuckled. "I can't imagine her here either. You think she wears a tiny leather skirt and a torn rock band T-shirt."

"Okay, that's a weird image. Have you been thinking about it much?"

He shoved her arm, and they both laughed. Kenna got out of the car. "I have to admit, there isn't much that smells better than the air in the mountains."

"Beer, exhaust, and puke?"

"Pine trees. Fresh mountain air."

"Right." Ramon slung an arm around her shoulder. "If you're gonna leave that ring on your finger, we should act like a couple. Otherwise, you're gonna get propositioned by every biker in there."

"Because I'm irresistible? They'll be falling over themselves to snatch me up." Kenna chuckled.

"I'll make it clear you're an acquired taste. More trouble than you're worth. I'm doing the world a favor keeping you off the market."

"You should tell Jax that. He can add it to his wedding vows."

Ramon pulled the front door of the roadhouse open while laughing out loud. It set the tone nicely, and they entered grinning at each other as if they had a shared secret —something that would sell them as being in a relationship.

The place was packed, wall-to-wall bodies but concentrated on the right with rows of pool tables all lined up. Opposite the front door, the bar stretched across at least twenty feet in width. Two bartenders manned the counter, and they seemed to be male identical twins.

Ramon pretty much dragged her—given his arm around her neck—to the corner, where they settled at a small round table in a sea of tables. She clocked the two bartenders, one with long dark hair tied back and the other with his head shaved. Both had sleeves of tattoos and distinctive clothing styles. The long-haired twin had a white shirt and black vest, and the shaved-head one had a tight T-shirt on.

A blond woman who was barely drinking age came over with a notepad. "What can I get you folks?"

Ramon ordered two beers and a basket of fries.

Kenna had to explain her glancing around so much, so she said, "This place is great. Is it always this busy?"

The blonde cocked her hip. "Best fries west of Nebraska."

Kenna grinned, and they shared a smile.

The waitress said, "I'll be back."

"Thanks." Kenna held up her phone and took a few pictures like a tourist or someone who had to update their social media every time they breathed. In reality, the pictures would go to Maizie as soon as she took them, uploading to their shared folder so Maizie could see everyone present in the room. She and Stairns, back at the campsite, would be able to run some of the faces and see who might be a threat. Or an asset.

The waitress delivered their drinks and food. By the time Kenna was done with her scan and had found Miller over at one end of the bar parked on a stool, Ramon had finished half his beer.

She switched his bottle for hers, so it looked like she was drinking, and took three fries from the basket. Hot. Greasy. "Okay, she was right about the fries. Maybe they're the reason Roxanne wanted to be here."

Ramon took another swig, looking around.

"See her yet?" Her back was to the room, so no doubt he'd see Roxanne come in before she did.

"She just walked in."

Kenna shifted in her chair but caught herself.

"Whoa." Ramon put his hand over hers.

She held on for an anchor, leaning on her partner in the way she was supposed to. Making their relationship sell to the people around them and keeping it platonic between them. Not that she had ever had feelings for Ramon, and if he'd had any for her, then he'd kept them to himself.

When was Jax coming up here, anyway?

"You good?"

She rolled her eyes. "Fine. What's she doing?"

"Doesn't matter. She tried to take Maizie. She's not going anywhere until she answers for that."

"Good. Then we're on the same page." Kenna squeezed his hand, then pulled hers back. "She doesn't leave."

"She approached Miller."

Kenna shifted again, bringing the half-drunk bottle of beer with her. "Good. Let's go."

"You gonna keep saying 'good'?"

"If I want." She grabbed another one of the fries and stuck it in her mouth. "Let's see if there's an open pool table. After we say hi to our friends we're about to bump into."

Ramon's expression no longer had any affection in it. He was a predator with prey in his sights and zero intention of letting that prey get away.

Kenna threaded through the tables, Ramon right behind

her, heading toward the pool tables. She glanced at the guy at the bar. "Miller!" She tried not to be *too* loud, but she needed Roxanne to see her.

On the stool at the bar, Miller lowered his bottle from his mouth where he'd been about to take a drink. He set the bottle down and slid his hand to his hip, keeping it there, out of sight. "Hey, Kenna!"

Roxanne stood beside him. She stiffened and turned to Kenna and Ramon, a calculated expression on her face. Her eyes dark. Her makeup heavy. Roadhouse Roxanne wasn't impressed.

"Gotcha." Kenna couldn't resist saying it. She stood a few feet away from Roxanne with Ramon by her left shoulder. "You're coming with us. It's best to do it quietly, with no fuss."

"I'm being arrested?" Roxanne glanced at Miller, then back at them. "You really think that'll stick when you have no warrant, no charges, no evidence, and no reason to take me anywhere."

She spoke with an American accent, a decent one. Not much trace of the British accent Kenna had heard her speak with so far.

Ramon said, "You ran from the car with Maizie in it."

"She's the one who crashed. I was scared for my life." Roxanne played innocent.

Kenna shook her head, not buying it for a second. It was clear she'd thought this through, working out ahead of time what her defense was going to be. "We aren't going around and around on this. Let's go." Her voice cracked on the last word, and she cleared her throat, which was suddenly starting to feel thick. "We don't need to make a scene—" Her voice quit, and she swallowed, sucking in air.

"You okay, Kenna?" Ramon shifted beside her.

"Not sure."

Roxanne's expression changed to one of immense satisfaction.

Miller slid off the stool. "What's going on?"

All around them, people started coughing. Doubled over, sputtering, and trying to breathe. Kenna watched them, trying not to panic. She slid her phone out and called 911, but she couldn't say anything. They could use all the help they could get with this, so having every emergency department respond wouldn't be a bad thing.

Roxanne glanced at Miller. "You always have the fries."

But not today? That was the implication of her words—that and the fact this was happening to those who had eaten the fries. Like Kenna.

Miller said, "I didn't have the stomach for food. When I knew this was coming?" He looked around. "What did you do to these people?"

Kenna cleared her throat. It didn't alleviate the feeling that something was lodged there. She sucked in a long breath, keeping it easy. Getting as much air as she could. Freaking out wasn't going to help anything.

"You're going with them," Miller said. "Because I can't even look at you. I guess I'll be here cleaning up this mess."

"Yes, well," Roxanne said, her accent back to British. Evidently, she didn't feel the need to keep up the ruse now. "When you never see me again, perhaps you could ask these two where they've buried me. Leave some kind of marker so people can pay their respects."

Kenna's head swam. She needed more air than she was getting. She strode to the bartender and motioned for a drink. He gave her a bottled water, opening the cap for her.

Kenna handed over her phone, already connected to 911. He took the phone and spoke to the dispatcher.

The water had better help. She couldn't think of anything else and didn't want to have a tube shoved down her throat. She hadn't eaten that many fries. Surely, it wasn't as bad as it could have been otherwise. Not like some of the people in here. As she drank, she took in the whole roadhouse and the carnage from...it had to be poison.

Whatever Roxanne had introduced into the fries was causing people to collapse because they were unable to breathe.

"You're murdering a room full of people," Miller said, standing close to Roxanne.

She hadn't moved, surveying her handiwork. Satisfied with herself.

"And for what?"

Roxanne turned to him, but only a fraction. "Because I can. Because my job is to slow you all down as much as possible."

Ramon shifted, threat in every line of his body. He was going for his gun.

As he drew it out, Roxanne moved fast. Her arm flung out, and she tossed something at him.

She ran in front of Kenna toward a side door.

Ramon stiffened, his body jerking as a pocketknife embedded in his chest. Kenna dropped the bottle and went to him.

Miller sprinted after Roxanne. "I've got her."

Kenna grabbed Ramon's waist. The handle of the knife was at least three inches. It wasn't long enough to be deep, but still... "You've been stabbed."

He muttered something that didn't sound good.

"You really do need to fix that language issue you have." But he didn't live by her tenets, so she wasn't supposed to force him to an ideal she'd chosen, which he didn't believe in. No one needed to be hit over the head with rules when they were missing the heart change that came with embracing the God who loved them.

Ramon spoke through gritted teeth. "Why are you crying?"

"I feel weird." But the water must have helped since her throat was letting out just enough air for her to speak. She looked at the knife. "We should take that out. It's hurting you."

"It'll hurt worse if you take it out." He led her to a stool. "Sit."

"I need my phone." She twisted to the bartender. "We need...stuff. Things. For the..." She waved her hand.

He held out her phone. "Cops and ambulance are on the way. I'll get the first aid kit for your boy here."

"Thanks." She had to brace herself on Ramon's shoulder, or she was going to fall over.

"Keep holding on."

"You've been stabbed. I should be helping you."

"Partners, remember? We help each other." He looked a little sad.

The same way she felt sad that he didn't know Jesus like she did. How was she supposed to tell him? She'd tried, but he always shut her down. She wanted to respect his wishes and not put a wedge between them, not make him feel as if he was letting her down—or not living up to her standard.

"Partners."

"Until Jax shows up and I don't exist."

"As if I'd forget about you." She touched her hands to his cheeks, but one had the phone in it, so he ended up with her phone to his ear.

He said, "Copy that. Tell them to hurry."

She stared into those dark eyes. "You've seen the worst

the world has to offer. You have every right to be angry and want revenge on everyone who wronged you. But you're here, helping me keep Maizie safe. Working cases."

"I lived in the darkness until you found me. Now, it's time to live in the light."

He was working his way back.

She had no doubt then that, eventually, he'd see faith the way she did. "Lots of people don't think what I do is in the light. All we see is death and destruction."

"Bringing light to the darkness. Isn't that what you're supposed to be doing?"

"We're supposed to be catching that woman." Except she couldn't breathe all the way, and people around them might be dying. "We need to help them."

"Here." The long haired bartender stood on their side of the counter and set a kit down. "Gauze? Until the paramedics arrive?"

"I don't need help," Ramon said. "What's your name?"

"Cliff." The bartender pulled on rubber gloves. "Sure, you don't need help. That's why you've got a knife in you."

"Gauze, Cliff," was all Ramon said.

The bartender pulled a packet open and held out a square.

Ramon whipped his hand up and slid out the knife, doing a good job of keeping it straight on the way out. He let out a breath, grabbed the gauze, and pressed it against the wound. "Thanks." He looked at her. "Give me your hand."

He placed it over the gauze. "Lean. I need pressure on it."

"One day, a woman is going to fall hopelessly in love with you, and I'll be there to say 'I told you so.'"

Ramon grinned, lines of stress around his eyes. "We'll see."

Cliff grunted. "Figured you guys were together."

"We're friends. Partners. Siblings. All of it." They'd pretended to be a couple for the purposes of bringing down Roxanne. They needed to know if Miller had caught her. Hopefully, Bruce was outside helping with that. The people around them needed medical help, but she could hear sirens in the distance.

Ramon's lips curled up slightly. "What she said. Family you don't know you need, then you realize you can't live without it."

"Why?" Kenna looked at Cliff, her mind connecting random pieces of this puzzle of a case and coming up with an odd conclusion that was probably nothing. Unless it was something. "You know anything about couples and motel rooms?"

Cliff frowned. "What?"

"Tell me." She shifted so she wasn't leaning so close to Ramon, kept pressure on the wound, and cleared her throat, looking at Cliff. "Maybe you tell couples who come in what motel they should stay at that you recommend, and when they're picked up, you get a cut of it."

Ramon flinched. "Seriously?"

"It's just a text." Cliff moved away slightly.

Ramon grabbed him, swinging the guy between them so that his forehead slammed into the bar. Thankfully, she'd backed up in time, or she'd have been caught in the crossfire. As it was, he slammed into her forearm, and Kenna had to let go of the gauze, crying out.

"Hey!" The other twin jumped over the bar, swearing at them and rushing over, ready to fight.

That was when things got interesting.

Chapter Eighteen

Ramon groaned. Kenna sat up on the hospital bed and looked at him, still holding the ice pack on her face. "You good, bro?"

He exhaled, coughed, and groaned some more. "Should've hit that guy again."

"I kicked the other one pretty hard." Soon as the police showed up, the twins had run out the back door. "We held our own." But what would they have done if the cops hadn't come in?

Stairns and Maizie rushed into the urgent care ward. This was the closest medical center to the roadhouse, which happened to be some small-town setup. The doctor hadn't even blinked when fifteen people were walked in with split lips and black eyes, having trouble breathing. Someone had broken ribs, but it wasn't Kenna or Ramon. Their fight with the twins spilled out to other people, and it all got pretty intense before the cops busted it up.

Maizie walked over, frowning. "What did you guys do?"

"We didn't start it." Kenna lowered the ice pack.

Maizie yelped.

"Is it that bad?"

Stairns moved to the end of the bed. "Your eye is swollen."

"Long as it's not purple."

Maizie went over to Ramon. "Did you really get stabbed?" As if he didn't have a bandage across his bare chest. High up and close to his shoulder. "Are you okay?"

Ramon said something in Spanish, and Maizie nodded. She swung the backpack off her shoulders and pulled out a T-shirt. He said, "Help me get this on?"

Kenna watched closely, making sure Maizie didn't have a reaction to being so close to a man with no shirt on. They kept it efficient, getting Ramon's arm through the hole before Maizie stretched the shirt over, and he ducked his head.

"Thanks, Maze." He got his other arm through himself.

She set a hand on her hip, like he was a wayward soul she needed to keep on the straight and narrow. "Why did you let yourself get stabbed?"

Ramon nearly smiled but didn't, probably a good idea. "Poison. She caught me off guard."

"Good thing she didn't put poison on the knife."

Kenna frowned, which made her face hurt even though the doctor had *stuck her with a needle.* She was going to leave him a one-star review online. "I didn't think of that." She had to cough again.

"What was it?"

"Some drug that closes up your airway like an allergic reaction," Kenna said. "The doctor explained it but..." She shrugged.

"I'll find out." Maizie folded her arms. "And Roxanne? And Miller?"

"Where is Bruce?" Stairns asked.

Kenna glanced around. "Huh. Think we lost track of him in the confusion. Miller ran after Roxanne, but she got away in a car. He got a partial plate, so he went back to the FBI office to run it. He's gonna tag team this with the police because they've got a suspect in an attempted mass murder."

"That's what they're calling it?" Stairns pulled out his phone. When Kenna nodded, he said, "I'll track down Bruce."

"I'm ready to get back to work." Ramon shifted to the edge of the bed, holding his left arm cradled in his right.

"You can get some rest." Maizie lifted her chin.

Kenna felt her lips twitch.

"So can you." She pinned Kenna with a stare. "Stairns and I will find Bruce. Tomorrow, we can figure out what to do next." She looked exasperated.

Kenna's phone rang. She reached all the way back to the bedside table and grabbed it. Jax was calling. "Hey." She held the phone to her ear and found her shoes by the bed.

"Ramon got stabbed?"

"Yeah, can you believe he didn't stop it?" She had to cough.

"Poison, really?"

"I ate like four fries."

"To be honest"—he sounded as exasperated as Maizie—"that's a miracle."

Kenna's mouth dropped open. "I..."

"Tell me I'm wrong." He paused. "I'm glad you're all right. That could have gone very badly."

Fine, she couldn't argue with it. She'd have dusted off that whole basket of fries if they'd been there any longer. "We've lost all our leads, and a bunch of people needed medical help. It did go badly."

"I'm gonna hand in my notice tomorrow. I'm done being in Phoenix."

"Don't quit over one bar fight. You'd be throwing away your career."

"My heart can't take this, Kenna." He sounded like he might be joking, but only a little and likely only to keep himself from getting overwhelmed by the fear.

"I'm good, just banged up." She had to cough again, but the meds the doctor had given her started working right away, so she was only a little short of breath. "Ramon is okay. He just needs to sleep. If your mom and your sister are fine, then we're good."

Stairns walked back over to them, talking on his phone. "Got it." He hung up. "Bruce is fine. But I can't believe Miller walked you into that."

"It was my idea," Kenna said. "I can't blame a guy for being mad that he got duped by a beautiful woman. She's a professional at this."

"This woman gets away a lot. It's time to lock her down."

She didn't explain that the woman was a genetically superior asset of a deadly organization...but she was thinking it. Kenna ducked her head. "I love you."

"Mmm. Love you, too." He hung up.

"He's mad. Kind of." She lowered her phone, aware it wasn't that he was angry with her for getting hurt. More like angry with himself for not being here to help. She'd be reacting the same way if he was out working cases miles from her. Even if he had a team of capable people watching his back.

Stairns said, "Bruce will meet us back at the campsite. Said he has something to show you."

"Let's get out of here." She kicked her foot so her shoe

slid on all the way and stood while also watching Ramon get up to assess his ability to move around. "How are you? Apart from the split lip, you look like nothing happened. I've got a swollen face."

"Practice? Not like it's the first time I've been stabbed."

Yeah, she'd seen the scars on his upper body. Even the doctor had blinked at the sight of them.

"I need a caramel milkshake." Kenna slid her arm through Maizie's. "Are you driving?"

"Um, no."

"Whatever the doctor gave me, it's good stuff."

Maizie chuckled.

Kenna fell asleep in the car, and when Stairns pulled into the campsite, she woke up with her forehead against the side window. She winced, a cold spot on her face from the glass, and groaned. "That's the worst way to sleep."

Stairns put the car in park. "Bruce is in our rig. He said to come see him."

"I'm going back to work." Maizie pushed the door open and got out. "Which is what I should've been doing this whole time."

Kenna nudged Ramon awake. "Time to switch to your bed."

He groaned, pushed the door open, and stumbled out.

Stairns met her at the rear of the car. "Maizie talked to Jax. She's fine. They were both worried about you guys."

"What does Bruce have?"

"A lead." Stairns pulled the Class C door open, and she stepped inside, spotting two unexpected men sitting at their table. "It's going to get crowded in here fast."

Bruce stood by the sink, drinking from a short glass. "Our friend next door?"

"Went back to work." She moved by him and got a water bottle out of their fridge.

Bruce pulled out his phone and sent a text.

Ramon eased by her. "I don't wanna know, and I've been stabbed, so I don't care."

She glanced at the two bound men at the table. Their wrists and feet were taped together. Their eyes widened, watching Ramon, and Cliff appeared to be breathing hard underneath the tape stretched over his mouth.

Worried about what was going to happen next?

Bet you didn't expect to get picked up by the same people you started a fight with, then ran from.

Ramon's retreat made her wonder how bad he felt that he didn't want in on what was going to happen next. Kenna watched him roll onto his bunk, halfway down the hall before the bedroom section. She held the water bottle to her face. "Cliff. And your brother. How fortuitous." With her other hand, she tapped out a quick text, took their picture, and included it.

It would probably take Langford half an hour to get over here, which would save this situation from a turn that wouldn't do any of them any good.

Stairns closed the door and set his elbow on the counter. The two men at the table both had bloody knots on their foreheads. In about the same spot. Bruce must have used the same tactic to take them both out.

"How'd you know we'd need them?"

Bruce lowered his glass. "Watched them run out the back. They were taking a path into the trees, so I followed. When I scoped it out before, I found a cabin up there. These guys chatted while they were walking." His tone flattened. "Heard them talking about you and Ramon."

The two men at the table started to breathe harder.

"Okay," Kenna said to draw their attention to her. "Who wants to talk about the motel?"

Both of them looked from her to Stairns, then at Bruce.

Definitely, the kind of older men a fool might underestimate.

But Bruce had taken them both down, subdued them, and transported them here.

"As you can see"—Kenna motioned to where Ramon was now snoring—"we're not interested in a fight. We only want information, and then you're free to go." To jail. "Whoever talks first gets to ask for something."

Cliff's unnamed brother lifted his chin.

Stairns leaned over and tore off the tape. "Your name?"

"Elyan Cartland. Cliff and I weren't doing nothin' but protecting our place. That's the price of business."

Kenna said, "Recommending to couples that they stay in a certain motel. After that, you...what? Send a photo of them to someone. So they know who to expect?"

Elyan winced. "It's just business."

"I'll say." Kenna stared at him. "I'm sure your mother is so proud of the two of you, being part of the organ trafficking world."

Elyan flinched.

Cliff fought against the tape around his hands and feet, moaning behind the tape. Bruce took a half step toward him, which Cliff assessed as the threat it was, and Cliff stilled, breathing hard.

"Organ trafficking?" Elyan sputtered. "That's crazy. It's just about ripping off tourists. Catching people with their pants down and blackmailing them."

"I'm not sure you know exactly what they're doing. Maybe you asked, and they gave you some half-baked ideas.

I think you should've dug a little deeper. Actually found out what they are doing."

Elyan said, "We do what we've gotta do."

"I can see that." Bruce had his attention on his phone. "Got yourselves into some gambling debt, probably owe the wrong person. These guys swoop in when you're desperate, and you think it's the answer to your problems."

"How much did they pay you?" Kenna asked.

"It doesn't matter now," Elyan said. "Just kill us and be done with it."

Cliff didn't seem to like that idea.

"We aren't going to kill you," Stairns said. "It would ruin the resale value of this rig."

Elyan's attention shifted to him, over by the door. "You're gonna let us go?"

Kenna said, "Sure. After you tell us where to find these people. How you get paid. All communication back and forth. Everything."

Elyan pressed his lips together and looked away.

Kenna went over and tore the tape off Cliff's mouth. "Your brother thinks we should just kill you."

"I saved a picture of them from our cameras, just in case."

"In case you needed insurance." Kenna stepped back into the aisle between the sink and the slender pantry cupboard. "Right? Let me guess, a man and a woman. But not the woman I was talking to earlier at the roadhouse. Someone else."

"Give me my phone. I'll send the file."

Bruce handed two phones to her. She handed them to Stairns, who ducked out the door. Elyan and Cliff both looked confused when the screen door snapped shut. Cool air from outside came through the open doorway, and in the opening, she spotted a car easing down the lane from the end of the row where the campsite main drag was.

Langford.

"You're in the middle of something, and you have no idea who these people are." Kenna glanced between the brothers. "You think organ trafficking is the worst of it? I'll tell you now it's the surface of what this is. Beneath that is so much more."

Her phone buzzed with a text from Maizie.

Got them.

She stowed her phone. Langford approached the door, followed by two uniformed officers whose car she hadn't even seen. Apparently, the detective wasn't taking any chances with this.

"Are they involved with the poisoning?"

Kenna said, "I thought it was attempted mass murder?"

Langford rolled her eyes. "Sounds like federal jargon to me. Who's your friend?" She motioned to Bruce.

"My associate, Bruce."

"You the one who brought in the infamous Cartland twins?"

Bruce took a sip of his drink. "Why? Is there a reward?"

Langford chuckled. "That's funny." She motioned behind her. "These officers will take the twins off your hands, given they have half a dozen outstanding warrants between them."

"Probably why they were hiding out at an out-of-the-way roadhouse." She was definitely going to find out why Miller hadn't realized the bartenders were wanted men. Too focused on Roxanne to pay attention to a bartender and his twin. Surely, he wasn't in on it, though it was almost worse that all this happened under his nose, and he never realized.

They were going to have a conversation.

Tomorrow. After she'd slept.

Bruce watched the cops load the twins into the back of their black-and-white patrol car. He muttered, "You never let me have any fun," and closed the door.

Kenna turned to Langford. "Thanks for the assist."

"Interesting friend you have there," Langford said. "And you're welcome, but I think I owe you a thanks for capturing them."

"All in a day's work."

"Believe me, I'm counting on it." In the dim light, her expression shifted.

"What is it?" Kenna asked her.

"Pressure from my captain. If we don't get a lead and there are no new victims soon, the case is getting put on the back burner." Langford shook her head. "Office politics."

Kenna wasn't going to let these people get away with this and hurt someone else. "I'll get you another lead."

Chapter Nineteen

"Way to get yourself some goodwill with the local PD." Stairns glanced over at Kenna as they walked down the drive to Chief Hadley's house. "Handing over those two wanted criminals to Detective Langford was a good idea."

Kenna shrugged. Bruce hadn't been super excited that she didn't allow him to "have some fun" as he'd said.

As they walked, she surveyed the front yard with its mature trees and tidy landscaping. Spring flowers had been planted on the edges of the walkway and along the front of the house on either side of the door. "Are we entirely sure Bruce is on the level?"

Stairns said, "He's just not the kind who shares. Some people can't handle not knowing every detail because they want to control everything around them."

Kenna tipped her head to the side. "I've had team leaders who were like that. You had to report in every time you made a move." She didn't mean Stairns, just other people she'd worked with. Guys who had been like Miller— at least before. He seemed different these days.

"Depends on how you feel about being responsible for the outcome of the situation."

Not too long ago, Kenna would have had a finger on the pulse of everything going on and what every member of her team was doing. She still hadn't quite finished wrestling with being responsible for the lives of everyone around her or the risk she was taking by caring about what happened to them. "I think I should trust people until they prove that I shouldn't."

"If you're going to give someone the benefit of the doubt, Bruce is a good guy to do that with."

Good. She surveyed the house in front of them. "I don't want to judge the size of his house and presume he's on the take or anything..."

"And anybody who is a first responder shouldn't have to live in poverty just to satisfy people's assumptions about where their money came from."

Kenna said, "Who knows, maybe his wife is super rich. Or he just had a run of good fortune in his investments."

"Exactly." Stairns knocked on the front door.

Ramon had stayed back at the campsite with Maizie, who was working on getting more from the brothers' cell phones, Hadley's activity online, and the reports they had received from the forensic analyst. What would help most of all was to know how Cliff contacted whoever it was he informed of a couple at the motel. If they could trace back that communication to whoever received it, then they would have a lead to follow to bring down the couple who were kidnapping people.

Whether they were the center of this operation or just a small part of it, Kenna would at least be one step closer to ending this. Finding her sister—cousin—and getting the chance to have a relationship with her.

Stairns knocked again.

Hopefully, Chief Hadley would be able to share some more information about where he was before he was kidnapped or if he knew anything else about the people who took him.

From deep in the house, she heard a long, high-pitched cry made by a man. A scream of pain. Kenna drew her weapon before she had even registered the fact it was likely Chief Hadley, full of fear and torment. Beside her, Stairns pulled his gun out also. Kenna lifted her foot and kicked the door by the handle, ramming her foot against the wood several times before she managed to get the door open.

It swung back to reveal a tile entryway and a small dog with long hair barking loudly at them. With each yap, it lifted its front paws off the floor.

"Sorry, dog." Kenna raced past the animal into the house. "Living room clear."

"Dining room clear."

She heard movement down a hallway and paused at the corner before looking around, gun-first. A woman ducked into a side room, blond hair flying. She had seen a photo of the wife that Maizie had found for her online. It could be Mrs. Chief Hadley, but unless she saw the woman's face, she couldn't know for sure.

Kenna raced to the room with the door open, keeping herself back from the door so that she didn't put her vital organs in the line of fire. Maybe she should start wearing a bulletproof vest, just on regular days. Every day. There was probably a high-end version that was a lot thinner than the bulky vests worn by first responders.

The room was empty.

Kenna stepped back, frowning. Where had that woman gone?

She kept going, opening another door along the hallway. This one led to a study with ceiling-high bookshelves and a ladder. It looked like a very female space, with lots of well-loved novels on the walls. In the center was a sofa, an armchair, and a coffee table. Apparently, the wife liked to read all kinds of popular novels.

She left the door open and went to the next room. Behind her, down the hall, maybe even on the other side of the house, she heard a crash. It sounded like Stairns had started to fight with someone. She was about to turn back to him when she caught sight of who was in the room.

Chief Hadley was tied to a rolling office chair in front of the fireplace in this very masculine office, with the huge TV over the fireplace and a ratty armchair that probably reclined. His wrists had been secured to the arms of the chair. Duct tape had been wound around his chest and the back of the chair so that he wasn't able to go anywhere. The wounds on his face were extensive, making her swollen cheekbone throb.

She went over and touched two fingers to his neck but felt no pulse. Kenna grabbed her phone and got on the walkie talkie app. She told Bruce to send a text to Langford explaining what'd happened. Then she went to the hall. "Stairns!"

A crash sounded from the other end of the single-level house. Maybe the bedroom? Something shattered like it was made of glass.

"Stairns!"

She took two steps before she was shoved from behind. Kenna stumbled, glancing off a side table in the hall and knocking over a vase. She spun around and saw a blond woman duck into another room. Kenna whipped the door open, going gun-first into the room.

The woman grabbed her arm.

Kenna planted one foot, still moving into the room, and kicked the woman's legs out from under her. *Mrs. Hadley.* With the hold the woman had on her arm, Kenna had to go down on top of her, otherwise Mrs. Hadley would've pulled on her injured arm too much.

They tumbled to the floor, and Kenna landed elbow first on the woman's chest. Her bumps and bruises—and the swollen side of her face—smarted. She kicked off the floor and rolled, but Mrs. Hadley put her strength into it, and they went too far.

The woman launched off Kenna and ran through the room. Kenna lifted her shoulders off the floor, pointed her gun at the fleeing woman, and moved her finger to the trigger. She didn't squeeze.

Mrs. Hadley pulled open a closet door at the back of this small bedroom and ducked into it.

Kenna frowned.

She went to the closet, opened the door, and found... nothing. Just a rail of clothes in front of her and a shelf above. Nothing moving. Was she was hiding? There were no legs under the rail of clothes. No attic access above her. "Secret door."

Rather than chase a woman through passageways she didn't know, Kenna retraced her steps to find Stairns in the dining room. His gray hair was rumpled, he looked flushed, and his shirt was askew. The woman in front of him held a kitchen knife, and he had found some kind of cloth—like a fabric place mat—and had it wrapped around both hands to ward her off.

Kenna stepped into the room with her gun raised. "Put the knife down or I shoot."

The woman breathed heavily through gritted teeth.

Behind her was a window, between them a dark wood table. Two chairs were knocked over. Stairns was over to the left, giving Kenna a clean shot.

Problem was, why did she look like Mrs. Hadley? Kenna had been fighting that woman—this woman—in that room down the hall, and she'd run into the closet. And yet, Stairns had been in an altercation with this Mrs. Hadley since before Kenna found the husband dead in that chair.

"Twins."

Stairns said, "Huh?" not moving one muscle, ready for whatever this woman was going to do next.

"There's more than one of her in this house."

Mrs. Hadley—the one Stairns had been fighting—threw the knife at Stairns. In the split second she took to swing her arm back before she launched the blade forward, Kenna squeezed the trigger on her gun.

The bullet slammed into Mrs. Hadley as she turned, embedding in her upper arm. She fell, or dove, toward the window. Kenna's next two bullets shattered the window. Mrs. Hadley ended up on the outside in a deafening explosion of glass. Kenna glanced at Stairns. "You good?" And ran to the window.

He groaned. "She's vicious. You should catch her."

Kenna looked outside to where Mrs. Hadley was up and running across the grass. "How about Bruce? He could use the steps." She breathed hard, pulled her phone out, and keyed up the walkie-talkie app. "She's coming to you."

"Copy that. Circling back."

Kenna frowned. "Whatever that means." She went over and helped Stairns up, though he didn't tug on her arm, so it wasn't really a case of her helping him. But she made the gesture anyway.

"She nicked my arm." He held the outside of his elbow.

"We need something to wrap it."

"I'll do that. You go after her."

"The cops will be on their way. Hadley is dead in the other room. Grab a towel and get out. And watch for the twin or you'll get a repeat of that." She motioned to the opening, then went over and climbed out of the big bay window, which was covered in glass. It embedded in the rubber soles of her shoes as she crunched over it, onto the grass.

Kenna jogged after Mrs. Hadley, trying to figure out what had just happened. Maizie had enough things to do, so asking her to find out if the chief's wife had a sibling would only slow her down. Or make things take longer. Maybe Ramon could look it up. Or they could contact somebody in the resistance. Given what happened here, she couldn't help thinking the chief's wife was an asset—like Preston's wife—placed with him to keep an eye out. Or to keep him in line.

In the end, whether there was one or two of them, it would be more important to confirm they did work for the "company" she was fighting against. If she was going to have even a slim chance of finding them and stopping what was happening here, then she had to catch the woman. And this time, she wouldn't be turning her over to the police.

Kenna jogged across the lawn in the same direction she'd seen the woman run.

Behind the house was a fence, and beyond that, she knew there was a road with a golf course on the opposite side. A wide open space where it wouldn't be so easy for her to hide.

She checked bushes and trees and shadowy corners back here for someone waiting to pop out and tackle her, but nothing moved. Kenna climbed up on the cable box, tucked behind a bush so the unsightly thing wasn't visible in the yard. She grabbed the top of the fence and spotted Mrs. Hadley.

Kenna clambered over, landing on both feet and bending her knees. She raced after the woman. Bruce was coming from the other direction down the street. That put their target in between them.

She would have nowhere to go but over the golf course, and eventually, they'd catch up to her.

A car turned the corner of the street about a quarter mile back behind Bruce. Kenna lifted her gun just in case the woman tried to commandeer it.

Bruce kept running, his focus on the woman.

"Car!" Kenna yelled.

The vehicle swerved around him, and Kenna spotted a female driver with dark hair. Bruce lowered a backpack from his shoulders, slowing his stride. The car pulled up on the street beside the woman, and she saw the driver yell to her. As if she was here to rescue the woman.

Kenna stopped, planted her feet, and squared her aim on the windshield. But she couldn't pull the trigger. Not if she didn't want to hurt the driver. She would certainly shoot Mrs. Hadley if she did anything to the driver. Then, the driver's face came into focus—Amara.

Amara hit the gas, driving toward Kenna.

Bruce lifted a weapon, wide in the barrel. No bigger than a compact submachine gun. What on earth was he...

Bruce aimed at the rear tire and fired. The projectile hit the wheel and launched the back end of the car up but didn't flip it. Amara fought the swerve, but the car was out of control. She bumped the curb at the golf course, went over the sidewalk, down the berm, and toward a sand trap that was probably there to keep balls from going into the street.

The car came to a stop with the front wheels still spinning.

She keyed her phone and contacted Stairns. "We need the car around back."

He responded, "On my way."

Bruce jogged over. "You hear sirens? I told Langford. She probably sent a car."

She could make out the tones in the distance. "Hadley is dead." She opened the driver's side door. "Bruce, get the other woman. Don't let her escape."

Kenna bent to look at Amara. The airbag had deployed, so she holstered her gun, found a knife in her pocket, and deflated it. "Time to go, Mom."

Bruce lifted up to look at her over the roof. "That's Amara?"

"Yep."

Amara groaned. "Kenna?"

"Sorry to break up the party. Time to go. Can you walk?" She gathered her mom out of the car. "I can't carry you."

"I know." Amara tugged on Kenna's shoulder and stood, leaning on the car. "Let's go."

"Bruce?" She helped her mom walk. With each step, Amara was more able to carry her own weight until she was walking on her own.

"Got her. She's out cold."

Stairns pulled up at the curb, and the sirens a street over got louder.

Amara said, "We should put her in the trunk, or she'll kill all of us."

Chapter Twenty

A mara turned to look out the window. "A rest stop?"

Kenna sat beside her on the back seat. They'd circled around, and Bruce had jumped in his vehicle, thankfully remaining behind them. For the sake of speed, they'd taken Amara's advice and dumped the other woman in the trunk of the car.

"Good place to talk and no one will look twice at us," Kenna said.

In the parking spot next to them, Bruce shoved the driver's door open and got out. She saw a gun in his waistband for a second before he moved his jacket to cover it.

Langford had called twice, but Kenna didn't answer. She sent the detective a text now and told her she'd connect later about Chief Hadley's death but was working a lead right now.

The detective probably wasn't happy with that answer.

Kenna got out, motioning for Amara to slide over to her. "Come this way."

Her mother—because she'd always thought of this

woman that way, even if she'd been dead all these years—didn't say anything. They went to the front entrance of the diner. A semi honked its horn, passing the rest stop but not pulling in. The parking lot had a line of semis and RVs, cars in rows, trucks and SUVs pulling vacation trailers. Families. Singles. The place bustled with people.

"Hopefully, we'll get a table."

Amara stopped by the door, flushed and a little rumpled but otherwise fine. "I'll talk to you, but your *friends* aren't part of our business."

Kenna held the door and glanced at Stairns who waved off any concern she might've had. He said, "We'll be close, and we'll keep an eye on the trunk. Make sure we don't lose anything."

The hostess took them to a table by the window, and Stairns and Bruce to the one behind it. Amara slid in, her chin up. Looking like the lady of the manor, which wasn't really necessary in a place where half the people in the restaurant had recently showered in the gas station next door. Who would sleep tonight in the cab of their vehicle and didn't mind that the coffee smelled burned.

Kenna ordered a plate that came with two eggs, bacon, potatoes covered in country gravy, and a slice of toast on the side—not that she would eat the toast. Amara asked for oatmeal.

"The woman you picked up? She killed her husband earlier today. Tied him to a chair and tortured him." Kenna took a sip of coffee, then added another little half-and-half pod to it.

"She's a means to an end, that's all you need to know."

"I get that you don't want me in your business, but you're not seeing that we could help each other."

Amara said, "You think I'm going to sign up for your team? I've been doing this alone for nearly three decades."

"Yeah. Me, too." She tried not to get irritated. "Only I thought you were dead, and there was no hope I'd ever see you. Turned out you just didn't want to see me."

Amara took a sip from the water glass on the table. "There's no point in dwelling on the past. It was impossible for me to see you. Much easier for you to believe I was dead."

That was her justification? "Dad saw you. Why was that not too much of a risk?"

"I never would have seen him. I'd have continued to let him believe I was dead." Amara glanced at the car, and the trunk that remained closed. "Only he figured out the truth."

Kenna stared at her.

Of course, her father had looked into it, refused to believe what he was told. Chased down the answers he needed.

Amara said, "I refused to see him if he told you I was alive, so he kept it from you, and we only saw each other a few times. It's not like we had some lengthy sordid relationship."

"I don't think it's sordid if you're married."

"You know what I mean."

Kenna sipped her coffee, sat back while the server delivered their plates, and put ketchup on her eggs. She ignored the look Amara gave her. "Why did you show up to pick up Mrs. Hadley? And don't tell me she is a means to an end."

Amara took a tiny bite of her oatmeal.

Kenna figured this was a lot like looking in a mirror of what she'd look like at fifty. Tiny silver strands at her temples and a trim figure. But Amara needed to be in peak condition to fight the fight she had spent her life and all her happiness on. Kenna wanted her future to be different—a husband, probably kids—at least eventually—and the ability to rest and let herself be happy with everything God seemed insistent on giving her. The Lord had decided to overwhelm her with the things He gave her. The people, the life she lived. All of it was His blessing after so many years of walking through the wilderness, being lonely. Working cases by herself.

She rubbed a hand over the top of her forearm, creating some friction between her long shirt sleeve and her scar, because the warmth of blood flow helped it to keep healing.

Amara watched her do it, but she said nothing.

The fact she wasn't curious at all about Kenna's life hurt a little, she could admit that to herself at least.

"How do you know her?"

"I don't know Clare Hadley."

Kenna swallowed a bite of potato. Stairns answered a phone call but spoke low while he ate big chunks of his omelet. "Why did you pick her up?"

"If I want Zeyla back, I'll have to trade something they want for her. Make an exchange."

"You're bargaining?" Kenna set her fork down. "Did they agree?"

"I'm going to make them an offer they can't refuse."

How very mafia of her. Kenna said, "Then you probably need both twins."

Amara frowned. "Twins?"

"There were two of them in the house. One disappeared into a closet, which I assume had some kind of hidden passage. The other is the one we chased out." Kenna studied her mother. "She didn't call you for a ride?"

"I was a passing Good Samaritan."

Hmm. "Would that have lasted long once she figured out you're one of them?"

"I can convince the younger ones what I need them to believe. It's why none of them have managed to kill me yet."

"Good for you." She tried not to make it sound sarcastic. Kenna really didn't mean it to be. She was actually glad her mother was still alive and that there was still a chance they could have a relationship. Unless her mother told her in no uncertain terms that there was no chance. "Tell me, is this organ trafficking thing connected to the company?"

"Most likely." Amara took another bite of her oatmeal.

"Do you know where they moved the operation? They cleared out of the abandoned hospital where Hadley and Zeyla were taken, and the place was destroyed." She explained about the field of shallow graves.

"The police are identifying all the victims?"

"If one is Zeyla, I'll make sure her body is released to you."

"It isn't." Amara sniffed. "I would know."

Kenna pressed her lips together. "Was Zeyla trying to do what I'm doing now and take them down? Did she get herself caught so she can fight back from the inside?"

"I'm certain that was her intention."

It seemed like maybe some of Amara's tactics had rubbed off on the daughter she'd had with Malcom Banbury. "Where was she staying?"

"I've already looked through her things. There was nothing there."

"How long has it been since you saw her?"

Amara shrugged one shoulder. "A couple of months, maybe longer. She was working here, and I've been on a job in Germany. Trying to do our part to take them down from different angles. It puts both of us in danger to spend too much time together."

"Because they don't know she's your daughter?"

"The way assets are raised…they don't spend much time with their biological parents. That way, there can be little emotional attachment. I raised her. I made sure of that. But she was in the care of an older woman, a former asset. I trusted her, but the company believed they'd placed Zeyla with Olivette. They had to believe things were above board—the way they wanted them to be."

"And under the surface, you live your life in a way that weakens what they're trying to do."

"You make it sound ineffective. We have dealt serious blows to the company, and they have never discovered it was us. Which is why Zeyla and I remain alive."

"But if you try to trade one of their assets back to them in exchange for her, it will all be over."

"She will expect me to not make the trade." Amara fiddled with her spoon but didn't take a bite. "To maintain our covers and let her dig herself out of this alone."

"So why aren't you?"

"The same reason you refuse to give up hope. I'm not going to abandon her. Not ever."

Kenna stared at her, wondering about that. It was true that she never gave up hope. She just hadn't ever thought of it like that. As if she somehow had the ability to be relentlessly hopeful. "I've seen what happens when hope dies. I don't want to feel that. It doesn't end well."

"And so you cling to your hope in the face of…everything. That kind of determination is what Zeyla and I bring to the fight against the company. Because we can do nothing else but try to fight them. Try to *weaken* their operation. One day, we will succeed in taking them down."

Bruce shifted in his chair. Kenna refocused on Amara. "Why don't you just tell me where their headquarters is or who is in charge? Give me a list, even. I have people who would work their way down and destroy everyone. Precise, strategic. There would be no company when they're done."

Bruce settled in his seat.

Stairns, across the table from him and facing Kenna, didn't seem to approve. But if Bruce was all in on taking down the company in a way that would mean total destruction with little collateral damage, then she was willing to consider mocking up a plan to get that done.

"I'll get you a list."

It was a testament to how she felt about her likelihood of success or how tired she was with the length of time this was taking or her optimism that she would, in fact, get Zeyla back.

Kenna wouldn't let the moment go. "I can help you. If you let me."

"And give me more to lose?" She pushed the oatmeal bowl to the end of the table.

"I've discovered that even after loss, there's still far more to gain. It's a little overwhelming, actually. I thought I was fine living alone in my RV, solving cases by myself. My parents were dead. My fiancé and my baby, my career. Everything I thought I was going to have in my life was gone. I was completely alone, trying to keep my sanity. So, I can understand being desperate to keep what you have. Or not knowing that when you lose things, God can give you back more than you ever dreamed you'd have."

"You think I'm part of what He gave you?"

Kenna wasn't going to say what she might be thinking. Not when Amara's tone sounded like that. "I guess we'll find out."

Amara didn't smile, but a smidge of humor lit her eyes for a second.

"So, you're taking Clare Hadley? The police will be looking for her. Should I tell them to call you to find out where she is, or do you expect me to lie and say I don't know whose car she got into?" That would be a risk, given some homeowner around the golf course could've seen the crash. "I'm assuming you don't need help making the trade."

Part of Kenna quaked inside. What if she went with Amara to make the trade and ended up as one of the traded pieces given to the company? All so her mom could get Zeyla back.

"Maybe they'll find the twin you mentioned, and she'll be arrested." Amara shrugged. "You could help with that, right? Point them in the direction."

Kenna said, "Why trade one twin when you could offer two?"

"I already have a second asset."

Kenna bit the inside of her lip.

"Your friend, Roxanne. I caught her last night while you were tussling at the roadhouse, getting that." She motioned to Kenna's face with her water glass.

"I caught an elbow," Kenna said. "You have Roxanne? In your custody?"

Amara shrugged. "She's going to garner me a whole lot of goodwill when I tell them how thoroughly she screwed up infiltrating the Federal Bureau of Idiots."

Stairns' head whipped around from watching the window.

"Easy," Kenna said. "I was FBI, and so was my father. This family doesn't disrespect the bureau." They might not always get along with the feds, but they weren't going to be disparaging them.

"In answer to your question, yes, I'll be taking Clare. I'll trade her and Roxanne to get Zeyla back."

"I wanna to talk to Roxanne before you do the trade."

Amara chuckled slightly. "If she had planned to tell you anything, she'd have said it already."

"Get me that list of names." She could tell their conversation was coming to an end before Amara shifted in the seat and began to slide toward the end of the bench. "And locations. I want everything you have on the structure of the company and who is in charge of every division."

"Some things are beyond even my extensive knowledge. It's why they've existed for so long."

"Give me what you have."

Amara said, "I'll need the car keys."

Stairns shook them.

Amara glanced at Bruce. They exchanged an inscrutable look. She took the keys and went out the door.

"Please tell me we have a tracker on that car."

Stairns said, "It's *my* car."

"We can follow it?"

He reluctantly nodded. "Maizie set it up. Just in case. Who knew it would be just in case your mom borrowed it?"

Bruce shifted in his seat again.

He'd seemed surprised when she referred to Amara as her mother. Hesitant to acknowledge her now. "You two know each other, Bruce?"

"We met in the woods by the roadhouse." He cleared his throat. "Last night."

"That's why you didn't show up to help." Kenna pulled out some cash to leave on the table to cover the bill. "Are you the reason Roxanne got away?"

"Nothing happened. Don't worry about it." He headed for the door.

Outside, Amara pulled from the space and drove toward the exit that would get her back on the highway.

Kenna stared after him. "Why does him telling me not to worry fail to fill me with confidence?"

"Because you're smart, and you have good instincts." Stairns grinned. "I guess we're riding back in his truck. Let's make sure he doesn't leave without us."

"I'll call Maizie so we can find out where she goes."

Chapter Twenty-One

"This is the address?" Kenna pointed at the screen of Maizie's laptop. They were on the picnic bench between the two vehicles with Ramon sitting across from them. Bruce was asleep in a plastic Adirondack chair by the fire pit, his hood up on his sweater mostly covering his face —or shading his eyes from the sun—and Cabot curled up on his lap snoring even though she didn't really fit there.

The air had a morning chill, but there was no breeze moving the trees. All was still at the RV park except for a lone older man walking a tiny dog. The sight of them made her want to contact her friend Dixie, whom she hadn't heard from in a while. And Forrest Crosby. Maybe even Taylor, her psychologist friend at the FBI in Salt Lake City.

Friends. People who had influenced her life in the last few years and stuck around in emails and texts and infrequent phone calls. Women she would go to for advice or just to chat.

Was she really going to invite them to her wedding?

She didn't even have a wedding date. When Jax got here, they could probably figure it out. But when one of them was constantly in the middle of a big case, it was hard to find time to plan like that. Even just thinking about getting married and the overwhelming amount of decisions involved made her heart start to beat faster.

Ramon asked, "Why are you freaking out?"

"I'm not. I'm just thinking about wedding planning."

Maizie and Ramon shared a cryptic glance. She was about to ask what it meant when Maizie said, "I don't think you need to worry about that right now. I mean, we've got so much going on with this. You have your dress, so you're good."

"Weddings are more than finding a dress. There are a *thousand* things to figure out."

Ramon shrugged it off. "You have time, right? You'll figure it out."

"Do you think your mom will come?" Maizie asked.

Kenna groaned. "Great. Now I'm thinking about that and how awkward it's going to be. I mean, it's not like she'll be all overwhelmed and happy for me."

Ramon's expression softened. "She's not going to get emotional. How can she when her existence is life and death, protecting her children. Keeping people alive and safe, and trying to take down the company. She's been at war her entire life. No rest. No downtime."

"She had it with me."

Ramon nodded slightly. "That's true, but that might be exactly why she knows it won't work. That taking time off costs someone their life. She may not be prepared to go so far as to take a day off because it could have disastrous consequences."

Kenna looked away, watching the tall pine trees around them. The mountains in the distance, and the expansive

Colorado sky with the sun rising, bringing with it an orange glow that stretched across the horizon.

She could understand what it felt like to know to your soul that letting go of the struggle for even a second would cause someone pain—most likely her. She'd felt that way about letting people in, going it alone for two years after she left the FBI. She had needed that time to heal. To figure out what she wanted. To process all the things she was feeling after losing Bradley. She'd worked out what she wanted the rest of her life to be and pieced together a life she loved out of the ashes of what she'd thought she would have. Who she thought she would be. The years she thought she would live.

God had directed her back to Salt Lake City, giving her that Joseph moment where what had been intended for evil He had used for good. Her good. She'd met Jax, reconnected with Ryson and his family, and started working with Stairns. Maizie had come along. Her friends, Dixie and Forrest. Then Ramon. Now Bruce as well. And Jax's family.

That was a lot of people to add to her Christmas list.

It was enough to make her want to shed a tear of gratitude that she had so many people in her life. Even if occasionally she needed a break from them in favor of some solitude.

Ramon continued, "And her daughter is missing. She managed to save you, but this girl might as well be everyone she's ever loved. If she loses Zeyla, then she loses *everything*."

"I get it."

"Do you?"

Kenna rolled her eyes. "Maizie, tell me about the house.

If Amara is going to try and trade Clare and Roxanne for Zeyla, I want to be there."

Maizie looked at her, tucking hair back behind her ear. "Are you going to call the cops or the FBI?"

"I'm not sure yet. Tell me what you've got."

Maizie looked back at her laptop. "Okay, from the top. The company we infiltrated has properties owned by companies, shell corporations, subsidiaries, all those words that mean they're companies inside of companies that are parent companies of other—"

"We get it," Ramon said.

"So I have a list of addresses of places they own. The address Amara sent is on the list. I'm still working through Hadley's information and the phones those two brothers had on them. All communication was on the dark web, so it's not searchable, and the threads are gone now. The number the brothers contacted is a dead end. The phone is unregistered, and it's either off or out of battery. My guess is they turn it on periodically when they're expecting contact."

Kenna shrugged. "They have Zeyla. She got Hadley out but was recaptured, and they burned the location and went somewhere else. I think it might be about drawing out my mother so they can have Amara *and* Zeyla."

Ramon said, "What about moving vehicles? If they had to transport everything and everyone—because that hospital was cleaned out—somewhere else, to the new location, that means they'd need vehicles to put the stuff in. At the last minute, they had to have hired transportation. There could be a paper trail."

Maizie said, "I'll see what I can find. We know it would've been contracted from the building we looked through, with all the bodies. Want me to pass on what I find to the police?"

Kenna said, "Langford is probably mad because we left Hadley's house. She isn't responding to my messages."

"She's probably at the DA's office getting a warrant for your arrest." Ramon smirked.

"That isn't actually so funny," Kenna said. "I'd rather not end up in jail."

Ramon shrugged. "It happens."

Kenna frowned. She wanted to ask what he was talking about, but they were better off focusing. "What else do we know?"

"According to social media..." Maizie's voice trailed off.

The Class C screen door snapped back on its hinges. Stairns rounded the hood of the vehicle and came over, holding a thermal cup and his phone. His gaze met Maizie's, and he nodded slightly.

Kenna asked, "Is there something I'm missing?" Everyone was sharing looks, and she was evidently not privy to their private conversations.

"Don't worry about it." Ramon waved a hand. Then to Maizie, he said, "What did you find online?"

Stairns sat beside Ramon with his coffee. He'd gone to talk to his wife when she'd called, and apparently, it put him in a good mood. Made her want to call Jax just so she could hear him say something sweet.

Maizie said, "They're having a party tonight at that address. A big fancy fundraiser for a local charity. It's black tie, and there are three hundred people on the guest list."

"I have a swollen face," Kenna pointed out. "And Ramon doesn't look much better."

"You could cover it with makeup," Maizie said. "Or wear a wig that falls over your left cheek."

Ramon said, "You could tell Langford. She could take Miller."

Stairns shook his head. "Terrible idea. They'll get outed as cops in five minutes, and we won't manage to find Amara in the crowd."

Ramon said, "I hate to be the one to suggest this, but given the crowd they'll be going into... What about Stairns and Maizie?"

Kenna and Stairns both said, "No," at the same time.

Ramon lifted his hands.

Maizie looked disappointed. "I have black eyes, but I could cover them with makeup."

Kenna turned on the bench seat to face the teen. "You absolutely could go to something like this. It has nothing to do with your age. It's about training and knowing what to do. Then, you go in with confidence, not as a ball of nerves with no skills."

"I don't mind being in the van. It's like being home in the Airstream."

This was new. "You like being there?"

"It's not like I'm scared to leave. I've been to Mexico and England. This is Colorado still, so we're not even that far from home, but I wanna go back there when the mission is over. And I don't want to spend more time on the road than in the Airstream at Stairns' house."

Kenna squeezed the girl's shoulder. "That's good to know. For now, it works, and if you want to change things in the future, we can make sure you have the skills to do what you want to do."

Maizie kept her expression impassive. "Bruce said he'd teach me how to interrogate a suspect. Like with pliers and a car battery."

Ramon busted up laughing.

What could Kenna say to that? Bruce was going to teach her *enhanced interrogation* tactics?

Maizie grinned, then laughed out loud. "He said to tell you that so I could see your reaction." She kept laughing. "That was a good one."

Bruce opened one eye under the hood. "Did I miss it?"

Maizie kept laughing.

Kenna said, "I'd throw this mug at you, but it would be a waste of good coffee and a good mug."

She saw Bruce's grin flash under his hood.

Maizie leaned against her shoulder, still chuckling.

"Let's all focus, shall we?" Because if Maizie was going to get them into this party, they needed an invitation, their names on the guest list, and fancy outfits. "Actually, I have an idea. Bruce? Why don't *you* go with me tonight? I could use some of those CIA spy skills of yours."

Bruce sat up, nearly dislodging Cabot from his lap. The dog didn't really fit there, but she curled up and made it work. "What are we doing?"

"Going to a society party. You'll need a tux."

He sat back in the chair, groaning.

The sounds of his displeasure continued through shopping at the mall, all the way until they were driving to the property in a rented supercar.

"You should've let me drive." Kenna smoothed down the skirt of her dress, which barely touched her knees.

Bruce barked a laugh. "No chance, honey."

"Excuse me? Is this some sexist thing?"

"Can't drive a car like this in heels."

"These shoes were a dumb idea. I'm going to fall on my face."

"Can't wear Converse to a black tie." Bruce glanced over. "Not even to make a statement."

"They're on the back seat. The minute I get outed as me, I'm coming back to the car to change them." At least, it had sounded like a good idea in her head. "Now, tell me about Amara."

He glanced at her again. "What about her? She's your mom, ain't she?"

The use of "ain't" was like a tell in poker. But Kenna wasn't going to point that out. "You saw her in the woods behind the roadhouse? She ended up with Roxanne in her custody, but you didn't report that you'd made contact with anyone."

"I don't do reports."

"Neither does Ramon, and what's the point of papers and papers and more papers anyway? We won't have anywhere to put them. That's why we add it to the message board. I updated everyone with my note." Not a report, just a little FYI. After all, if she didn't do it, then *none* of them would. "But you said nothing about seeing her."

"Fine." Bruce pressed his lips together. "She got by me."

"I know she's a highly trained asset. Maybe being out of the CIA for a while made you lose your edge, some of your skills are rusty." She would've continued but got the desired response already.

He cut her off, blustering. "You think I'm rusty?"

"Then how'd she get by you?"

"Maybe Amara hypnotized me. Does the company do that?"

"Probably," Kenna said, shuddering a little at the thought of it. "But why would she?"

"How should I know?"

"So, a beautiful woman bewitched you, and you lost your mind...as it were. I guess it's good to know your weakness." Even if the object of his desire was the woman she'd considered her mother for years.

Bruce sighed. "Roxanne will recognize us both."

"I'm more worried about the other people at the party." Her phone rang, so she slid her thumb across the screen. "Yeah, Maze?"

"I got the guest list. I'm adding your names, but you're not going to like this."

Kenna frowned. Out the window, the sky was more clouds than stars. The road was darkness and headlights. Brake lights. Streetlights. All of it ruined what nature should look like at night.

Maizie might need the Airstream, but Kenna needed open sky. Maybe Wyoming or Utah. Someplace with no one for miles and nothing but stars overhead.

"Senator Woodford is attending, which you might think is a big deal, but also on the list is Adrielle Jaxton and Elaine Caliveri."

"Laney?" Jax's sister and mom would be at the party? "Are you serious?"

Bruce pulled off the highway.

"They're on the list."

Kenna said, "They're supposed to have protection on them, and they're walking right into the lion's den?"

Bruce gripped the wheel. "It's their world. Isn't it?"

Maizie said, "I should call Jax and tell him what's going on."

"Thanks, Maze. Anyone else on the list I should know about?"

"A federal judge. The lieutenant governor from Wyoming. Business leaders. College professors. Stairns said 'captains of industry,' whatever that means."

"Law enforcement?"

"Maybe. I'm still running names on the... Yikes, this guy is the general of the Colorado National Guard. When I saw Adrielle's and Laney's names, I called you right away."

"Thanks. I'll make sure they're safe, and I'll get them out. Bruce can take care of Amara."

Maizie said, "Stairns said if you come across the Colorado Bureau of Investigation, give them a wide berth."

"Copy that." She spotted the turn up ahead. "We're here."

"You have comms." Maizie hung up.

Bruce pulled into the drive and went through the open gate between two brick pillars with stone lions on top. He slowed to go down the long drive lined with cars. The drive circled at the end, with a fountain in the center. The two-story house was lit up. A valet took guests' keys at a stand out front.

"Guess this is it." She tucked her phone into the glove box.

Bruce said, "Try not to stab anyone."

"That's it? That's your advice."

"You go for the family. I'll take care of your mom." He pulled up at the valet stand.

Kenna said, "Try not to get hypnotized again, or I'll stab you."

He just grinned.

Chapter Twenty-Two

Bruce escorted her through the front door. She half expected someone to announce their names to the ballroom, but with the number of guests here, that would become tiresome.

The expansive ceiling had arches several feet apart, all the way down to two halves of a staircase that met on an upper level opening to the right. It seemed the party was going on up there also. People were moving up and down the stairs, and music was coming from the center of the room, where a stringed ensemble played in front of the fireplace.

To the left, the high wall had a number of tapestries.

"Are we in Colorado, or did we flip back to Europe again?" Bruce muttered.

"It does look like the inside of that house we toured."

"They wish. It's not the same."

She smiled. "You liked it there."

"But the US is home. Or it was, now it's the place I can't leave." Bruce patted her arm. "Don't worry about me. I'm just a nostalgic old man having a moment."

There was a lot she could say, but not much that would be helpful. He'd signed on to be a CIA officer knowing the risks. He'd been burned through no fault of his own, as far as she knew. Left in England with his government denying all knowledge of him. A burned spy could be killed by any foreign government, and the US wouldn't bat an eye—or retaliate.

Now that he was back in the US, at least he could be home, but it probably did feel a lot like being trapped.

"You ever want a change in your job, you let me know." She glanced at him. "And if you wanna go after that guy you saw. The one who got you burned? I'm all in."

Bruce grinned. "You say the sweetest things."

She smiled.

"You're probably gonna have Stairns do it, but..."

"What?" She shook her head.

"If you needed someone to walk you down the aisle, I'd do it. I wanna do it."

She didn't know what to say.

"It's fine, though." He patted her arm. "You have other people in line in front of me."

She squeezed his hand because he was right. "Thanks for offering."

Bruce cleared his throat. "I'm gonna go do some work now. Maizie gave me some gadgets, and I wanna try them out." He lifted his brows. "I'll be back. Maybe."

Kenna chuckled.

He leaned down and kissed her cheek. "Knock 'em dead."

"That is the plan."

Bruce wandered off, and she heard him chuckling as he moved away from her through the crowd. Kenna turned toward one of the two bar stations and asked for a soda. She needed to find Jax's mom and sister in this ocean of people. Or her mother. Maybe Zeyla or Roxanne or Mrs. Hadley. Maybe she had no idea what she was doing here. It was only a fishing expedition.

Better yet, she could trust Bruce to do his job and find Amara, and she could safeguard the people who would be her family when she said, "I do," to Jax.

Kenna sipped the soda. The sleeves of her dress hooked over her thumbs, and the material bunched up at her elbow when she lifted her arm, but buying a dress with sleeves had been more of a reflex than anything else. No one needed to see her scars. In a room like this, full of power brokers, that sign of weakness would let them know she could be devoured like prey. She needed every way she could find to level the playing field.

Maizie had sent photos of the key players on the guest list—the ones most likely connected to the company they were fighting. She flipped through the images once more, then decided to do a circuit of the ballroom.

"If you want an introduction to the senator, I can make that happen." His voice was like syrup that was a little too sweet.

She turned to him, standing far too close to her, and lifted her gaze. Maybe twenty-five at best, slicked back hair, and a tailored suit with a silk tie.

"Is that right?" She lifted one brow and tried to pretend Jax was being enticing about going out for Mexican food.

It worked if his smile was anything to go by. "I work for the senator. I have all year, since I graduated from Harvard."

"Wow. That's impressive."

"I'm Charleston Whitworth-Harrow. My friends call me Charlie." He held his hand out.

She shook his oddly smooth skin, wondering what he thought of her hand. That was only the beginning of the differences between them. "Kenna Banbury."

She waited to see if he recognized her name. It wasn't impossible. When he didn't react, she figured she was in the clear. He wasn't going to drug her and take her to some cell in the basement where they would remove a kidney and half her liver—or whatever was on the menu.

At least, not in the next ten minutes.

"Kenna. That's a great name." It was a little too rehearsed. "Let's go find the senator. Last I saw, he was holding court upstairs. It's quieter in the billiards room, but mostly, they just prefer to camp out close to the cigar cabinet."

Kenna smiled like he couldn't possibly have said something more interesting if he tried. In her ear, through the comms earbud she'd inserted in the car, she heard a snort.

Bruce said, "This guy. Where'd you find him?"

She cleared her throat.

"Yeah, yeah. I'm searching the lower level. Catch you later."

Charlie had said something.

"Sorry." Kenna shook her head. "I'm a bit mesmerized by this place. I didn't catch what you said."

He reached the stairs first, grasping the thick dark wood handrail and stepping up onto the red floral pattern carpet. He paused. "I asked what you do for a living."

"My father was an author. He published a number of books and movies. So long ago no one nowadays has seen them. But I don't have to work. This is going to sound terribly entitled, but I have a trust fund." She tried to blush but doubted it actually happened.

"How scandalous." He chuckled. "A trust fund. What is the world coming to?" His grin spread wide.

She laughed, trying to sound like a delighted college-age girl. *Kill me now.* Surely, he knew she was too old for this. But it was easier to act like a vapid person with no job who failed to contribute to the world than it was to pretend to be a physicist. There were less questions to answer.

"Yes," she said. "I'm afraid I'm one of *those* people."

"We should form a club," he said as they ascended the stairs. "Tell me, what did you buy with your last check?"

She smiled, as if delighted to be asked. "A dress. It's pretty fabulous, if I might say so. I'm saving it for a special occasion." She quoted the retail price with alterations and the shoes.

Charlie whistled. "I bought a yacht. It's in Virginia Beach. I think I'm going to sail down to Nassau. Spend some time in the Caribbean this summer."

"Will the senator give you the time off?"

He waved a hand. "Doesn't matter. I'll be ready for a change of direction by then. How about you? What would you say if I asked you to go with me for the summer?"

They slowed at the top of the stairs.

"I'd say you should ask someone you know. Otherwise, you might find yourself stuck on a boat with an axe murderer and no way to save yourself."

Charlie tipped his head back and laughed. "An axe murderer. That's a good one."

Two women stepped out of the upper room. Laney and Adrielle. Kenna gave Laney wide eyes that hopefully said, *Save me.*

"Charleston Whitworth-Harrow, are you bothering my dear friend?" Laney picked up her pace, came over, and kissed Kenna on the cheek. She whispered, "You owe me."

Kenna said, "So good to see you, Laney." She reached out to Jax's mother and said, "Adrielle."

The older woman squeezed her hand. "I didn't expect to see you here, dear."

"You know me. I like to party." Kenna chuckled.

"I'm going to introduce Kenna to the senator," Charlie said, motioning to the door.

Adrielle frowned.

"I've always wanted to meet a senator. Charlie here is so sweet to offer to let me meet his boss." She lifted her brows a couple of times. "Maybe I'll get an internship, too."

She squeezed Laney's hand and whispered, "Love you guys, but you should leave this party." Then, she kept going up the stairs. If only she could escort them out.

Laney gave a subtle nod. Good. She got the message.

Kenna went with Charlie, sliding her arm through his. "Can you believe she wore that dress? Green is so last season." Kenna had no idea what she was talking about, but people in this echelon of society bonded over the failure of others. Pretty much like most echelons of society. She was guessing Charlie would be receptive to it.

He snorted. "My father's housekeeper wore a green dress on New Years Eve. It was a monstrosity. You should've seen how hideous it was. I'll show you a picture after I introduce you to...oh, there he is."

The man in question, Senator Woodford, sat on a wingback chair in the corner, surrounded by people on the edge of their seats leaning toward him evidently enraptured by whatever he was saying.

Charleston Whitworth-Harrow was apparently the kind of intern who could motion with one finger, interrupt the entire conversation, and have Woodford lifting his drink for a last sip, leaving his cigar in the ashtray, and coming over to them.

"Senator, this is Kenna Banbury."

That was the introduction that got her a reaction. "Is it really." Statement, not a question. The senator had some years on him, but the advances of modern cosmetic medicine had smoothed out the rough edges. His nails were buffed. His top button was unfastened, and his eyes were slightly glassy, making her wonder if it was only the drink that had him in this fuzzy, altered state.

The senator looked her up and down, then said, "Get lost, son."

"Yes, sir."

He barely glanced at Charlie as he disappeared into the crowd. He stared down at her from a height at least two inches taller. He wasn't thick in the chest. He had slim hips and slender legs under those well-tailored pants, but she wasn't going to underestimate him. It took considerable grip strength to whack a golf ball for hours every week and a keenly deceptive mind to operate in political circles.

Best to do this the easy way. "I won't be calling you *sir*."

"No, I don't suppose you will." His expression gave away nothing. "Pretty brazen of you to simply walk in the front door."

"No one stopped me."

"They were instructed not to bar your entry."

And her companion? "So, your people clocked me from the moment I entered and have had eyes on me ever since." She hoped Laney and Adrielle were out. And that no one was going to snap a trap shut on Bruce and end whatever snooping he was doing right now.

She had to trust he had the skills to evade capture because there wasn't much else she could do to help him.

This would become an elaborate exchange of assets if it came to it. She wasn't above bartering. Did Amara even know all the ways this could go wrong?

In her ear, Bruce said, "Don't worry about me."

The senator said, "We should go somewhere less busy. Then we can have a conversation."

She didn't like the sound of it, but Bruce needed more time with Amara. It wasn't like they would simply allow her to walk out the door. "Lead the way."

He took her to the back of the room and a doorway where he entered a code. She didn't catch all the numbers, but just enough she could get through the door if she had a few minutes. The dimly lit hallway was lined with wood paneling that added to the darkness.

Another room off to one side held an office with a single desk and a high-backed chair. Walls of bookshelves. Artwork above a fireplace that looked like it had been carved out of a single piece of stone. Real wood logs, now ashy in color, on a metal grate. A wide window covered by floor-to-ceiling heavy drapes.

"Nice office."

Woodford went to the credenza, opened it, and drew out a glass decanter with a stopper on top. He motioned to her with it.

"No thank you."

"I'm sure you aren't here for my decorator's number."

"How do you know?" She folded her arms loosely so they didn't hurt but enough to look as if she intended to be defiant. "Maybe I am."

He chuckled, pouring himself a hefty serving of whatever that was. "You walked in my front door. You could've called. What do you want, Kenna Banbury?"

"Zeyla."

He simply stared at her.

"Which begs the question, why would I rescue one woman and leave an organ trafficking operation to continue? Not really my style to live and let live, is it?"

"So, we're to be at odds?"

"Depends," she said. "Are you the one kidnapping people and taking their body parts out?"

He sat on the edge of the desk like a pompous rich guy who'd become a senator purely so he could feel like he ruled the world. "Me? That's amusing. You won't find me getting my hands dirty, I can assure you."

"Yeah, I bet." She lowered her arms, feeling a little exposed in a dress. Not that she'd left her weapons behind, they were just concealed a little better than normal. "Give me the people who are responsible, and I'll be on my way."

He seemed amused for a moment, took a sip of his drink, and then shrugged. "Very well. You have a deal. I'll give you the couple."

"And Zeyla."

"That will be a little more difficult, as I have no idea who that is."

Great. He could have nothing to do with the company, or he might be up to his eyeballs in the whole thing with no intention of admitting that to her. "Don't worry, I'll find her myself."

Chapter Twenty-Three

Kenna stepped out of the little office, wondering how much of a chance she'd have to snoop in these back halls before someone discovered her.

She was about to ask Bruce what was going on when Charlie stepped into the hall at the far end.

"Come to escort me to the ballroom?"

He walked toward her, intensity in his stride and shadows on his face.

"Charlie."

"It isn't like we can have you wandering around the house," Senator Woodford said from behind her.

"Is he okay?" She motioned to Charlie, who stopped in front of her.

"Charleston knows to do as he's told," the senator said. "Now escort Ms. Banbury to the ballroom before things get...interesting."

Charlie grabbed her arm above the elbow and started for the door at the end of the hallway.

"It's been a pleasure. Shame it had to be cut short," she said over her shoulder. Trying not to trip on these shoes.

Despite what Bruce said, she should have worn her Converse. These weren't her people, not even if she was going to marry Jax and his family ran in these circles. Kenna had no need to impress any of them. "Hope you keep your end of the bargain."

"Don't worry. Our arrangement will be pleasurable, for both of us."

Now she regretted saying anything at all because that just sounded gross. Why did smarmy bad guys always have to make things weird?

She pressed her lips together. He didn't have to drag her; she could walk. She was perfectly capable of leaving this party on her own. But Charlie looked like an automaton right now. Someone brainwashed, trained to do his master's bidding like a puppy dog.

Was this a substance the company had created? One that had suggestive powers or gave someone the ability to control another. There was a terrifying thought. She wasn't drinking or eating anything for the remainder of this case unless she had made it herself or the container had been sealed.

He dragged her through the door.

"Let go of me, Charlie."

His glassy gaze slid over to her. "Ask nicely."

Kenna shifted her weight and brought her knee up between his legs. She knew she'd hit the jackpot when he doubled over and collapsed onto the floor. "Sorry, but it's effective."

He grabbed for her foot, anger suffusing his features. Crying out.

She jumped out of his hold and wound up kicking off the shoes. They'd been expensive but ridiculous. Not pricey enough for her to risk going back and retrieving them. She ran the few feet to the next door, the one that would get her into that back room at the top of the stairs.

Hopefully, Laney and Adrielle had managed to leave with no trouble. Her partner tonight was the first priority. "You read me, Bruce?"

"Loud and clear." He sounded distracted.

"We're bugging out."

"And things were just getting interesting," he said. "Thought that guy was going to proposition you right then and there."

Kenna made a face. "I'm spoken for."

Bruce chuckled. "Good for you, kid."

They could talk about him calling her that later. After they got out of this. "What are you working on?"

"A treasure trove. I'm getting it all photographed so it uploads to Maizie or whatever y'all have setup."

"If you're in a lower level, it might not transmit until you're topside. How far down did you get?"

"Subbasement four."

Kenna blew out a breath. "So this place is even bigger than we know." She ducked into the VIP room, trying to slip through without causing a scene. No one followed her from the hall, so she eased the door closed quietly. "Any sign of my mom?"

"No. Hang on. Someone is coming."

"Forget what you have and get out. This situation is getting too hot." He'd come here knowing that their enemy, this company, might be aware that he'd killed one of their high level assets. Considering she'd been trying to murder Kenna and Jax at the time, it was justified. But the company might hold a grudge against Bruce for protecting her the day she got engaged.

He would tell her he didn't much care about the threat.

He cared about the mission and their little group being safe. After that, he was going to take care of his own business with his former partner, or handler, whoever that guy had been. The rest of them would help, but they all knew this took precedence.

Through her earbud, she heard someone talking in a higher tone, like a woman's voice, but couldn't make out what they were saying.

She eased through the VIP room all nonchalant and got to the top of the stairs, scanning the room. As if she would find Laney and Adrielle in the ballroom somewhere. They should be long gone by now.

She held the rail and descended the carpeted steps like it was perfectly normal to do that in bare feet and an expensive dress.

When she was almost to the bottom step, the front doors of the building flew open and crashed against the wall. Police in bulletproof vests and waterproof jackets strode in, followed by armed tactical officers. She rounded the stairs at the bottom just as they announced themselves.

"FBI! Nobody leaves, nobody causes a fuss. Everybody stays where they are." The guy in charge wasn't Miller, but she figured he would be here.

No one paid any mind. Most of the crowd jogged themselves out of their surprise and started to head for the exits.

Kenna glanced over her shoulder and saw local police and state cops. Mostly feds, though. But local SWAT were good and not to be left out of the fun. The cooperation between agencies was heartwarming.

She found a door under the stairs and tried the handle, finding it unlocked. She nearly thanked God, but considering she was fleeing the police, maybe that wasn't the best idea. *I always need help though, and that's what You do. So,*

I'm asking for wisdom. This thing could go sideways so easily. Maybe it already did, and I just don't want to admit it.

She ducked through the door, and a few people rushed after her, trying to get away from the cops.

Kenna spotted a kitchen, all brightly lit, at the end of the hall. She smelled cooking meat, and the top of the wall at the ceiling seemed a little hazy with smoke. The people with her pressed against her back, so she stepped to the side and let them pass.

An open door opposite her, halfway down the hall, led to a lower level. She slipped into the stairwell, pulling the door closed behind her just as a cop came into the hall. He didn't notice her. She shut the door silently and felt for the wall, picturing the stairs in her head. Dark wood, about two feet wide, a little spiral staircase for staff to use to get around the house. For all she knew, down here was only a food pantry kept below ground so it remained cooler.

She eased her way down in the dark, tuning her senses to the sounds around her. The muffled swipe of each footstep. Nothing above her, but then that quiet was severed by a thud and a distant shout.

She kept going, winding around. Until she was certain she had gone several floors.

If someone was down here, she didn't want to alert them to her presence by talking to Bruce over the comms. She didn't hear anything on his end.

What had happened?

He'd indicated someone was going to discover him. But a trained spy would be able to evade being seen—unless his intention was to be caught.

Where was her mother and Zeyla? She could help them, but if her mom didn't let her in on the plan, then there wasn't much she could do. Who wanted to insert themselves into a situation where they weren't welcome. It hurt her feelings a bit. But maybe there was a reason her mom was keeping her out of this. Like she was proactively trying to save Kenna from these people.

Her feet touched flat tile, colder than the wood of the stairs.

Kenna ran her hand over the wall, trying to find a light switch. She found some kind of switch and flicked it on. Overhead lighting flickered and then stuck in a dim yellow glow that switched on closest to her first. One by one, lights on the ceiling illuminated going away from her. A long hallway that took a minute to light up all the way down.

Her eyes widened.

In front of her was a dining table and chairs set up, and to the left, behind a glass wall with a door in the center, she could see racks of wine. Kept in a temperature-controlled environment.

Past the table, stacks of barrels used to age wine and other drinks were lined up. She didn't know a whole lot about that process, but some of the barrels were stained red where the wine seemed to be leaking out.

If she wanted to cause a big problem, she could knock some shelves over. But right now, that would only be out of spite.

Upstairs, the police were already rounding people up. Arresting whoever they'd come here for or searching the place. Or were they commandeering equipment and documentation? She let out a frustrated grunt. Not being in the know was the worst.

Since there was no one around, she said, "Bruce, do you copy?" Her voice echoed in the open space, bouncing off the stone walls and wood barrels.

She sensed someone else, like she wasn't entirely alone.

Bruce never responded.

She took a step into the open room and looked around for another door...or a person. "Mrs. Hadley."

A woman stood beside a pedestal table, pouring herself a glass.

She wore a white pair of slacks and a white blouse that fit her loosely. Plenty of gold bracelets, and white sandals on her feet. She laughed a little. "Want some? We can toast that man's demise."

Kenna stared at her as she turned, then had to keep her gasp to herself.

"As if you don't have an injury." She motioned to Kenna with the glass nearly overflowing. Half the side of her face was angry with welts and bruises, and something wept from her left eye. She lifted her sleeve and wiped at it. In spots on the side of her head, it looked like her hair had been pulled out.

"Did Hadley do that?" Kenna asked. "It's Clare, right? Is that really your name?"

"That would be my sister. My dead sister."

"Sorry for your loss."

She shrugged and took a sip of the drink. "It's the one left alive that you should feel sorry for. The one who has to explain, justify, and suffer the consequences of that loss."

"Amara traded you back." Her mother had been coming here with Roxanne and Clare to exchange them for Zeyla. Kenna wanted desperately to know if that had been success-ful. "Isn't that right?"

Or was it the reason her sister was dead.

This woman could either be the one she'd fought with in Hadley's house or the one Stairns had tussled with.

"Maybe I will have that drink. After you tell me your name."

"What does it matter who any of us is?" She turned back to the bottle on a tray with a circle of short glasses. "But for what it's worth, I'm Garnet."

"Like the gem? That's a nice name."

"I sound like a stripper. I don't use it." She handed Kenna the glass.

Kenna sniffed it and discovered it was brandy, not whiskey. She didn't like one and had never had the other. But if she needed a quick weapon, tossing this thing at Garnet was the fastest way to distract this woman so Kenna could either subdue her or make a run for it.

"So, you displeased them, and this is your punishment." Kenna motioned with her chin at Garnet's injuries. Kenna had covered the swelling on her face with makeup, and it was less noticeable than it had been the day before, but it must be clearly visible if Garnet picked up on it. "I know more about your life and how things work than you probably realize."

"I know you think you do." Garnet sipped her drink, turning to survey the barrels and then the wine behind the glass. "But if you did, you'd want what I want."

"And what's that?"

"To set fire to this whole place."

"So you can escape, free and clear?"

Garnet glanced at her. "I'll be in here burning along with the precious drinks. The priceless bottles that should be in a museum."

"Will it put a dent in their operation?"

"Nothing will do that. I'll be an inconvenience at best, but I'll have made my point."

"What if I can make you a better offer? The chance to

take them down once and for all. To stop this company from continuing to victimize people and make the world what they want it to be."

Garnet said, "You think you can do all that?"

"I know trying is better than the life you lead now."

Garnet huffed, almost laughing but not quite. "And the punishment for failure will make me wish I was never born. I should know. I've already experienced it."

She was trapped, defeated by a lack of hope—because it had been extinguished. There wasn't much Kenna could offer that would change her mind. But she had to hope because if she lost that, then she was no better than this woman.

Out of options.

Forced to live a life by someone else's dictates.

"They need you. That's why they have to keep you in line." Kenna let that sink in for a moment. "Otherwise, you would mean nothing. The things you do wouldn't be important. Now that there's only one of you, you're doubly valuable."

"After I've proven my loyalty to them."

"So fight back. Live your life your way."

Garnet said, "That sounds like a great idea."

"Come with me. Help me take them down." Kenna moved to the table so she could set her drink down. So they could get out of here and make a plan to finish this.

"My way. Remember?" Garnet tossed her glass at the table, shattering it across the surface and spilling alcohol. She grabbed Kenna's cup and did the same thing. "I think I have a lighter in here somewhere." She rummaged in a clutch on the stool.

"You can't—"

"My way." She whipped around and stared at Kenna,

rage in her expression. "Remember?" Garnet lifted a lighter and flicked it on. "I'll give you a one-minute head start. There's a door at the far end of the room."

"Don't kill yourself. Help me stop them." What more could she do to implore this woman? To convince her to help?

Garnet tossed the lighter at the table, and the alcohol went up in flames. "Run, little mouse."

Chapter Twenty-Four

Kenna stumbled out the door, onto gravel. Tiny, jagged-edged rocks cut into her feet. She raced across the gravel behind the house, past a huge set of stone steps that came out from the door and split at a balcony to hug the wall. A person could descend in either direction. Or simply stand at the rail and look out over the expanse of the back lawn.

She reached the grass and slowed to a stop.

A cop raced down the steps after her, hand on his gun. She lifted her hands, palms out. "I don't have ID. I just have no shoes, and those rocks hurt."

He was younger and had an FBI vest on. "You were at the office talking to Miller."

"I was. Is he here tonight?"

"He's taking lead."

"What about Detective Langford?" She patted her hips as if looking for something. "I think I lost my phone." And she'd lost Bruce, plus where were her mother and sister? "Among other things." She coughed.

"Is there a reason you smell like smoke, ma'am?" He glanced at the back door.

A small group stepped out and came down the steps toward them.

Smoke continued to pour from the door she'd come out of. "Someone should probably call an ambulance. I didn't start the fire, though. Just so you know."

Senator Woodford, two women, and three other men. One of the women held the other up so she could walk.

Kenna gasped. "Zeyla! Amara!" She moved toward them, but the FBI agent caught her.

The senator and his men escorted Amara and Zeyla down the steps and across the gravel.

"Let me go. That's my family."

"Don't make me draw my weapon, ma'am."

"I'm not the criminal here. He is!" Kenna pointed at the senator, who looked over at her.

"Lewis?" The senator called over—to the FBI agent.

The agent said, "There's a Jeep just past the tree line. You need to hurry."

"You're letting them go!" Kenna shoved the agent and started running. "Amara!"

One of the men with them pulled a gun and fired wildly in her direction. Kenna ducked her head, covered it with her arms—as if that would help shield her from bullets—and went to one knee.

"Kenna! Run!" Amara yelled at her.

"We had a deal, Woodford!" She didn't move, but she wasn't going to let them just leave without putting up some sort of a fight.

The agent slammed into her from behind, and they both went down.

Her face hit the ground and pain flashed through the side of her face.

"You asked for someone else! That was our deal!" Woodford sounded amused, but she couldn't see his face.

Her head was turned toward the building.

The agent on her back secured her hands behind her, and she heard the clink of cuffs before cold metal snaked around her wrists.

"Get off me." She winced, his weight pushing her hips against the ground.

"You have the right to remain silent, remember?" He pulled her hair, lifting her face off the ground, and leaned close. "You might want to use it before I find a creative way to shut you up."

She wanted to smile.

She nearly did, and if he'd seen it, he would have known exactly what it meant.

He lifted off her. Backed up, but she didn't look to see.

Kenna moved slowly, curling her legs and lifting up so she could sit. The basement was well and truly on fire.

Which meant it wouldn't be long before Garnet's life was swallowed up by the flames, and she ended it all. Kenna didn't want to carry the weight of another suicide. Garnet had made her choice, and Kenna lacked the strength to bodily force her out of that room. She had opted to save herself, sure. But what were the alternatives? Life in a psychiatric facility where they ensured Garnet didn't kill herself. Misery. If the company took her back, she would endure even more pain and humiliation.

Unlike what Bradley had done, taking his life, Garnet hadn't chosen hope because she'd had none left in this life. What she'd done was make a calculated decision to use her death to deal a blow to these people. Even in a small way.

The agent stood over her.

"I'll need your card. And your badge number." She turned her head to the side and spat on the ground.

"Good luck with that, considering I discovered you aiding the escape of the subject of a federal warrant."

"Senator Woodford? Who knew?" She would've guessed, but that wasn't the point. Playing dumb meant he'd say more because explaining things to her proved he was smarter than her. "I thought he was such a nice guy. One of those family values politicians you'd never suspect."

Kind of like the way this agent would never suspect that his boss's boss was likely friends with her fiancé, if not an associate of his. She was going to enjoy him finding out that arresting her and blaming her for what he was into wouldn't go far.

Was he really just going to stand there?

Seemed like he was waiting for something, or someone.

"You gonna call the fire department? That blaze could get out of hand." And her backside was starting to get wet on the grass.

He unclipped his phone from the side of his belt and looked at the screen. "Okay, let's go."

She shifted her weight on her legs and rocked to standing without assistance. Not just because she didn't want him to touch her, but also because she had to know she could get up without the use of her hands. "Lead the way."

He snorted and grabbed her arm.

"Gravel and bare feet do not mix."

He didn't listen. He walked her across it anyway to the stone steps where she had to rub the soles of her feet on the worn stone to dislodge the rocks embedded in her skin. "Quit messing around."

"I'm also eager for you to present me to your superior.

It'll be the highlight of my week. But we should do it out front since the building is on fire." She spotted a couple of cops in the wide entryway just inside the door. "Hey, Sarge! The wine cellar downstairs is on fire. We probably need fire and EMS unless they're on their way."

The agent looked at her, suspicion dawning, hopefully.

"Hey, Detective Davis." That was Langford's partner. "How are you? Is Naomi here?"

Davis frowned. "Special Agent, why is that woman in custody?"

"Caught her aiding the escape of some fugitives."

Kenna lifted her brows. "Downstairs is on fire. We need to get everyone out."

The agent tugged her along, not willing to stop. "She probably set the fire as well, just to confuse us. She allowed the senator and a few others to run for it across the lawn."

They moved through the archway into a smaller sitting room.

She spotted a couple of state police and nodded. "Guys. How are you?"

The agent said, "Shut up."

"Right. Right. Supposed to be silent. I remember now. I'll shut up."

He tugged on her arm and walked her into the ballroom with no shoes on her feet and dirt on her face. Probably grass in her hair, not to mention the smoke smell from fleeing the cellar while the flames licked across the floor. Thankfully, she hadn't been burned. That hurt even when it was a tiny singe from the oven.

A collection of agents and officers huddled in the middle by the front door. Rounding people up. Interviewing guests and taking statements.

"Hey, Miller!" she called out as loud as she could, drawing as much attention as possible.

"Shut up!" He pulled on her arm, *hard*.

She cried out because it hurt. "Someone, pull the fire alarm. The cellar is ablaze." She breathed through the pain in her arms. "Miller."

He strode toward her, glancing around. "Everyone outside! Langford, get the fire alarm." His expression washed with the kind of thunder that preceded a bolt of lightning that cracked across the sky and the kind of storm that destroyed entire towns. "Got yourself in trouble."

"Woodford left with my mom and my sister and a few goons. One of them shot at me."

"Not having a very good day, are you?" Miller looked her up and down. "You look a bit..."

"Don't finish that."

The agent holding her arm said, "Sir, she's under arrest for aiding and abetting."

Kenna frowned. "Is the senator who you were looking for? What are the charges?"

The agent shook her arm, but not super hard. "What did I say about keeping your mouth shut?"

Miller looked at him. "You can let her go. I'll take it from here."

Kenna studied the agent as well. "You might want to check his creds. There's something definitely off, at best. At worst, he's in their pocket."

The agent exploded into movement, drawing his weapon from its holster on his belt. Everyone around them reacted. The agent's face twisted with rage.

Miller strode to him, grabbed the guy's collar, and walked him back. Away from Kenna. All the way until he had his back up against the wall. "Put your gun away. Chief Richards!"

A uniformed older police officer strode over. "You need some help, Special Agent Miller?"

"Yes, sir. If your men could take this man somewhere quiet and have a conversation with him, that would be appreciated."

Two cops walked the agent away. Kenna didn't move from her spot, hands still cuffed behind her. Miller turned to her, and she said, "Bad day."

He frowned. "You can keep those cuffs on."

She bit her lip.

"Humor me and stick around. There will be paperwork, and you're not going *anywhere*."

She couldn't say, *Do you know who my fiancé is?* That wouldn't be professional. But she thought it.

Miller said, "We'll get to you."

He led her to the ballroom and sat her in a chair. Kenna protested, "And we need to go outside, not sit around in here! This building is on fire."

Someone strode over to them, a dark-haired fed who was about forty. "Sprinklers are on downstairs. We're figuring out what happened."

She'd had enough of new people for one day. Where was Bruce? She needed to call Jax. Find out if his mom and sister were out.

Figure out how to find her own family.

Sleep.

Find some shoes.

Take a pain pill.

She sniffed back tears that wanted to flow and sat in the chair feeling sorry for herself. Tonight had not gone according to plan. In fact, it was kind of a disaster. But every time something like this happened, she wanted someone she loved to come and rescue her.

She wanted Jax to walk through the door and make it all right.

Or Stairns, with his connections and the respect he'd earned over a lifetime of service to the bureau. She would even take Ramon right now. Bruce. Maizie.

That was how she knew she was a lost cause.

She wanted her family. Lord, have mercy, but she *needed* them.

Which, of course, would only get worse. Eventually, she wouldn't be able to live without them. Then she would *really* be in trouble, because the moment one of them left for good or died, even in peaceful circumstances, she would be left suffering in the aftermath. Contending with grief all over again.

Langford wandered over. "You okay?"

"Sure. Peachy." Kenna wiped her cheek on her shoulder. Even just that made her arms ache. She bit the inside of her lip.

"This is where I remind you that you're supposed to be keeping me in the loop."

"Drive me back to my RV, and I'll tell you everything."

Langford chuckled. "Maybe later."

Kenna sat in that chair, her arms cuffed behind her, and there was nothing she could do but watch firefighters in their gear traipse through the house with axes and all kinds of cool things.

No one spoke to her for the first hour. After that, Miller had an officer move her cuffs to the front so she could rest her hands in her lap. He gave her a cup of coffee. As if that was going to placate her.

By the time the second hour had passed, Miller finally

came over. He handed her his phone. "It's for you. Don't think this means we're good."

She touched the screen and saw the active call was connected to *Jaxton.* "Jax."

"I just got off the plane."

"Can you pick me up?" She sniffed.

"I'll be there in half an hour."

She sagged back against the wall. "I love you."

He chuckled. "I'll be Oliver, your rideshare driver."

She frowned. "Oliver sounds weird. You've been Jax for two and a half years."

"And you've been trouble." He paused a second, then said, "I called Laney, but she hasn't answered."

"They were here, but I told them to leave earlier. I don't know if they got out before the cops came in. I need Miller to tell me what's going on."

"I can't throw my weight around until I'm there and I'm the ranking person on scene."

"I'll enjoy watching that."

"And you wanted me to quit my job."

She smiled.

"I'll be there soon." He said goodbye and hung up.

Miller came over. "Feel better?"

"Where are Adrielle Jaxton and Elaine Caliveri? Are they here?" She held on to his phone, needing to know what happened to Jax's family. "And I need to make another call." Allowing him to have Maizie's number was a calculated risk, but she needed someone out there looking for Amara and Zeyla. Where had the senator taken them?

He held out his hand. Guess she wasn't going to get another call.

"Answer the question." It was the first of many Kenna had for him.

"I'll find out."

She handed him his phone. "You do that. He'll want to know where they are when he gets here."

Miller frowned.

"Thirty-minute warning."

Miller bit off a curse and walked off, barking orders as he went. Which was kind of satisfying. She took an odd enjoyment about FBI agents snapping to attention because Jax was on his way.

A cop raced into the ballroom. "Sir!" He addressed all the cops like he didn't know who to speak to. "A helicopter just flew over and dropped two bodies in the pond out front."

Chapter Twenty-Five

Kenna felt her eyes widen. She ducked her chin a fraction so no one saw her face. Right now, she had zero ability to school her features. If anyone looked at her, they'd realize immediately she could guess who the two people were that had just been tossed out of a chopper.

But if it really was the two kidnappers, that meant Senator Woodford kept up his end of their bargain. But he'd taken her mom and her sister with him. There had been nothing she could've done to stop him without dying for her efforts.

Kenna tuned out the buzz of movement and conversation around her and closed her eyes.

"Bruce." She gave him a second, then said, "Bruce, do you read me?"

Nothing. And she'd tried more than once.

Woodford hadn't said anything about her mother. When she'd mentioned Zeyla, he pretended not to know her sister—cousin, whatever they were to each other. Then again, maybe he'd never heard her real name. Maybe he only knew her as Chimera.

Not only did she need to find Laney and Adrielle, but she also needed to find Amara and Zeyla. Mother-daughter pairs. Jax's family had him, and probably his father, and law enforcement on their side. Who did her mom have?

She opened her eyes and looked around. There had to be someone who worked for the senator still here. Not all of them could've made a run for it.

She scanned the guests, mostly just trying to find Mr. Whitworth-Harrow. Had Charlie run off like a scared little mouse when the police raided the place? She'd kicked him in a way that would have impeded his ability to sprint.

There.

He sat with his back to the wall on the stairs, way across the ballroom. Looking dejected. Probably because his favorite person had left and not taken him. Of course, she was just speculating. He could be tired and sad the party was over.

Miller came back over.

"Can I use your phone again?"

He ignored her question and stood there, towering over her. As if she was going to let him use his size to intimidate her. "Any idea why two bodies just dropped in the pond from a chopper?"

"You think I would know?"

He stared at her.

"Fine." Kenna rolled her eyes because all she had left was sarcasm. "Depends if one is male and one is female."

His eyes narrowed.

"Well?"

Miller nodded.

"The kidnappers." She shrugged. "Of course, I don't know for sure, but that would be my guess. Shame we can't ask Hadley and have him confirm their identities."

"What about the other victim?"

Kenna said, "I saw Senator Woodford escort her into the trees, thanks to your agent letting them make a run for it. I'd suggest you locate Woodford and ask him why he left during a police raid and where she is. But I wouldn't want to tell you your job."

Miller snorted. "Sure." He stiffened and muttered something.

Jax walked in the front doors. Badge on the lapel of his wool coat so that no one would be confused about who he was. A couple of the FBI agents across the entryway snapped to attention—former military guys, probably. The kind of people accustomed to showing respect to the chain of command.

Jax lifted two fingers in acknowledgment, scanned the room, and found her in the chair with Miller standing over her.

Miller stepped back, a pinched look on his face.

"Hey, buddy. How's it going?" Jax clapped Miller on the shoulder. "Good to see you."

"Sir."

Kenna bit the inside of her lip to keep from smiling. "Don't let that dirty agent go. You should get to the bottom of that."

"Right after he uncuffs you." Jax stopped beside her and stuck his hands in his pockets. Holding himself back from what he wanted to do.

Miller used a key to release the cuffs, taking them and walking away.

Jax held out his hand, and she stood, touching her lips to his. "You lost your shoes?"

She didn't kiss him the way she wanted to right now,

but it was enough in a room full of people where he had to be professional. "It's been an interesting night."

"You're cold."

"Can I have your coat?"

He smiled slightly, tugged off the badge, and slid his coat off. He helped her thread her arms through and then slid the badge onto his belt. "There isn't anything I can do about your shoes."

"You could piggyback me out to the car."

He smiled, then tugged the lapels of the coat toward him and kissed her. "Wouldn't that cause a stir."

"I didn't realize I was so cold. Your coat is warm." She wrapped the edges around her. The wool fell to her knees almost, heavy and warm. "We need to find people. Get moving."

"Maizie."

She nodded.

Jax pulled out a set of keys. "There's an Audi out front. I'll be there in a few minutes."

"Thanks." She took the keys and kissed his cheek.

Now that he was here, she had no desire to question Charlie or do anything else right now. But only in this moment. Tomorrow might be a different story, but right now she wanted to curl up in this coat and warm up. Afterward they'd all make a plan together.

She headed for the door. "Bruce." Kenna checked that the comms earbud was still seated correctly so she could hear him if he spoke. "Bruce, do you read me?"

Outside, a crowd of cops had gathered on the lawn, so she couldn't see the two bodies. Probably for the best. The human form didn't do well hitting water at terminal velocity. Things got messy.

She stepped as lightly as she could across the gravel

drive to the car that lit up when she clicked the button on the key fob. A man sat in the front seat. It took her a second to recognize Jax's father.

He'd sent her out here knowing his dad was in the car?

Kenna pulled open the rear door and slid in. "Mr. Jaxton, how are you?"

"Kenna." He glanced at her, twisting around a little in the seat so he could look at her. "I'm eager to hear word about my wife and daughter. Her husband is quite beside himself that he can't reach her, and I'd imagine the children are worried."

Laney's husband probably wouldn't have said anything that would scare them. "I lost track of them at the party. Perhaps they ran out of phone battery or got lost on unfamiliar roads." He'd had a security detail on them, hadn't he? Surely, they knew where Laney and Adrielle had gone. Or if they were still in the house. "Have you heard from the people who were protecting them?"

"They were dismissed for the evening." Seemed like he had to force the words out. Like he didn't want to tell her but knew he had to give her the information in order to get them back. "Adrielle didn't want to bring them to the party. They were nearby, expecting a call to collect the women and take them back to the hotel."

"So they could still be here. Do you have a way to track their phones and see where they are?"

"Both left the building earlier, and their phones stopped transmitting their locations just beyond the grounds of this residence." He shifted in the seat, looking through the windshield. "Oliver asked me to lend you his cell phone?" He said it like a question, handing over the device.

"Thanks." She risked overstepping and just touched the

shoulder of the seat he was in, patting it lightly. "Let's figure out how to find them."

She called Bruce first, but there was no answer. Her comms earpiece got in the way, so she took it out and slid it into the inside pocket of Jax's coat.

It took a second to find Maizie in his contacts. She was listed as "M," which made Kenna smile, despite everything that was going on.

Ramon was the one who answered. "It's me."

Kenna responded, "It's me. Is she okay?"

"Are you?"

Kenna frowned. "Talk."

"Maizie is fine. She's just in the middle of a hack. Trying to access the senator's information."

"That's good."

"And you?"

"We need to find my mom and Zeyla."

Jax's dad shifted in his seat. Reacting to something, or simply adjusting his seat? Maybe he thought they should be fully focused on their family.

"On it. Stairns will help."

Kenna asked, "Have you heard from Bruce? I'm starting to get nervous. The police weren't going to let me go room by room and search for him. I haven't seen him since earlier. We lost contact." At least if the police had rounded him up with everyone else, there would be a name on a list of guests somewhere when he was asked for his information.

Or, like the burned spy he was, he'd somehow managed to slip out. But if he'd done that, why hadn't he contacted her?

The guy could be lying somewhere in the house, dead or bleeding out.

She bit her lip. "Ramon?"

"I was checking. None of us have heard from him, and he's not transmitting. Neither of you were from the minute you stepped into that building."

"But we could talk to each other on comms." Through the window, she saw Jax come down the front steps and head toward them. But he passed the car and walked to the crowd of cops that had thinned out now that a coroner's van had shown up. "I wish I knew what happened to him. Not much of this makes sense."

Ramon said, "You should've taken me with you."

"Because you don't trust Bruce now?" More likely, he didn't appreciate being out of the loop.

"Maizie," Ramon said, not talking to Kenna, "that doesn't mean I don't want to stay here and hang with you. No, that's not what it means. I'm just frustrated." He grunted. "Fine."

She heard a shuffle over the line.

Then, "Hi."

"Hi, Maze."

"I told him to give me my phone."

"Good for you."

"I'm ready for Elizabeth to be done with her...vacation." She cleared her throat. "I'm surrounded by these guys practically twenty-four seven. I need to paint my nails and talk about cute boys."

Ramon made a strangled sound in the background.

"Go outside or something. I'm trying to work."

Kenna smiled. "Jax is here, but we have work to do."

"Too bad. There's a new rom-com at the movies. I think you'd like it. The woman character is a former spy, and the guy is a Marine veteran. They both—"

"Hey, can you tell me this later?"

"Sure, I was just talking until Ramon left the RV. He's gone outside with Stairns."

Kenna watched Jax walk back over to them through the other side window. Watching him move. Appreciating her fiancé for more than just his intelligence or professional skills for a second. It was enough to make her want to lift a hand and fan her face.

"Now, I can tell you what I found," Maizie said.

Kenna frowned. "What's that?"

"I didn't want to tell anyone else before I told you, but I have a connection between Jax's dad and the senator. Or, at least, a foundation that the senator launched. Maybe it's nothing, or maybe there's something sinister about it."

"Pretend we don't know for sure until we know for sure."

Jax climbed into the car, and she handed over the keys from her spot in the back seat. He spoke quietly to his father, sat in front, and turned on the engine.

Maizie said, "The foundation supports children looking for scholarships in the arts. So low income families can put their kids in competition dance or buy instruments. They even support youth sports leagues."

She said something else, but the sound deadened in the phone.

Then, her voice was coming out of the speakers. "If Woodford is all in with the company, and Jax's dad is funneling money into a foundation that looks good on the surface, but underneath, it's money for them—"

Kenna lowered the phone. "Maze—"

"What are we supposed to think but that Jax's dad is associated with them?"

Her stomach dropped. He was going to think she'd been investigating him.

She tapped the Bluetooth button on Jax's phone and lifted it to her ear. "I'll call you back." She hung up before Maizie could respond.

Jax let off the gas. She reached forward and slipped his phone into the cubby in the center console. "Sorry."

He sat stiffly in the driver's seat, both hands on the wheel. "Dad?"

"Yes, son?"

Jax didn't relax. He got to the end of the drive and pulled onto the street. "Mom and Laney weren't inside. They weren't on any list the police have of people in the building when they raided it, and someone I spoke to said she remembered Mom and Laney leaving shortly before that anyway. So where are they?"

"How am I supposed to provide an answer to that question?" His father lifted both hands. "Isn't that what we're here to find?"

Kenna eased back into her seat and clipped the seat belt. Was their disappearance connected to him and his relationship with the company, or was this was something else entirely? She needed her phone, but it was in Bruce's car, back at the house. If he needed a way to leave the house later, he would be able to take the car.

She jogged her knee up and down, trying to process everything and decide what to do first. Stairns and Ramon, Maizie. Some shoes and a change of clothes. Jax's dad needed to tell them everything he knew. Maizie needed to find the senator. Kenna needed to use the restroom, get a gun, and get ready to find her family.

Jax let out a grunt. "You need to tell us everything, Dad. I don't believe you're in bed with these people, but maybe you got in too far before you realized you're not into what they are. That you don't want anything to do with them. I want to give you the benefit of the doubt, but that means you need to be honest."

"So you can tell me what a mess I've made of everything?"

"That's not what this is," Jax said. "No one is accusing you. We just want to find Mom and Laney."

She heard a car rev behind them and twisted around. The car came up too fast, approaching the back end of this rental. "Incoming." She patted his shoulder. "Jax."

"Got it. Everyone buckled in?"

His dad said, "Yes."

Kenna said, "Don't worry about me."

He hit the gas, and they sped up, pushing her back into her seat. The car behind did the same. It put on a burst of speed and clipped the back end of their car at an angle from the license plate to the left corner, pushing them into a spin.

Kenna held on as her stomach swirled. The center median flashed in front of the car, then the trees on the side of the road. Cars around them honked.

The Audi clipped another vehicle and crossed the rumble strip at the shoulder.

And then, they were airborne.

She didn't know how long it was before she woke up, but when she did, it wasn't pleasant. Everything hurt. Like she'd been hit by a car and thrown through the air, inside Jax's...

Jax.

She tried to say his name and heard herself moan, but no real words came out. All she had the strength to do was take in air to keep her heart beating, at least until she became more aware of the world. Herself. The situation.

Jax had slumped over the airbag. In front of her, his

father had collapsed against the window, his head against the tempered glass. She unclipped her seat belt first. Then she would...

Someone hammered on the window. Kenna flinched around, which didn't feel great.

Roxanne stood beside her door, pointing a gun at Kenna. "Get out." The words were muffled behind the glass, and the company asset knocked on the window with the butt of the gun. "Now."

Kenna hit the button and grabbed the handle. She twisted around with her knees and kicked at the door so that it swung out fast.

It clipped Roxanne, and she stumbled back, surprised but also amused. "Nice try." She held the gun on Kenna and motioned for her to move. "You're coming with me before EMS gets here."

"I don't think so." There was no way she'd leave Jax and his dad unconscious. "You guys have taken way too much from me today. I'm done."

Kenna leaned against the side of the car and lifted her chin. Her feet sank into the cool earth, dirt and grass with some twigs and pine needles. She really needed to find a pair of shoes.

She looked around and saw a few people had pulled over to help them. Maybe only two cars since the third was probably Roxanne's.

The other woman took a step closer to her. "Move. Start walking or I start shooting places that won't kill you."

Kenna said, "I'm not leaving. You're gonna kidnap me in front of witnesses?"

Roxanne's expression indicated she didn't much care.

"Put it down!" A man roared, and Kenna looked to see

Bruce making his way down the grassy hill from the highway.

She ducked inside the car to see if Jax or his dad was waking up. They needed an ambulance for sure. So did she, probably, though she usually didn't like to admit it. Who wanted to feel helpless? Far too reminiscent of the worst day of her life.

"I said, put it down!"

A second later, a gunshot exploded.

Kenna flinched, turning back to see Roxanne fall to the ground.

"Let's go." Bruce walked all the way up to her, right in her space.

She needed Roxanne's gun just in case the woman wasn't fully dead. Though, from the look of her, Bruce didn't leave even a chance she was still alive. Kenna stepped toward the dead woman, hardly able to process what had just happened.

Bruce grabbed her shoulder, squeezing the side of her neck.

"What—"

Everything went black.

Chapter Twenty-Six

K enna came awake swinging her arms this time. In a full rage with no intention of letting up. Her wrist clipped the dashboard of a car, and she cried out.

Bruce reached over with his arm across her front, high up by her collarbone, and pushed her back against the seat. "Easy. You'll hurt yourself."

They were on the highway, driving somewhere.

"Go back!"

"No." He didn't even shake his head.

"I'm gonna kill you. Jax is back there!"

"Easy. The cops pulled up as we left. They'll get an ambulance out there, and your boy will be fine."

"And his father?"

Bruce asked, "His dad was there?"

She shifted in the seat, getting out of the cramped way she'd been sitting. He'd covered her lap and her knees with a jacket...after he'd pinched her neck and knocked her out. "Pull over."

"No."

"Stop the car, Bruce. I'm getting out."

"Not with no shoes on you ain't."

She should batter him until he pulled over, then kick *him* out. Only that was nothing but the bluster of someone who was mad but didn't have the physical strength to overpower the other person. Weapon. She needed a weapon.

Kenna searched around. Checked the hidden pockets of her dress... "You patted me down?"

"Didn't want you to run the risk of hurting yourself."

"I'm more likely to hurt you right now. *What* are you doing?"

He kept his attention on the road in front of them. "My job. Helping you solve your cases, and in this case, helping you get your family back. Isn't that what you pay me for?"

"Perhaps I made a poor choice."

"Don't think you wanna fight me in court for wrongful dismissal. You'll have to settle, and it'll cost you."

Kenna leaned over. "Your enemies would murder you before it even went to trial."

"We're doing this my way."

He knew she was right, but he didn't want to admit it. "Why would I go along with this when I just left Jax back there in who knows what state, along with his father?" She looked down at her hand and remembered she left her engagement ring in the dresser drawer in the RV. She hadn't even thought of it until now, but suddenly, it seemed like *everything*. One part of the story, but it seemed to linchpin the entire thing.

More important than a smart watch that would give away her location—which was not on her wrist. When was the last time she'd worn it?

Bruce didn't know about the necklace, or did he? She needed a second to reach up and flick the switch on the back to transmit her location to Maizie. But the battery didn't last for hours, so until Maizie knew to start looking for her, there was no point in wasting its life.

He glanced over. "You want your mom back, right?"

She stared at him, aware they were going out of Denver on the freeway. South? Or some other direction. She had no idea. Maybe they were going nowhere in particular. Could Maizie track them? Did the teen know what was happening? Until she got a call from Jax, she might not know that anything was wrong. She wouldn't think anything was off about Bruce being with Kenna, if she discovered they were together.

"Well?"

"Quiet. I'm plotting how to get away from you."

He reached over and flipped on the radio, which started playing last century's greatest rock hits for crusty old ex-CIA officers who were enjoying being back in the US after years of exile.

She waited a second, then turned it off. "My mom?"

"I knew you wouldn't leave Jax of your own accord."

Duh. "What about my mom?"

"I figured the easiest way to make a clean break from that car was to knock you out. It was expedient, so you don't need to be mad. I made the choice, it's done, and now we can move on."

"You're fired."

"I followed Roxanne from the house after you, and when she stepped in, I took her down." He paused for emphasis, then said, "Jax needs to find his mom and his sister, right? He's gotta focus on that."

"I was going to help."

"At the expense of yours." Bruce shrugged. "Now we can do both, and you can blame me. Doesn't need to put a wedge between you and Jax, and this way, his dad doesn't get in the way of our mission." He slapped his chest. "Jax's family is their business. If Dad screws that up, then it's on him. Nothing to do with us. Your family? They're our responsibility."

Did he hit his head and suffer some kind of injury or a mental breakdown? Maybe he had PTSD. His logic was sort of sound but also didn't make sense to anyone else.

Except that she had been trying not to wonder whether helping Jax find his family would mean she never found hers. Splitting up wouldn't have been her first choice. They spent hardly any time in person as it was—at least right now. She'd been content to just be with him and find out what his dad knew about the company, hoping that finding his sister and his mom would lead them closer to Amara and Zeyla.

But the reality was that she could easily be torn between the two.

She might have to choose.

She had no idea what the answer would be. "Where are we going?"

Bruce glanced over. For a while, he didn't say anything, and then he seemed to be admitting something that might be a secret. "Woodford has Amara and Zeyla."

"I saw him take them." But the way he'd said it made her wonder if he knew far more than she did. Though, he likely didn't know that Clare's twin had opted to kill herself with a fire. Or that Kenna had uncovered a dirty FBI agent.

Where had he been while she focused on the mission?

Seemed like he'd had a mission of his own the entire time. One she hadn't been privy to.

He said, "Your mom tried to exchange with his guys, giving them Clare and Roxanne. It went wrong, and Clare was killed. Roxanne knocked out your mom, and they put her in the cell with Zeyla."

"When the cops arrived, they left out the back."

Bruce grunted. "Figures they'd run."

"So where are they?" She looked around for a phone. His phone. Where had he put it? Or was he completely off the reservation, gone dark. No communication.

The glove box.

She pulled the handle, and it dropped down. Kenna's phone tumbled out into her hands.

He grabbed the phone, hit the button on his window, and tossed it out. As the window whirred back up, he said, "Too easy to trace. The company knows where you are all the time, and I'd be surprised if they haven't hacked you already."

"As if Maizie would let that happen."

"They've been in her system. You wanna tell me it's impenetrable?"

"Nothing is impenetrable."

Bruce said, "That's why we're going old school."

"Why are you doing this?"

"You and I paired up tonight. Figured we'd see it through, given certain developments. So let's get them back."

She shifted in the seat again, trying not to punch him. "What happened?"

This seemed far more than just a mission. In fact, it almost seemed as if it might be personal to him. Because of Amara? Like maybe they'd had some kind of...moment in the woods. One chance meeting.

When he said nothing, she said, "If I can't trust you, I'm not working with you. I don't care how helpful you'll be."

He'd already burned far too much of her goodwill tonight by leaving Jax behind.

"I'm doing my job. It isn't about trust. It's about finishing the mission while there's time. Waiting around only lessens the chance of success." Bruce leaned heavier on the gas pedal. "Strike while the iron is hot."

"Because you know...what?"

He pushed out a heavy breath. "Fine. Maizie ran my old handler against the company, Jax's dad, Woodford, and all of it."

"He's connected."

Bruce nodded.

"So instead of some altruistic, get the job done, help *me* out, it's actually about you getting revenge against the guy who burned you."

"Just a bonus."

"And my mother?"

"Can I help it?" He wrung the steering wheel in his grasp. "She got to me."

Kenna gritted her teeth. "Good to know that even though you're a trained spy, you're still a man who isn't immune to a woman's charms."

His phone rang once, then stopped.

Bruce lifted it from his jacket pocket, making her remember putting the earpiece in Jax's coat. While he looked at the screen, his wrists braced on the steering wheel, she ducked her hand in the inside coat pocket and then slid the earpiece in her ear. Hopefully, while he was too distracted to see. "What was that?"

"Address for the meet." He put the phone away. "It's far enough away that we've got to pick it up. No more delays."

She eased over to the door. "Who are we meeting and what for?"

"Depends how much you want them back."

"Can you just explain it?"

Bruce sighed. "I'd rather you didn't flip out."

"So, I'm going to think this is a terrible idea? There's a huge surprise." She shook her head, trying to figure out where they could possibly be going. "Tell me what we're doing."

He knew she wasn't going to kill him, even if she wanted to. This wasn't the world of international covert ops where people routinely disappeared—assassinated or kidnapped, then tortured and killed. Not between the two of them, at least.

"You said you want them back."

She didn't respond. It was far more complicated with her family than Jax getting his mom and sister back. Their relationship was nothing like that. He'd been raised by loving parents. His sister was amazing, a wife and mom in her own right.

Her mother had played dead for decades.

Her father had lied to her and had another child.

Her sister, cousin, whatever, she was nothing more than a stranger.

"Means you need to trade yourself for them."

Just like that? An exchange.

"Didn't you say Amara tried that? It didn't work." They wanted her mom and Zeyla, so why would they trade the two of them and lose what they'd finally gained after all these years? "They're valuable assets. If my mom is to be believed, they've been hiding from the company for years. Staying under the radar. There's no way these people are going to let Amara and Zeyla go."

"They're prepared to give them up. If they can have you."

She wasn't even going to think about that. "Why would they?"

"Who knows? I made the deal. It's set."

"It's dumb." How best to explain it to him? "Bruce, it's obviously a trap. They're going to have all of us instead because we walked right into it. None of us is going to go free. You'll probably get killed—or traded to your enemies—and we're all done. They won. Game over."

If only someone on the other end of the comms would contact her. She prayed Maizie realized what was going on and turned the system on so she could connect. The comms used the closest Bluetooth, which was Bruce's phone, unless he turned it off.

If his plan didn't work, she would be lost to the company. "Do you know what happened to Adrielle and Laney? At least tell me that."

Bruce shrugged. "I didn't see them, and I didn't ask."

"There's more going on than just Amara, but you've got tunnel vision." It was a chess game, and he was playing checkers with half the pieces. "You're not seeing the bigger picture."

"It's not that complicated, girl. You want them back, and I've agreed to trade you for them. They go free, and Ramon and Stairns get to finding you."

"You think I'll last longer than them?" Such a vote of confidence, though probably not a good thing.

"Zeyla, yeah. She was in a bad way. I could tell your mom was worried."

"She didn't want my help." Kenna folded her arms loosely. She needed him to let her borrow his phone. "She wanted to get Zeyla on her own."

"They're going to kill her. Maybe both of them. Make

an example to the rest of the resistance. You'll know you could've stopped it."

Kenna said, "And instead, I should trade myself so they can kill me?"

"I might be able to keep that from happening. If everything goes right."

"You have to understand why I have doubts." Not just about Bruce but about this entire plan. As soon as she could, Kenna was going to make a run for it. Go as far as fast as she could and try to escape. Then she would resolve this *her* way and not Bruce's. He could do what he wanted, but it wasn't going to involve trading her to the company.

"Yeah, but you'll live with it. They don't want you dead. They want you to be one of their surrogates."

Her stomach flipped over.

Bruce said, "You think I'm gonna let you stay in a place like that, let them do that to you?"

"It's exactly what you just said."

"That's what they're going to think. Your mom played it straight. We're now playing with dirty rules, and things are gonna get messy. I need to know you're on board."

"I won't be unless you tell me everything."

She was about to strangle him. Just reach over with both hands and make a point of throttling him with her bare hands, even if she didn't have the strength to do any damage. She could get her point across, regardless.

The earpiece buzzed, crackling a little. If the thing suddenly emitted a high-pitched sound, she was going to have to keep from reacting, no matter how bad it was.

Bruce jerked the wheel toward the right side of the freeway, taking the exit far too late. Another car honked at him. He braked hard and skidded to a stop at the red light, turning left as soon as it went green. Under the overpass for the freeway, he pulled to the side of the road.

"Was all that necessary?" She stared at him, biting her lip. Praying someone connected with the comms channel. Maizie could do it from the website. But she'd have to know there was a reason to log on.

Bruce put the car in park. "Here's what's going to happen."

Chapter Twenty-Seven

Bruce pulled into the entrance of the concrete plant under a full moon. In the white glow, she spotted two vehicles. Both of them were town cars—the kind hired by someone who usually had a driver and probably had a security detail as well. In fact, it had surprised her to find Jax's dad in the front of the rental Audi from that fact alone. He was definitely the kind of guy who sat in the back and was transported where he was going by someone he paid to do it.

"Guess there's nothing left to say."

She glanced over at him.

"Because you realize that doing this is the right thing. It gets them back, which is what you've wanted for them since you found out they were alive."

"Don't presume you know what's in my head. We haven't known each other that long."

Bruce shrugged off her comment. "I was trained to read people and to do it fast."

"You have it all figured out."

He reached behind their seats to a bag in the back and

rummaged before he pulled out a roll of tape. "Don't ever use this stuff to *actually* secure something. It's breakaway tape. You want to get free? Just pull your hands apart hard, and it'll tear. So, make sure you don't do it too early." He waved, motioning toward himself.

She lifted her hands, not exactly excited to be bound at the wrists. The state she was in—no shoes, wearing a dress, rumpled hair, and half her face still sort of swollen—she looked like the captive she was meant to be.

All because he figured she would be happy to trade herself so Amara and Zeyla could go free.

Which, to be fair, was a noble action. When it was her choice. Not so much when someone else did the deciding for her. She didn't like that.

"We aren't going to be friends after this."

"You say that now, but they'll be free. Isn't that the idea?"

"The idea is everyone walks away. Not just some people." Fine, she was scared. Who wanted to be a captive of their enemy? Especially one that was involved in organ trafficking. That, evidently, wanted her to be a surrogate for one of the next generation of babies—or more than one. She could be walking into a lifetime of captivity for all she knew.

"Idealistic. Never thought you were that kind." He pulled tape away from the roll and wrapped it around her wrists. "You, of all people, know things don't usually work out the way we planned. That's why we have things like breakaway tape and tracking devices in our necklaces. Comms earbuds." He reached to her ear and pulled it out.

Kenna pressed her lips together. *Great.*

"And hidden weapons." He dug something out of a pocket by his hip and tucked it into the hidden pocket at the back of her dress beside the zipper. Thankfully, he kept his touch brief, but she rolled her eyes anyway.

He said, "Time to go."

"Yeah, one sec."

"Make it fast." He already had his hand on the door.

She glanced at the cars. No one had gotten out, so maybe they were waiting for Bruce to move first.

Kenna said, "Once you make the exchange, you're going to contact Maizie and Ramon. Get them and Stairns tasked with finding me. You're going to locate Jax and his father, praying the whole time they aren't injured more than a bruise or two at most. And then—"

"I've got it," he said. "I'll protect your mom and sister, your friends will look for you, and your boyfriend will punch me in the face when I explain. But we'll work it out, and I'll help him find you."

She hesitated, but it might be best to just get out of the car and get this over with.

"I'll have to drive to the campsite. They're in my phone. They're in our whole system since we were hacked months ago. They know everything."

Kenna sucked in a breath.

"You knew it was possible, so there's no need to be surprised, is there?" Bruce shrugged. "We're going offline to solve this. Old school like the Cold War. And I'll take care of everyone." He tugged on the handle and got out, walking around the front of the car to open her door for her.

She stood on the concrete, gritty with dirt and pebbles that pricked at her bare feet. It was freezing, but she still wore Jax's coat. At least she had that one part of him to take with her. To curl up inside and try to find solace in her faith.

She had a feeling she was going to need it when the darkness fully descended.

"You'd better take care of all of them. I mean it, Bruce."

He gave her a sharp nod and dragged her by the elbow toward the two town cars. They walked to a spot about halfway between them and whoever this exchange involved.

One of the doors opened, the back seat of the town car on the right. A suited man got out. Not the senator. She recognized this man as one of the men who'd left the house with him. Not the one who pulled a gun on her, thankfully. That guy would be too hotheaded for something like this.

"I heard the FBI is looking for you." She lifted her chin.

Bruce tugged on her arm. "Shut up." To the other man, he said, "Bring them out, and we'll make the trade." He had one hand free, presumably in case something went wrong, he could reach for a weapon.

A warranted precaution as it turned out, but not quite enough.

The man in front of them pulled a gun and pointed it at Bruce. He squeezed off a shot. It hit Bruce square in the chest, and he fell backward.

Kenna ducked to the side a couple of steps.

The man was on her before she could react, and she was being lifted. He tossed her over his shoulder. Kenna kicked her legs and put up as much of a fuss as possible. She didn't have to dig much to find a genuinely scared reaction. But she did have to focus so she didn't pull too hard on the tape and tear her wrists free.

The trunk of the town car flipped open, and he tossed her inside.

The lid slammed, leaving Kenna in the darkness.

Bruce.

She might not agree with the guy and his tactics, which

made Ramon look like a boy scout at this point, but she didn't want him to die. She didn't want the team to lose him. Or for him to never have that shot at righting the wrong that had been done to him by his CIA handler. He'd only just come back to the US. He deserved a shot at a retirement, living the life he wanted.

The car set off, the engine vibration rumbling under her.

Kenna felt around for something—or someone. But all she felt was carpet, sticky in places. She curled her knees up and tucked them in the coat. In her heart, she prayed silently, crying out to the Lord for help. Even if she had kinda gotten herself into this situation. With a whole lot of help from Bruce.

She prayed for the mother-daughter pairs, held captive. In who knew what situation.

And for Jax and his father, that they hadn't sustained serious injuries in the crash.

She prayed for wisdom.

For Ramon, Stairns, and Maizie, that they would find her.

She prayed Bruce would live. Not just because if he did, then she could kick his butt for this.

They drove for a long time before the car slowed, rolling at a low speed down a road that seemed like gravel. *Lord, let this tracker in the necklace be transmitting somehow. Let it be the thing that leads them to me.*

She was fully in favor of a miracle.

"I'm probably going to need one."

The car stopped. She rolled a little in the trunk and had to brace herself to keep from smashing her face against the interior.

Finally, the trunk flipped open, but it wasn't that same guy she saw.

It was Amara.

Kenna said, "This was all you?"

"Of course not." She touched a thick collar on her neck. "I'm as much a captive as you are right now."

Kenna frowned.

"Get out of there." Her mom stood back.

Behind her, a huge house that looked like a mansion version of a log cabin stretched overhead. Some rich person had purposely built "rustic" and thought that meant they'd be roughing it with state-of-the-art high-end features and the latest appliances.

"I guess crime really does pay." She sat up. "I could use a hand."

The man who'd tossed her in came over and lifted her by her armpits, setting her down on the driveway. "Both of you inside."

Amara put her arm around Kenna's shoulders. They walked to the wide porch, which had brand-new-looking wood Adirondack chairs and barrels with profusions of spring flowers, like it was meant for a magazine photo shoot. Not comfy so a person could relax in a place they called home.

As they reached the first step, Amara whispered, "What was that man thinking?"

She glanced at her mother. "Bruce?"

"He's with us. Me." She winced.

The resistance.

Kenna asked, "All this time?"

Her mom nodded.

"I don't suppose you can—"

Someone grabbed her arm. The sudden hard pull caused the tape holding her wrists to tear free, and the thug whipped her across the porch into the house. She tumbled onto the floor of the entryway and slid across the floor on the small rug.

Kenna slammed into a table in the center of the entryway with its roof-height ceiling. A vase wobbled on the table, fell in front of her, and shattered. Water and pottery sprayed out in every direction.

She curled up.

The bright yellow lights of the interior of the house glared at her, probably highlighting all the fear in her eyes. She had no idea what was going to happen next.

Or if she would ever be saved.

She stayed where she was, on the rug half under the table. To her right, someone had hung a huge painting of a deer on a snowy morning above the double doors that led to a sitting room or living room. To the left was a set of closed doors. Stairs behind her.

"Bring them in, Holt," a man called out from where she couldn't see him—the living room, probably.

The big man who had just tossed her across the floor dragged her up by her arm. Everything he did was about proving to her that she had no power here. Reinforcing the idea that she could do nothing while they could do whatever they wanted.

It would've worked if she didn't believe that God was ultimately in control. He was the sovereign Lord of her life, and anything that happened to her was because He allowed it. No matter what it was or how awful things got, she could trust that He knew what He was doing.

It was the only thing that was going to hold her together.

Tucked away, deep in her soul. That sure and certain hope she had would keep her going so that she never fell into despair the way Bradley had.

Even if what happened tonight was far worse than facing down a serial killer.

Holt shoved her down onto a sofa. The kind with cushions that had no give, so you couldn't curl up and relax, but they looked good. As if that was the point of furniture.

Kenna blew hair off her face and didn't look at Senator Woodford. "I've never understood aesthetics. It needs to be comfortable and functional. Who cares if everything matches or it looks Instagram-worthy or whatever?"

Amara sat on the edge of the seat beside her, too far for Kenna to find any solidarity in their closeness. Which was what they'd had for years. Exactly the kind of relationship Amara had decided was best for them. That was the worst part. Her mother had just made the decision and never given Kenna the option. Not even when she came of age and could have chosen for herself did Amara tell her who she was—that she was alive.

And she had a sister?

"Where is Zeyla?" Kenna glanced from her mom to Woodford. "Don't pretend you don't know who she is."

Amara said, "Chimera."

Kenna frowned.

Amara glanced at her. "That's the name he knows her by."

"Ah," Woodford said. "My greatest disappointment."

Kenna said, "You'll find we're all like that. The whole family. You should just let us go. Save yourself the trouble."

"Unfortunately for your...I suppose you'd consider her your mother, is that right?" Woodford asked from his spot on a leather recliner.

At least one of them was comfortable.

"My mother died a long time ago. I only just met this woman." She motioned to Amara.

"Unfortunately for her, she isn't going anywhere. The collar she's wearing contains plastic explosives. If she goes even ten feet from the perimeter of the house, there will be a mess of brain matter to clean up."

"Good to know." Kenna tried to say it like she didn't care about Amara that much. As if this woman was a stranger to her. It was far better for Woodford to believe he had little in the way of leverage against her.

"If she attempts to remove it, that will trigger a fail-safe. If anything but the key in my pocket is inserted into the mechanism, it will blow up."

"Where's Zeyla?"

Amara stiffened, just a tiny bit but enough that Kenna caught it. Her sister was in a worse situation than she was? Not good.

Woodford said, "She'll make herself useful, as will the rest of you."

Great. So good. Kenna was super excited about that.

The goon—Holt—stood by the door like a sentry. She couldn't take them both out, and even if she tried, they'd have to subdue Woodford and get the key before they could leave. And there was probably more of his men in this house.

She needed firepower.

And a pair of Converse.

She would settle for tactical pants and a hair tie. She wasn't picky. Maybe a couple of Ibuprofen and use of a bathroom. A cheeseburger. One of Jax's hugs. A smile from Maizie, and Cabot's wagging tail.

Even here, with nothing but the necklace and whatever

Bruce had slipped into the back of her dress, she still had a whole lot. *Thank You.*

Kenna lifted her chin and looked at the senator. "What do you want with me?"

Chapter Twenty-Eight

"This way."

Kenna held the coat close around her, ignoring all the aches and pains. Although she could disassociate by cataloguing each one, that would likely lead to her curled up on the floor and crying because it all actually hurt quite a lot.

She followed Senator Woodford down the wood-paneled hallway. "How many floors do you have?"

"You saw on the way in, didn't you?"

Right. "What about below ground?"

Woodford chuckled but didn't turn. He kept walking. All that arrogance in the line of his shoulders, keeping his spine straight with the confidence that the man behind her would take care of any problems Kenna caused—or was about to cause.

She focused on walking. On the pinching pain with each footstep. Much better than thinking about people she knew who had been left for dead, women who had been abducted, or what was going to happen next.

He'd dismissed her mother, who wandered out of the room with her head bowed. Kenna might not do exactly the same with an explosive around her neck, but whatever she did do would probably get her killed for her trouble.

She needed to play this right.

If they wanted her subdued, she would act the part. Was that what her mom was doing? She could see the merit of playing along so that they believed they'd won the battle over her spirit.

He stopped at a double door in the hallway, made with the same wood inlay as the walls. Ornate. Dark and imposing. Woodford grasped both handles and pushed them inward, revealing a bright room with a medical suite. An older man lay in the bed, hooked up to all kinds of machines, unconscious or in some kind of coma.

It reminded her of the first time she had met her grandfather on the island of Crete in Greece. As soon as she'd found him and discovered he was alive, she had gone with Jax to meet him. She'd received a novel her father had never published, printed and bound. The old man had died since then, as if perhaps he'd only been hanging on until she came. Until his task had ended and the novel had been passed on.

The truth had been told.

Kenna's bare feet touched the cold white tile on the floor. It actually felt good on the warm cuts and scrapes. She didn't think she was bleeding, but she definitely had some abrasions. "Who is he?"

"I suppose you could say he's my uncle, after a fashion." Woodford walked to the left side of the bed, scanning the readings on the monitors. "He seems to be doing well today."

Kenna heard a shuffle, then saw a short, heavyset

woman in a maid outfit scurry from a corner. The woman had to be in her sixties. "Yes, Mister Woodford. The doctor say he respond well to the treatment. His body isn't rejecting the liver."

"That's good." Woodford ran his fingers over the old man's forehead, then down his cheek. "That's very good."

"Whose liver was it?" Kenna spoke before she could stop herself. She bit the inside of her lip.

"Your sister has proven very useful."

"I am going to kill you," Kenna said. "Just so you know."

Woodford actually chuckled. He straightened from leaning over the bed. "You and I are going to form a different kind of bargain."

"I'm not agreeing to anything."

"I think, in time, you'll come to see things from my point of view."

Kenna said, "I highly doubt that."

What she wasn't so sure of was their ability to drug her, coerce her around to their thinking, or generally torture her until she broke and did whatever they wanted. But right here and right now, in control of her own mind, she knew what was true—and what she wanted.

Woodford looked from the man in the bed to her. "My uncle is a powerful man whose will holds much sway in our organization."

"Not so much anymore, by the look of him."

She heard a slight shuffle behind her. Woodford lifted his hand, and the movement stopped. The man behind her wanted to lash out because she'd spoken disparagingly about the old man in the bed.

Kenna asked, "So who is he? Apart from your uncle."

"You might call him the Grand Master. Or so I've heard that's how the resistance has taken to referring to him. He raised me." Woodford glanced affectionately at the man in the hospital bed.

"Sorry for your loss."

"He is far from dead, I assure you."

"Because you're kidnapping people, removing their organs, and putting them in him?" She lifted her chin in the direction of the bed, still holding the coat wrapped closely around her. "All in a futile attempt to prolong his life."

"It's far from futile."

"Instead, you could just kill him and take his position."

Woodford moved faster than she expected. His hand swung toward her, and his palm cracked across her already swollen cheek.

Kenna looked at the floor, her chin almost at her right shoulder. "Or not." After a second, she straightened and looked at him. "So he lives. No matter the cost."

"Cost is irrelevant. There is only our will and nothing else."

She nodded as if that was fascinating, even though it seemed completely narcissistic in a weird, collective way. "And me? You're gonna carve me up?"

"We die so that others may live," Woodford said. "Isn't that how it goes?"

"Sounds familiar. But I think it might be a military, wartime thing. Not you choosing who sacrifices a piece of themselves for *your* gain. The people you take from aren't volunteers. They don't choose to give their lives for you."

"In the end, we all choose to give everything. As will you."

She just stared at him.

"In your own way."

"You can't force me to do what you want and call it a choice."

"You'll make the right choice. In the end."

"You can't force me to carry a baby for you people." She had to say it. He had to hear those words from her lips. "I'm not going to do that."

"I believe, in fact, that I *can* force you." Woodford stepped closer, and she thought she heard a grunt of humor behind her. Meanwhile, Woodford stared at her almost like he was entranced. "After all, you are one of us."

Kenna gritted her teeth. "Just tell me what you want."

"All in good time." He seemed to snap out of whatever spell he'd been under and motioned her toward the hall. "Come with me. There is more for you to see, and I believe it will change your mind if you allow yourself to see things as they really are."

Not likely, but moving was better than standing still. "If you want to try and change my mind, it would help if I had clean clothes, shoes, and some food. It's been a long day." And the more she was allowed privacy to change, or a minute to eat, the more time she had to figure out how to get her mom and Zeyla and get out of here.

She needed a phone line they wouldn't be monitoring. Or a cell they couldn't trace. A way to contact her friends—like via a computer. Something with a connection to the internet.

Leaving a note on a message board where Maizie would see it was far better than a text or call they could trace. The last thing she wanted was to endanger her friends.

Maybe that nurse/housekeeper lady would be amenable to helping her figure a way out of here. That meant finding a method for removing the explosive collar they'd put on Amara.

Odd that they hadn't put one on her yet.

"All in due time." Woodford glanced over his shoulder

at her. "In fact, I have the perfect outfit for you to change into."

Okay, gross. But she said nothing and continued to follow him. The guy behind her wasn't going to be easy to take down, even if she could reach the weapon at her spine and surprise him with an attack.

She kept the coat closed around her but found the cross of her necklace and flicked off the switch. Maizie had plenty of time to find her here by now. However, if the house blocked all signals in and out, effectively cutting off the transmitter, then she wasn't going to waste its short battery life by leaving it on when it meant nothing.

The first chance she got to go outside, she could turn it on.

He led her into a small study with a desk in the corner. She preferred her laptop on a picnic table, in the RV at the small dinette, or at some all-night breakfast restaurant with her friends. She would never have an office in her home. The idea of it repulsed her at this point after seeing so many men who thought their power came from subjugating others while sitting in their pretentious offices.

"Nice workspace." She put as much disgust into her tone as she could. "All the better for ruling the world."

"This is the Grand Master's room. I'm only keeping things running."

Seriously. "You've never thought of taking over? Not even once?"

"That is not how our world works. Self-promotion harms the whole. When one part seeks to function independently, the entire organization breaks down."

"Go team?"

He ignored that comment and opened a laptop on the desk, rotating it so that she could see the screen.

Kenna took an involuntary step forward. "Adrielle and Laney." They sat close together on a small couch, holding each other's hands. "Where are they?"

"A very nice five-star hotel. Which they will not be leaving until I'm assured you intend to cooperate."

"It's gonna be a long nine months waiting for me to give birth."

Woodford almost smiled. "Their safety isn't so much an assurance of your cooperation as it is ensuring we won't face others' interference."

"Others like who?" The guy wanted to talk all upper class, East Coast, snooty. She'd been raised by a rough man who worked rough cases and lived in a trailer.

"I'm sure you can figure that out. What I'm more concerned about is how much of a problem you intend to be."

Oh, he didn't want to know the answer to that. Just thinking about it made her smile.

"However, considering the parameters of your mother's existence and your sister's life expectancy, I'm sure you can be brought around to my way of thinking."

Kenna walked to a chair and slumped into it, exhausted by the endless talking around things. Bruce did it. Now Woodford. "What do you want, Senator?"

"A wife."

"I'm already engaged." Something he no doubt already knew.

"Really? I don't see a ring on your finger."

She rolled her eyes. "I'm not marrying you."

"Unless you want to witness the deaths of your mother, your sister, those two women in that hotel"—he pointed at the laptop screen—"and your friends at the campsite—"

"You say that word like it's dirty. Like campsites aren't *awesome*."

Woodford frowned a second, hesitating like she'd thrown him off.

"Awesome, like fast-food chicken restaurants and milkshakes at beachside diners. Those bags of popcorn you only get from gas stations on the highway between small towns. Meeting new people everywhere you go. Living a life that has nothing to do with social media and everything to do with face-to-face interactions with real people. Affecting their lives. Bringing justice. Finding people who've gone missing or been lost. Or abducted."

"Are you done?"

"Oh, buddy. I'm just getting started."

"Be that as it may. I'm sure you'll endeavor to make my life interesting."

"For as long as we both shall live?" She figured he understood the murderous look in her eye. "Sounds great."

"You can be sure I'll have certain...protections in place. If you're thinking about ending my life. I'm only one small cog in the wheel of this machine. You won't be marrying me so much as you'll be marrying the entire *Dominatus*."

That didn't sound so good. "Who?" She stared at him, completely confused. "What did you say? Dominoes? Like the game?"

"*Dominatus*. I suppose I can't expect you to be versed in Latin."

"Not unless you want to be exorcised. I can accommodate that." She wasn't going to back down. Married? As if. She was going to marry *Jax* and no one else. Ever. Thank you and goodnight. "What does it mean?"

"It is our organization. We are the power in the world. The ones in command."

"Oh, like world domination." She nodded. "Cool, cool. Good stuff. It's good to have goals."

Woodford sighed.

"What else?"

He stared at her for a moment, then went to perch on the edge of the desk. "We will be married in name only. You will bear the children of the *Dominatus*, and thankfully, I won't have to spend much time in your presence." A look of frustration, and maybe a little bit of disgust, crossed his face.

"You can't please everyone, I guess."

"Don't worry, I'll teach you how." He reached over and closed the lid of the laptop. "And you'll be well-versed in the consequences of disobeying me." Woodford glanced at the guy who stood by the door, then picked up a pouch from the desk beside her.

Heavy hands landed on her shoulders.

She stiffened, but he held her fast and didn't let her move. Woodford came over with a syringe in one hand. Kenna kicked at him. The man holding her didn't let go. She gritted her teeth and shoved at them both. He held her down, and the senator stuck the needle in the side of her neck.

The spot burned hot enough that she gasped.

Woodford said, "Why waste any more time?"

Warmth washed over her. Kenna tried to fight it, but eventually, the sensation crested over her like a wave that sucked her under a king tide. Deep into the water where she floated for a while.

She came awake, at least in part.

Warm.

Floating.

A man stood over the bed, a woman on the other side. Kenna didn't like hospitals—if that's what this was. She couldn't form the words to ask. Couldn't do anything but lie there on the cusp of moving, or speaking, but unable to do either.

Before she was sucked under again.

Chapter Twenty-Nine

The next time Kenna awoke, she was lying on a couch in a small office that wasn't a rich man's study, more like government chic. She could hear someone crying softly. It wasn't her.

She blinked and started to sit up.

A woman gasped. "Kenna! Don't try to move too fast."

She found the woman's face. "Laney." Kenna brushed back the hair that had fallen over her face and let out a groan, lying back against the pillow. This couch was hard and uncomfortable. "What happened?"

Before the drugs, she hadn't been with Jax's sister. His mom was here as well, on a chair beside the couch.

Laney crouched by Kenna's hip. "Stay where you are. I can explain but...they're watching."

"Talk fast." None of this made any sense.

Kenna reached out a hand and gently touched the collar on Laney's neck. The one with explosives in it that, if activated, would blow her head off and kill her instantly. "Laney." She groaned the word, then touched her own collar. Nothing. "Why don't I have one? You're both wearing them."

Adrielle looked away, a balled-up tissue in her hand. Anger was far better than sadness in whatever situation this was.

She sat up, a huge skirt moving with her as she lowered her legs to the floor. She was wearing... "Why am I in my wedding dress?"

Laney backed up and sat on the coffee table. Whoever owned this office, they might work for the government, but they were high up. Like a senator. "We have only been here half an hour, so we don't know much. They made us put you in that, by the way. We didn't want the senator's men doing it." She motioned to Kenna's middle.

Adrielle didn't look at them. Her body language screamed that she was on the precipice of losing all control.

Kenna gritted her teeth and shifted back on the couch. "Why do I ache all over?"

Laney shook her head. "They put these collars on us. They're explosive devices..."

Kenna was already nodding. "I saw my mom at the senator's house. They'd put one on her. This is about getting organs for his uncle. He's sick." Her voice broke, and she cleared her throat, hardly able to process it. "Zeyla."

She'd never even met her sister and had only seen her in person once.

Kenna didn't want to lose that shot at a sibling. But right now, there wasn't anything she could do about it.

Okay, time to quit ignoring the obvious. "He took my dress from Akira and put me in it because I'm supposed to marry him?"

Laney bit her lip.

Adrielle said, "If you don't, we all die. But we're probably dead either way. Once he has no need for us—"

"Mom."

Kenna glanced between the two women. "My friends will find us. Or we'll figure a way out of this." He'd had the collars' key in his pocket before. Or perhaps he had some kind of remote detonator, maybe on his phone. "We just need a plan."

She patted her lap. *Lord...*

All of it went unspoken, but He knew.

She looked around. "You took off my dress?"

Laney said, "Yes. It's there." She motioned to the basic desk and aging monitor.

Kenna stood. Pain whipped through her middle, and she sucked in a breath and sat back down.

"I'll get it." Laney went to the desk and brought it back.

Kenna clenched her teeth and turned the dress over in her hands, looking for the pocket by the zipper. *Please be there.* Whatever it was, she figured she would need it. "Do you know if Jax is okay, and your husband?" She looked at Adrielle.

The older woman only shook her head, pressing the balled-up tissue in her fist to her mouth.

Laney asked, "What happened just now when you tried to stand?"

"They did something to me. I don't know what." But she could guess well enough. Kenna wasn't going to think about it, though. She could do that later. After they all got out of this situation. "You've tried the phone on the desk?"

Laney nodded. "It isn't plugged in. There isn't even a cable."

"Ah." Kenna found the opening to the pocket and slid out a thin implement that didn't look like more than a hefty fountain pen. She removed the lid and found a wicked serrated blade, hiding it in the folds of her dress so she could look at it.

The handle had some curve to it. A slight guard around the middle, where the lid connected, would keep her from cutting her fingers when she thrusted forward and her hand slid. She wanted to swipe it through the air in her hand, to get a feel for the weight, but that would be too noticeable. Instead, she replaced the lid and slipped it into the front of the dress she wore.

She didn't have her necklace and wasn't sure where it was. At this point, if her friends couldn't find her, then they were in serious trouble.

But she figured she could stall. Give her friends the best possible chance of finding them.

Kenna looked at the window and saw daylight through the slats of the blinds but couldn't see outside. Just that little bit of light coming in, letting her know it was daytime. "Where are we?"

Laney swallowed. "The federal courthouse in Cheyenne, Wyoming. We were in Denver just a few hours ago. They loaded us into an SUV, and we came north. We didn't know why. They never told us anything until we got here. Just what these collars are. What they do."

Kenna reached over and clasped Laney's hand, holding on for a second. "Jax will come."

"I hope that's true." She looked rumpled. Exhausted. Scared.

"How are you, Adrielle?" Kenna looked at her future mother-in-law.

She couldn't think about Amara and Zeyla. Not when she was here with these women. Unless she got out of this situation, she wouldn't be able to rescue them. Even if she did, it might be too late.

"I'm scared."

Laney whispered, "She needs her heart pills."

Kenna said, "I'll put that on the list." She wanted to make light of the situation and joke. Find her bravado she always seemed to be able to draw from. But it wasn't here. It was gone, along with her strength and her ability to stand up.

What had they done to her?

They could've taken an organ from her. Or extracted her eggs.

Okay, focus.

She couldn't think about that, or she'd spiral with the endless possibilities and drive herself into a tailspin. Instead, she could ask Senator Woodford. Preferably at a time when her friends and family were safe, and she had that knife to his throat. Just a tiny bead of blood weeping from the spot where she was poking him.

She wasn't normally the murderous type, but that would be satisfying.

The door opened before she could say more or decide anything. Woodford strode in. "Good. You're ready."

"Ask me if I can stand up." Kenna stared at him from her spot on the couch.

He lifted a remote. "Test me and I'll turn this on. It's a dead man's switch. You know what that is?"

"You take your finger off the button, and it activates."

"Kaboom." His brows rose.

"Why don't you just give me a logical reason why I should cooperate, and then there's no need to endanger people or make threats? I'll cooperate."

He stared right back at her.

"But you never asked. You're so used to threats and terrorizing people you forgot diplomacy." She looked away, effectively dismissing him. "You forgot about negotiating."

"My way is more expedient." He came over, grabbed her upper arm, and hauled her to her feet.

Kenna screamed in his face, pouring all the acknowledgment of her pain into the cry. Plus, a whole lot extra just because she could.

A tendon in his jaw flexed.

"Sorry, am I not supposed to let you know that whatever sick thing you guys did while I was unconscious still hurts?" She clasped her hands together in front of her in a prayer position. "If you wanted demure, you chose the wrong girl."

Adrielle let out a whimper.

Woodford ran his hand down over her elbow to her wrist, holding it so tight it felt as if her bones were going to slam together. He studied the scars on her arms. "Disgusting. But I suppose you can simply cover them with sleeves, and no one needs to see."

She lifted her other hand and held her forearm up. "I've started to not mind them."

Not that she would be explaining to him what they meant to her. Or how far she'd come in her acceptance of the things that had been done to her and the grace given to her by Jesus.

Thank You. Also, some help would be awesome. If You're not busy. Now was definitely the time for casual and close for her prayers. Not distant and formal. *Anytime now would be great. Not telling You what to do or anything. K, love You. Bye.*

Some in the world considered that sacrilegious, but if this was going to be a relationship, she was going to be real. Kenna would accept nothing less than a dependent relationship that was deep and honest. Not a formal agreement based on mutual respect.

"They're ready for us." He dropped her arm like it stank and stepped back. "Ladies, if you would come with me?"

Laney and Adrielle both stood. Laney held out her arm, and Kenna snaked hers through. They weren't going to hold each other up, but they could walk together.

The federal courthouse in Cheyenne.

Kenna figured they had a judge in their pockets. If it was a weekday, there would be people here. She actually had no idea what day it was. There could be staff in the building. Would that mean all of them were on the company's payroll? *Dominatus.* The word dropped into her mind unbidden. She had a name for them now, and if Woodford had told it to her, that meant he didn't expect her to live to tell anyone else.

He expected to control whether she lived or died.

Two armed men stood in the hallway. They walked behind the group down the hall to a pair of wood doors with an opaque glass window that had gold lettering. "Is that the judge in your pocket? Or did you coerce him as well?"

"Everyone who is here today is here because they've made the choice to participate. Even you." He pushed the doors open.

Laney slid her arm down and held Kenna's hand and, on her other side, took her mother's hand as well.

Kenna glared at him. "Really seems like I chose this."

"It's the prudent course of action." Woodford stepped into the courtroom. "If you don't want to die."

Kenna spotted a couple more guys, including the one from the cabin. But not her mother or any other women except the ones with her. Charlie sat in the front row of the gallery, and the judge in his robes arranged some papers on the defense table. The older man had a string tie and cowboy boots, his robes drooped off weak shoulders. He turned to them with tiny reading glasses perched on his nose.

She wanted to find fault with him or see some indication he was part of this evil organization. But he just seemed like someone's grandpa.

"I see our bride has woken up."

Kenna said, "I thought marriage licenses took a few days. Don't some states require a blood test?" She thought of something else. "I don't have my driver's license, so I guess we can't do this after all. So sorry you all wasted your time coming here."

The men around the room said nothing.

Charlie didn't stand up. He sat there with a pinched expression, looking a little bit...scared. Because he thought she might kick him again?

"How are you, Charlie?" She shot him a look, full of mirth because she was so over this, ready to flip out and start raging as loud as she could.

Anytime now.

The senator grabbed her arm and shoved her toward the judge. "Shut up."

She looked back to see him turn to Laney and her mother.

"Would one of you care to remind her what happens if this doesn't go forward?"

Adrielle whimpered.

Laney said, "Kenna," and it sounded like a moan.

"Sorry." She stood between the judge and the senator and counted six guys. Four goons who probably had guns, Charlie, and the judge. She probably couldn't take them all out, but she could kill the senator with the knife tucked down the front of her dress.

Woodford studied her. "They should've fixed your hair."

"You should've given us more time."

"Let's just say I'm...eager to go through with this."

"Gross." She turned to the judge. "You're really fine being complicit in this? Isn't it against the law that you agreed to uphold?"

"Weddings are happy occasions for everyone."

"Sure they are." This guy seemed like he was on something. He couldn't seriously be this delusional, could he?

Woodford moved to stand next to her, and she heard a beep. When she looked over, he had his hand around the dead man's switch. "Just in case."

"Why do you even want to be married to me? I'll make every day miserable for you, relentlessly, until you're so tired of it you want to drive your car off a bridge."

Someone snorted.

Woodford ignored it. "As enjoyable as it would be to take you to every society party I can get an invitation to, I'm sure you'll much prefer spending your life in a comfortable room. With padded walls. Bearing my children." He leaned close. "All of them."

"Two...seven...twenty? How many are we talking?"

Woodford glared at her. "As many as I like, until you die."

"Seems inefficient."

"On the contrary, it will serve a great purpose and keep many of our women in line. You will be the example to all of a life well lived."

Kenna pressed her lips together.

"Silence is a wise choice. Until you say, 'I do.'"

"You can't make me say it."

Woodford waved the switch in his right hand. "I think I can. Unless you want to say it with brain matter on that dress."

It was already ruined just by the fact she had to wear it standing with this guy. A man who seriously thought she was going to agree to this?

But her defiance would cost Laney's and Adrielle's lives.

He grabbed her shoulders and turned her to face the judge, who cleared his throat.

"Dearly beloved, we are gathered here today…"

Kenna bit her lip. *Anytime now, God.*

Chapter Thirty

Kenna stopped short of tapping her foot. The judge might think she wanted him to hurry things up, and in reality, she needed this to take as long as possible.

The door handle rattled.

She twisted around to look over her shoulder, but the senator didn't let go of her arm. Tomorrow, she would have a bruise there from the strength of his grip. Hopefully, that would be the worst of her problems, but that was unlikely to be the case.

A brunette teenage girl in a pizza delivery uniform came in, carrying a stack of two pizzas, a ball cap low over her face. "Shoot. This isn't the accounting group? Did I get the wrong floor *again*? My boss is gonna *kill* me."

Kenna bit down hard on the side of her lip. Maizie.

"Leave." Woodford looked at his men. "Get rid of her."

"Is this a wedding?" She slipped into one of the rows and sank into a chair. "I love weddings. I won't disturb nothin'. I just want to watch." She handed the first guy who approached her the pizza. "Hold this. I don't wanna smell like pepperoni. This is a special occasion."

"What are you doing?" The guy tossed the pepperoni aside and pulled his gun out.

Kenna gasped. "She's just an innocent pizza delivery girl. Let her go. You don't have to hurt her."

Kenna couldn't look at Adrielle and Laney, sitting in the row in front of Maizie with their backs straight. Trying not to get caught in the crossfire. Hoping they wouldn't have to watch anyone get murdered today.

She didn't blame them. Anyone in here was at risk of their life ending in a messy way before they even realized what was happening.

In order to even try and save their lives, she was going to have to get her hands around that dead man's switch and make sure Woodford didn't let go of it.

Maizie said, "I'm just recording on my phone. Or is this secret, like no pictures? Are you guys famous? Are you in *witness protection?*"

"You wanna get shot, girl?" He grabbed her arm and hauled her out of the chair. "Get out of here. It ain't none of your business."

"Okay, gees. You guys are serious." She stumbled but caught her feet under her. "Fine, whatever. Tell accounting you took their pizzas."

He shoved her toward the door.

"Ow, gees. I'm *going.*"

The doors flew open in front of her. Someone tossed a small canister across the floor. Kenna swung around to face Woodford and grabbed his right wrist, ducking behind him a second too late. But she already had her eyes closed.

The room flashed with light so bright it was like lightning inside the room, filling it for a split second. The accompanying sound was so loud it eclipsed everything in her ears. In a second, they were completely deafened, and she could hear nothing, quickly replaced by sharp pain in both ears and a loud high-pitched ringing sound.

She grasped Woodford's hand. He flinched, his knees buckling from the sudden noise and the bright light. He'd been looking at the door when it went off, which meant he was disoriented now. But she couldn't allow him to let go of the dead man's switch.

Whatever he did, she had to keep his hand on the button. Even transferring it to her grip would be too risky.

He collapsed onto one knee. Smoke filled the air.

She spotted flashing lights, bobbing up and down. People moving through the cloud from the flash-bang. Her ears rang so sharply all she could think about was the pain. Woodford listed to the side. She had a dress on, but instinct rode out above all other things.

Kenna dropped to her hip, swung her leg over, and hooked it around his neck. She pinned his upper body and his head to the floor, twisting his arm around his back so he was locked in place.

He fought her hold, but her legs were stronger. Even if it hurt. Even if she wouldn't be able to hang on forever.

Muzzle flash erupted in the room.

Kenna held on for dear life while the cops or whoever had come in cleared the room and took out everyone who fought back. She saw white letters on a black vest but couldn't make out the words. The person came down the center aisle.

Charlie dove out of the row he'd been in and slammed into the person, knocking them into the opposite row, colliding with chairs that went flying. She couldn't hear anything except the ringing in her ears.

She watched for them to rise up above the chairs so she could see what was happening. But they didn't.

Kenna looked back behind her for the judge, but he was nowhere to be found.

If they were raiding this room, what about the cabin? What about her mom and sister? By doing this, they could be signing the death warrant for her family if Woodford had left instructions that they were to be killed immediately if anything happened.

Hot tears rolled down her face.

Her hold on Woodford must have slipped a little because he shifted. His hips came up. Then his foot swung up, and he kicked up toward his backside. His shoe caught her shoulder, and she cried out, moving out of his reach. She didn't let his head up. He would probably bite her.

Out of the smoke, Maizie moved to the chairs over where Laney and her mom had been. She might've said something to Kenna. All she saw was mouthed words tossed in her direction with a glance. She heard none of it.

Kenna kept up her two-handed grip on Woodford's fingers. He thrashed again and stilled. Passed out? His hand would relax, and he would let go of the switch if she wasn't careful. But it would be far easier to keep the button pressed down with him no longer fighting her.

She allowed her hands to relax a little but didn't let go of the button. She put all of her attention on holding it down.

Listening to the ringing in her ears.

Keeping Laney and Adrielle alive.

Someone touched her face. She lifted her chin, tears still rolling down her face. Jax spoke to her, but all she could do was shake her head. He frowned.

"It's a dead man's switch." She spoke slowly, forcing the words out. He had to know what was happening.

Jax flinched. He reached back on his belt and pulled out

plastic ties, which he used to circle Woodford's hand and keep his fingers on the button.

Finally, she could let go.

Kenna slumped back, moving her leg off Woodford's shoulders. She had no strength to get up and laid on the floor instead, staring up at the ceiling. She turned her head to see Jax shouting orders to others. Maizie ran over with her phone, typing on the screen. She held it close to the switch in Woodford's hand and glanced at Jax, saying something. He squeezed her shoulder.

Kenna couldn't hear what they were saying and couldn't get up. She couldn't ask where Stairns and Ramon were or what had happened to Jax's dad—and Bruce, who'd been shot in the chest and left for dead.

Tears leaked from the corner of her eye.

Jax glanced at her for a second, then said something to Maizie.

They weren't going to be able to take the explosive collars off. Not without...the key. Kenna rolled over and pushed up. Her arms didn't like that, so she just scooted along the floor in the wedding dress. Probably getting it dirty.

The whole getting married business was ruined for now anyway, so she didn't worry about it.

She tugged his suit jacket out from under him and dug in the closest pocket.

Jax set his hand on her arm. She looked at him, and he shook his head, silently asking, *What?*

She motioned turning a key, then touched her collar, then pointed to where his mom and Laney were.

"There's a key?"

Jax helped her search the senator's pockets. The guy

was unconscious, but she didn't want to be next to him when he woke up. Not without the knife in her dress.

She patted her front and made sure it was there.

Jax came up with the key from the senator's pocket, touched her cheek, and leaned across the unconscious man to touch his lips to hers.

Woodford shifted.

She fell back, and the senator lifted a gun with his left hand. Jax's holster was empty.

The senator brought the weapon up. She dove for his arm, shoving it aside, and felt the gun go off.

He slammed the gun at the side of her head, his other hand still holding the switch with his grip zip-tied into place. Both hands swung at her. Pain exploded in the side of her skull.

Kenna fell back again.

She dragged the knife from her bodice, tugged off the lid, and swung it at the senator. The gun muzzle flashed over and over as he fired wildly around the room. Jax lay on top of Maizie, covering the teen with his body.

Kenna jabbed the knife into the side of the senator's neck.

The gun slipped from his hand.

Woodford reached up and clutched the knife handle on his neck, drawing it out as he gasped and choked on his own blood. The knife fell to the floor. He clutched the blood seeping from his neck and fell back.

What would happen to the dead man's switch if it became soaked with blood? She pushed the zip-tied hand out farther from the senator's bleeding body.

Kenna gathered up the stupid dress and clambered over him. She fell to her knees by Jax and turned his shoulder. His head came around, and Maizie blinked up at them from the floor. Kenna touched the teen's head. Jax had a gash on the side of his face, across his cheekbone. A graze from a bullet.

She gasped, then coughed out the grit and smoke still in the air.

The key.

She looked around, found the key on the floor, swiped it up, and stumbled across the room. Langford swung around, crouched by Adrielle. Yelling to someone.

Mrs. Jaxton needed her heart pills. That was what Laney had told her.

Kenna unlocked the latch on Laney's collar. Laney took the key and did her mother's. Kenna took both collars and threw them to the far corner of the room.

Only then did she let out a breath.

Every part of her body hurt.

She slumped to the floor. Laney tried to catch her, but pain flashed in Kenna's forearms, and she couldn't hold on.

Then Jax was there, gathering her to him.

She buried her face against his shirt, wrapped her arms around his waist, and prayed for her mother and sister.

She felt Maizie touch her arm.

Two EMTs came in and crouched by Adrielle. Kenna hung onto Jax, leaning against him until he scooped her up with one arm under her knees and another behind her back. He lifted her, carrying her like a terrible facsimile of a bride over a threshold. The whole thing was ridiculous anyway.

She looked over her shoulder.

Woodford lay dead on the floor. Along with all his plans and his attempts to terrorize people. At least this small part of the *Dominatus* was gone.

It was over.

Chapter Thirty-One

Kenna woke up warm again. Which wasn't good last time, so she came awake far too fast. Sitting up in a hospital bed. But with a heavy weight across her front that she had to push against.

"Whoa, whoa. It's just me."

She held on to his sleeve, lying down again so she had to roll slightly toward him and look up. "Did we get married? Is that why you're in bed with me?"

He grinned. Fully clothed, on top of the blanket. So she guessed the answer was no. He smiled slightly. "They said they were bringing me a chair, but it's been a couple of hours, so I figure they forgot. If I ask, they might kick me out because visiting hours are over."

Kenna moved her arm and realized she had an IV needle in her elbow. She looked at the clear bag hanging on the hook. It would be easier to bury her head in the sand and not deal with the hard emotions, but doing that wasn't going to get her answers to any of her questions.

She ducked her head and pressed her forehead against

his shirt, wanting to wrap her arms around him. Stay there forever.

His fingers slid into her hair, and he held on to her.

"You got shot." Her ears still hurt. "I can hear now."

"I figured the flash-bang would knock you out."

"I saw it coming and hid behind Woodford." Talking was tiring her out. "Tell me all of it. Tell me you got Amara and Zeyla."

"Ramon and Stairns covered that part. They got your location from the necklace." He shifted. "I don't know where it went, but when we find it, we're keeping that thing because it saved your life."

She agreed. "They're okay?"

"Zeyla is here in the hospital. She's in a bad way, and your mom is with her."

Kenna let out a long breath.

"Ramon is fine. Stairns got grazed. They found Bruce nearly dead in a parking lot."

Her hands tightened on his shirt.

"He's alive, but it's critical. He lost a lot of blood." Jax dipped his head. "Did he betray us?"

"I don't know. I need to figure it out in my head, but I can't do that right now."

"Okay. Get some sleep?"

Kenna asked, "Your mom and sister are okay?"

"They'll be okay."

"And your dad?"

"He's with Miller."

"There are more loose ends. People. Parts of this. So much more."

"And we'll tackle all of it together. Okay?"

Kenna nodded against his chest. Part of that was what they'd done to her when she had been unconscious. She'd taken a pregnancy test before in her life, and it had been positive. She'd lost that baby. If she was pregnant again, she would deal with the change in direction her life would take. In the end, the answer was that simple. She'd escaped, and her baby would live free of the *Dominatus*. Not captive. Not bred for their purposes.

She needed to talk it over with someone, and the best person might not be Jax. He was just a little too close to the whole thing. "I need my ring."

He let out a breath that sounded like a note of humor. "Where did you leave it?"

"My dresser in the RV."

"I'll have Maizie bring it when she comes back. She and Ramon were working with Langford on picking apart Woodford's life so they can prove a tie to the judge. The one that was going to perform the wedding...he was caught by one of the Denver FBI agents, but he's claiming he was coerced."

"I guess he might've been, but he didn't act like it."

"They need to prove it if we're ever going to set the record straight about what's going on."

Kenna let out a long sigh.

He chuckled. "I know. The whole thing sounds exhausting. It's been a long week, so close your eyes, and I'll be here when you wake up."

"Thanks."

"You're welcome."

"For saving me, I mean."

He said, "You're the one who saved me. You killed Woodford. With...whatever that knife was."

"Bruce gave it to me. I have no idea."

"Oh. I think I know."

Kenna shook her head. "What do you mean?"

"We had a tracker on you. We followed you from the cabin to the courthouse, the whole way."

"I had the necklace." She frowned. "I turned it off to save the battery, but I turned it back on?" She tried to think if she'd had it at the courthouse but couldn't remember exactly. All of it was so foggy. And terrifying.

Jax rubbed a hand up and down the outside of her arm, infusing her with more of his warmth. "Maizie said the signal was being blocked. We tracked you with that pen... knife...thing."

"Then we owe Bruce."

"We never would have found you otherwise," Jax said. "I'll be praying he pulls through."

"When I'm up and back to work, I'm going to help him figure out what happened when he got burned and if there's a debt he needs to pay back."

"Revenge. Sounds fun."

She lifted her chin and looked at him.

"You think I'm leaving again?"

Given the expression on his face, she guessed the answer to that rhetorical question was no. "I'm feeling the sudden urge to spend some time in Phoenix."

"Your team can have the RV at a campsite. You'll be at my house."

"How presumptuous."

"Get used to it. I'm not feeling the need to be apart for a *while*. We've got cases to work, a revenge plan to enact, and...some other things."

She had no idea what to guess first. None of it would be unpleasant. "Good thing I didn't just marry some crazy senator from Colorado, then."

"We're not joking about that for at least ten years."

"Good to know." A yawn overtook her, and she relaxed after it. Closed her eyes.

"Go to sleep."

"Yeah, yeah."

But she did.

For some time to come, Kenna wasn't going to wake up without panicking at first. Wondering if she would see those people standing over her bed. Wondering if being rescued had been a dream. That Jax wasn't here. That she was still captive, and the world hadn't been put back to rights by her team. Her friends. Her family.

But Jax wasn't here.

She shifted in the hospital bed and saw that the IV had been removed. Kenna started to sit up.

"I'll help you." Amara moved to the bedside, pressed the button to raise the head of the bed, and fluffed Kenna's pillow. "It's nice to be able to do something."

"How is she?"

Amara smoothed down the blanket over Kenna. "How are *you*?"

"Answer my question first."

"Your father always avoided the painful subject in favor of something else. Like working a case."

Kenna pressed her lips together.

Amara sighed. "Thank you for sending your friends. I know you weren't able to organize it, but they came to us because of you."

"They're good people." She wanted to hug them, but she also needed more information. Answers. And Jax. Not necessarily in that order. Jax could come in anytime.

Her engagement ring glinted on her left hand, and she

smiled at the sight of it. He must have fetched it, or had Maizie bring it as he'd said, while she was sleeping. He probably thought she wanted time alone with her mother.

"This isn't over." She had to say it. Out loud. "At best, we took down one part of their operation."

"I pulled the plug on the Grand Master." Her mother looked at her own hands on the rail, grasping the metal as if she needed to cling to it. "Before we left the cabin, I made sure he was dead."

Kenna laid her hand on her mom's. "That's good."

She lifted her gaze. "I'm sorry for what they did to you."

The not knowing was terrifying her.

"I know they put something inside you."

"A baby? Mom, did they impregnate me?" Her voice broke, but she got the words out. "I need to know."

Amara shook her head. "I don't know. It's not the only thing they're working on, researching, and building in those labs. They don't just create the next generation and find a surrogate. They are into all kinds of genetic research."

"So it could be a virus for all we know? I could be patient zero about to start a worldwide plague."

Amara held her hand. "We don't know, but we can run some tests."

Kenna leaned back against the pillow and groaned. "This just gets better and better."

"Have the doctors tested your blood?"

"For what? We have no idea what they should look for. It's too early to tell if I'm pregnant."

"Then have the doctor give you something to prevent pregnancy."

Kenna let go of her mother's hand. "I lost a baby once. I'm not killing one just because it didn't show up as part of a plan."

"So you'll just do nothing and let this destroy your life?"

"I guess so."

The door opened, and Jax glanced between them. "Is everything okay?"

Kenna pressed her lips together.

Amara said, "I'm glad you're feeling better."

"But you aren't going to tell me how Zeyla is. And you say I avoid answering questions." She had to take a breath. Try to settle her racing heart. Was she really pregnant? That might be better than any other alternative.

For now, it would be a "wait and see" exercise. *Maybe it could be nothing, Lord. Can I ask for that?*

Amara said, "She needs two transplants to be stabilized. Maizie is doing some of the legwork to get things moving along."

"What does that mean? My people aren't here to break the law for you."

"No, only for you." Amara moved to the end of the bed. "I'm glad you're all right."

"Am I? I have no idea."

Jax stepped into the room. "The two of you can finish this conversation later."

Kenna sniffed. She didn't want to cry. It was supposed to be a happy time, with all of them free. They could heal, given the space to do that. Recovery took time.

Amara stopped at the door. "If Zeyla lives, it will be thanks to you and your team."

Kenna watched her leave.

"Hey." Jax settled on the edge of the bed.

She shook her head. "Don't."

He hesitated. "Don't what?"

"I don't know. But don't." She held out a hand, braced against his chest. Pushing him away. Holding on. Either.

Both. She had no idea. "I could be a ticking time bomb for a contagion. Or I could be carrying the spawn of *Dominatus*. Or something else entirely. You have no idea. I could kill you."

He covered her hand with his on his chest. "That's the point. Whatever happens to you, I'm there for it. Whatever happens to me, you're there. No matter what, we stick together."

Tears rolled down her face. "I don't like crying."

Jax chuckled. "Laney said she just has to get it out, then she feels better."

"She's pretty smart."

"So are you."

"Says the guy who always says the right thing."

He chuckled.

"Where are Maizie, Ramon, and Stairns? I half expected Langford to come by. Or Miller. Is everyone..." She didn't even know what to think about what they were all doing.

Jax winced.

"Are they afraid they're gonna get infected? Am I in quarantine or something?" She looked around but didn't see any infectious disease things. Whatever those would look like.

"It's not that. The doctor is going to check you out in a little while, and if you're up to it, you can be released."

Kenna waited for the rest of it.

He almost seemed nervous.

"What did you do?" She narrowed her eyes.

"It wasn't just me. Maizie helped."

"Jax..."

"Elizabeth is back from her trip. It wasn't a cruise. She went to the small town where her uncle is the pastor of that little country church, and she was setting up the whole thing. But it's moot now. You're not well enough. It doesn't matter."

"Explain better than that."

He winced again. "I figured you didn't want to do the whole invitations, guest list, packed church with people we hardly know. And months of waiting. *I* didn't want to wait months. We only needed a pastor, our friends, and a cake."

"You planned our wedding?"

"It was supposed to be on Saturday. Since you got the dress and all, I figured everyone shows up at the church, and we just do it." He hesitated. "It was a good plan, but the week got away from us."

"I'll say." She tipped her head to the side. "When were you going to tell me I'm getting married...whatever day is Saturday?"

"Actually, it's today."

"Sorry, I was busy nearly marrying someone else."

He leaned forward and touched his lips to hers. "There's nothing to apologize for. You saved lives this week, and you stopped some very bad people. There are corrupt cops, feds, and government officials who aren't operating now because what you did exposed them."

Kenna said, "You really planned the whole thing?"

He made a face, looking unhappy. Because the plan didn't work. "Forrest Crosby flew in from Wisconsin. She's with Maizie in the cafeteria. Ramon took one look at her and nearly tripped over his feet. Your friend Dixie is in Denver with her husband and their son. The Rysons are at a vacation rental in Aspen that I booked for them."

Kenna swallowed against the lump in her throat. "Thank you."

"You're not mad?"

"That you thought of everything, and you were going to make it as easy as possible for me? No, I'm not mad."

Jax let go of some of his tension. "I wondered a few times if it was going to backfire on me."

He'd had everyone she cared about come to Colorado so they could get married in a simple service with as little fuss as possible. Giving everything so she could have what she needed, as well as what she wanted.

Kenna said, "I love you, you know."

Jax smiled. "I was hoping you'd say that."

"I still have a dress. But it's dirty." The reality of her situation settled on her like a shadow over her heart. "I could be pregnant with someone else's baby, or a hundred other terrible scenarios. It isn't exactly the start either of us had planned. You probably don't want—"

He touched her cheeks. "I want you."

More tears trailed down her cheeks. He swiped them away with his thumbs. "It could get worse before there's any better."

"We never know what might happen. We have to leave the future in God's hands."

Kenna said, "Maybe you could help me figure out how to do that."

"I'd love to."

He slid his arms around her and kissed her, lingering in a place where she could be swept away in the promise of what was to come. The reassurance of his strength wrapped around her. She'd found home in the person God had brought to her when she needed him most. The future He had prepared for her.

One with Jax by her side.

No matter what happened.

Chapter Thirty-Two

"We should get you another dress." Maizie stood in front of Kenna, her hands on her hips, in the hallway of the hospital. Nurses sat behind their desk. A TV played some daytime comedy show, and the audience's laughter drifted down the hall to them.

Talk about spur of the moment. "Everything is set to go. Why waste time getting another dress? This one still has some life in it."

She looked at Ramon for support, but all his attention was on his phone. Everyone had pitched in helping out, getting things ready, and he'd been tapping away on that thing doing something.

Kenna wasn't so sure about herself and whether she had much life left in her. But that was defeat talking. There was a whole heap of worry in her heart and mind over what was going to happen next. She and Jax had prayed together about it. She'd prayed while she showered, and he went to do...something, and then she put the dress back on. Trying to find peace and let things go that she couldn't control. It was time to live the life she had while she had it and let God take care of tomorrow.

The doctor had taken vials and vials of blood and run all kinds of tests looking for antibodies, bacteria, viruses, indications she might be pregnant. They'd done an ultrasound and hadn't seen anything—it was far too early anyway. She would have to wait at least a week for another blood test to determine if she was pregnant and longer than that for a more definitive answer.

But God knew.

It was all in His hands.

"I'm not getting married in scrubs."

Maizie was about to say something else.

Kenna cut her off. "Love you, Maze."

She rolled her eyes. "I refuse to believe anything is going to happen to you. Let's just enjoy the day, all right?"

"That's what I've been trying to tell you." Kenna didn't like sitting in a wheelchair for this discussion, being at such a disadvantage. But she was going to walk down the aisle of a little country church, so she was saving her energy.

Jax and his father stepped out of the elevator.

Ramon slipped his phone into his pocket. Jax came over, swinging an arm around Maizie's shoulders. "Ready, kiddo?"

She smiled up at him. "I'm ready, but Kenna is wearing a dirty, torn dress."

"Don't worry about it," Ramon said. "It'll be fine."

Maizie frowned at him.

"Don't we need to go?" Ramon came over and grabbed the handles of the wheelchair, pushing her toward the elevator.

Jax walked with Maizie behind them. His father hit the button for the elevator, and they all got in.

Kenna said, "It's going to be a long drive to the church, right?"

"Need some coffee?" Jax asked.

She smiled.

Before she could say anything, a hand waved in the door to keep it from sliding shut. Amara stepped on. "I'm coming. Is that okay?" She looked around, but her gaze settled on Kenna.

"That would be nice." She shared a smile with her mom.

Jax's dad cleared his throat.

Maizie said, "We aren't driving!"

Kenna glanced at the collection of guilty faces. How many more things had they planned without telling her? "What? How are we getting there? Dog sleds?"

Maizie giggled.

Jax smiled.

She couldn't see Ramon behind her.

Jax's dad said, "There's a helicopter on the roof for us." He rocked back and forth on the balls of his feet. As if he was nervous—or felt guilty. "I wouldn't want the two of you to be late to your wedding."

"A helicopter?" Her brows rose.

She knew he'd spoken to the feds at length and given statements about the *Dominatus*. They weren't shut down, just a small fraction of the organization here locally had been terminated. But he had told the police everything he knew.

Miller had been tasked with the case against the federal judge, something Maizie had been helping him and Langford with. Maizie had told Kenna that she'd seen the two of them *look at each other*. Evidently, it was significant enough to imply a relationship—and also, evidently, it was something that Jax and Kenna still did.

She'd liked hearing that.

His dad nodded. "A helicopter. If that's all right with you."

She held out her hand to him. When he clasped it, she said, "Thank you."

"You're very welcome, Kenna. I know what you did for my Adrielle and Elaine. You saved their lives. It's the least I can do."

Amara watched the interplay. Kenna looked at Maizie and Jax, standing close and sharing an inside joke. Even Ramon, back on his phone. Amara tried to see what was on his screen, but he moved it away.

At the top floor, they went up a short flight of stairs and across the rooftop to the chopper. The kind with rows of cushy white seats that her dress was going to get dirty. There was even blood on one part of her dress, but it was what it was, and there wasn't anything she could do.

She sat in the chopper between Jax and Maizie. Maizie wanted to watch out of the window the entire ride. Kenna leaned her head on Jax's shoulder and looked at the mountains as they went south from Cheyenne back down to Colorado and the small town where Elizabeth's uncle pastored.

The pilot set the helicopter down on the lawn behind the church.

She watched the back door open, and a crowd of people came out while Kenna took off her headphones. They all piled out of the chopper onto the grass. Her Converse sank into the soft earth.

Jax interlaced his fingers with hers. "Are you as nervous as I am?"

"At least you've done this before."

"Nothing that happens with you is anything like what I've done before."

Kenna laughed. "I guess that's probably true."

She leaned against him and looked around, seeing her RV parked in front of the church. The Rysons came down the steps from the church, their toddler running straight for Maizie, who scooped her up and spun her around.

Stairns walked with his arm around Elizabeth.

Amara headed into the church alone while Forrest Crosby and Dixie—and her family—stopped to speak with Ramon. Bruce was still in critical condition, or no doubt he'd be here as well.

Kenna watched them all. "They're good people."

"So are you."

She looked over. "I know."

Jax motioned to the church with his chin. "You should go see what that is about."

Ramon stood on the back steps, hands folded across his chest.

"Think he'll be my bridesmaid?"

Jax laughed. "I think he'll stand up with you if you ask. He and Maizie were arguing about it earlier."

She frowned. Jax walked with her to the back door of the church. As they crossed the lawn, he asked, "Feeling okay?"

"I think so. It's too early to tell anything, but as far as I know at this moment, it's all clear. Nothing to worry about. Yet."

Jax gave her a squeeze. "I'll be there no matter what."

"I know." They climbed the steps. "Why do you look mad, Ramon? It's a happy occasion."

He lifted one brow. "You owe me."

"For what?"

"I have to go on a date with...that woman." He unfolded his arms. "I'll show you to the room. Akira had another dress that's the exact size as that and as close as she could get to the same design. She's waiting for you."

"You called her?"

"I'm not going to let you get married with mud on your dress," Ramon said.

"It's probably blood, actually."

"Whatever. Come on."

Jax scratched his jaw, looking like he wanted to laugh. "Guess I'll see you in there."

She grabbed his cheeks and kissed him. "I'll be quick."

"I have to change as well."

She lifted her brows.

"See you in ten."

Kenna went with Ramon. He led her to a small library where Akira had a huge white garment bag. Amara was there, and Dixie.

Kenna hugged her friend. "Thanks for coming."

Dixie leaned back, still holding on to Kenna. "Girl, I wouldn't miss this for the world." She stepped by Kenna and held her elbow out for Ramon. "Let's go find Forrest."

The look on Ramon's face upon hearing that name wasn't lost on her. Ramon and Forrest Crosby? That could be an interesting combination.

Akira spread her arms. "Let's get you out of that thing." She didn't sound happy about the state of it.

Kenna said, "Sorry. It was a rough week."

Akira laughed, unzipping the dress so Kenna could step out of it.

Amara produced the replacement. Kenna went over to

her, hugging herself so she didn't freeze while wearing next to nothing. "It's beautiful."

Her mother nodded. "You'll be beautiful in it. But it isn't the dress; it's you."

"Thanks, Mom."

Kenna stepped into it, and her mom zipped the dress.

Akira came over with white silk gloves in her hands. "Ready for these?"

Kenna held her hand out. "I think I'm going to go without. I don't need to cover up my scars."

"Why not?" Amara said. "You don't need to be reminded of them every time you look at the photos."

"Maybe I do. They're a part of me, aren't they?" Perhaps her mom was ashamed of them somehow, but Kenna wanted this chance to explain how she felt. "They represent what I've lost, sure. They remind me of everything I should've had. But they also represent the things I have now. Things God gave me because He wanted to pour His grace into my life. I could be living alone in my RV solving cases by myself.

"But I have Maizie, Ramon, Stairns, and Elizabeth. Friends. Family. There are little kids out there who are a part of my life. Good people who could've chosen anyone to be friends with, but they chose to stick with me. And what does that say if they're the best kind of people. Maybe it means I'm something good, something special, like they are.

"Jesus has scars like I do. He sacrificed. He gave everything for me. So why would me having scars mean something bad? To me, they remind me to look at what I have now." She swiped a tear from her cheek. "I have so much. More than I ever thought possible. And that includes you, Mom."

"I love you, Kenna." Amara gave her a hug.

"I missed you." When her mom leaned back, Kenna said. "I always missed you because you're my mother. Even if it's not biological, you're the one who was going to raise me. I want you in my life. I know you need to be with Zeyla and help her. She has a long road to recover from everything they did to her. But I'd like to see you."

Her mom said, "That would be nice."

It seemed her mom was done fighting the company, the *Dominatus*. But maybe it was more like passing the torch and allowing someone else to take up the cause while she fought a different fight at home for her family.

"Okay, let's do this."

Across the room, Akira wiped a tear away. Kenna went into the hall and found the lobby of the church. A lone man in a suit stood there, waiting for her.

"Ryson." Kenna picked up her pace, lifting the front of the dress.

He frowned. "Converse?"

"No one will see them under my dress."

"I just did."

Kenna waved a hand, dismissing his concern. She gave him a hug. "It's so good to see you."

"Free vacation and the chance to see you in a dress? I wouldn't miss it."

She leaned back. "Are you walking me down the aisle?"

"If you'll let me."

"Sounds like a plan."

Ryson grinned, then surveyed her head. "Sure you don't want to do something with your hair?"

"What's wrong with my hair?"

He frowned. "Just...fluff it or something."

She backed up, tipped her head forward, and ran her fingers through it. Okay, fine, it was pretty tangled. She heard a door open, and when she flicked her hair back and straightened, Valentina Ryson, his wife, stepped out of the sanctuary.

She said, "I have a comb and a hair tie."

Kenna took both, ran the comb through her hair, and secured it in a high bun. Valentina pulled it out.

Kenna was about to object when Valentina said, "You gave me an idea."

She stood behind Kenna, twisting and turning pieces of hair and gathering them. She secured it into a bun as Kenna had done, but with loose pieces that hung down by her ears. She ran to a water fountain, wet her fingers, ran back, and curled the pieces so they hung in ringlets.

"Take a look."

Kenna walked to the mirror on the wall and saw her hair had been twisted back and curled into a bun that seemed easy and natural. "Thank you." She cleared her throat.

Valentina kissed her cheek, swiped the spot with her thumb, and disappeared into the sanctuary.

"Ready?" Ryson held his elbow out.

Kenna blew out a long breath. "I'll never be more ready."

"So we might as well get it over with?"

She laughed. "Now or never."

If she was going to live her life the way she wanted, it meant not giving in to the fear of what the future might hold. That would lead her into a depression or grief. She'd had enough of those to last a lifetime. Things with Jax wouldn't be perfect by any means. But they would be good if she kept looking for the good every day.

If she gave of herself every day, the way he would give of himself. Both of them working to make their marriage—

and their life—a place the other would always want to stay. A place they would call home. Together.

Wherever that would be.

A piano started to play melodic notes. The tune was familiar, but she couldn't place where she'd heard it. The handful of people in the church stood. At the altar, Jax stood beside the pastor. Her husband-to-be wore a dark suit, white shirt, and no tie.

She lifted the edge of her skirt and showed everyone her Converse.

Laughter erupted around the church, and Jax grinned.

Kenna looked at her friends, her family, and the life she'd always wanted. No matter what happened, they would be together. Through her health journey or theirs. Through ups and downs. Cases. Investigations. Working to take down *Dominatus* here and across the world.

Whatever came, this family would face it together.

Ryson asked, "Ready?"

Kenna took the first step down the aisle.

Toward the rest of her life.

Keep Reading For...

- Where to find more great Lisa Phillips books.

- How to sign up for Lisa's newsletter and get a FREE book.

- Where to find Lisa on social media.

About the Author

Find out more about Lisa Phillips at her website, where you'll discover more romantic suspense fan-favorite series and heart-pounding thriller novels.
https://authorlisaphillips.com/

If you loved this book, please consider sharing about it on social media. Or leave a review at your book retailer website, on Goodreads, or on Bookbub. Your review will help others find great books to entertain and encourage them!

Signup for Lisa's newsletter by scanning the QR code below to stay updated on sales, new releases, and recommendations for your TBR pile. New Subscribers even get a FREE book!

Find Lisa on Social Media!

facebook.com/authorlisaphillips

instagram.com/lisaphillipsbks

bookbub.com/authors/lisa-phillips

Also by Lisa Phillips

Find out more about Brand of Justice at my website:

https://authorlisaphillips.com/product-tag/brand-of-justice/

Book 1: Cold Dead Night

Book 2: Burn the Dawn

Book 3: Quick and Dead

Book 4: Over the Limit

Book 5: Skin and Bone

Book 6: Dust and Ashes

Book 7: Long Road Home

Book 8 : Dead to Rights

Book 9: Fear No Evil

Book 10: Out of Time

Book 11: Every Which Way

Book 12: One More Chance (June 2025)

———

Other series by Lisa:

Last Chance Downrange

Chevalier Protection Specialists

Last Chance County

Northwest Counter-Terrorism Taskforce

Double Down

WITSEC Town (Sanctuary)

Numerous other titles including several with *Love Inspired Suspense*, find the complete list here (or scan the QR code):

https://authorlisaphillips.com/all-books/